一次就考到

雅思閱讀

總是提前答完且答好每一題

韋爾 ◎ 著

7+

MP3

三大學習特色 破解各篇章閱讀架構／閱讀重點核心／活化思路

時間統籌：包含最基礎的閱讀時間控管，把點滴流失掉的時間找回來，依序拆解試題，每篇閱讀都於時限內答完，更能隨意組織並同步答多個題型，迅速**優化閱讀速度**。

剪枝＋跳讀的掌握：除了剪枝技巧外，附加**「跳讀段落」**的提醒跟理解每篇文章框架的設計，減掉更大幅度不需要閱讀的部分。

語法強化：包含詳盡的語法補充，讀完文章立即就能判別且定位答案，有效**縮短思考時間**，秒答各類型考官改寫後的試題。

PREFACE 作者序

　　這次雅思閱讀的題材中選用了常見的主題，商業類、心理學類以及生物類，每篇搭配特定題型，像是摘要題出了**不同類型**的挖空方式，就這樣完成了浩瀚的這一本書。在題材中收錄了三篇三國演義的文章，精選大家熟悉的：**貂蟬的美人計、孔明草船借箭和三氣周瑜**。雅思閱讀是檢測考生對於語文的掌握度，而非對內容了解度的一項考試，加上雅思考試有判斷題（Not Given 的選項），所以一定要根據閱讀文章有提到的來作答。**「語文技巧」**的掌握度和**「高階同義語句理解」**比起**「背景知識」**和**「機經」**的掌握更為重要，所以有些對**「語法」**掌握良好的讀者，就能迅速答好某些題，且贏過那些對三國演義劇情都熟悉或者是中、英文版都看過的讀者，在寫相關類別的試題中能答對更多的題數。

　　在寫解析時，筆者有陷入掙扎和考量，有時候教學者沒有考量到大多數的學習者，所以大概一句「以關鍵字定位回去...」就打發了，或者是在一個長句中出現好幾個近似或同義表達，覺得學習者應該可以辨別的出來就略過了。好像數學高手在教學時略過太多步驟，結果學習者還是不懂，這些在解析中都有一一列出，也有試題和原文文章的對照，考生可以清楚看到哪些字作了同義轉換，學習起來能更快的作出定位（畢竟每題的答題時間真的很有限）。

解析的部分還有提供考生一個依據（考生常陷入到底該先讀題目根據關鍵字定位，還是一段段文章接續閱讀邊寫邊答的窘境），這部分真的很重要！（這牽涉到**時間統籌**）因為有時候你採用了閱讀題目後根據題目關鍵字定位回去找，都找不到對應訊息，又改成採用一段段接續閱讀邊讀邊寫試題時，無形中造成了答題慌亂和時間無形的浪費，繼而影響在其他篇的答題心情。也有解析是「**涵蓋同步答兩個題型的**」或是「**順讀**」邊讀邊寫的題型（當然已經具備一定程度者，就能先掃描所有題目後邊寫邊答所有題型，因為有時候題目出的很散），書籍中也有提供考生針對「出題很散」的答法。

出題的部分則**完全根據歷屆劍橋雅思官方版（劍橋雅思 10-13 以及劍橋雅思官方指南）**，例如在 Which paragraph contains the following information 的出題中就參考了劍橋雅思 11 等的相關出題，加入提升讀者將「讀過的訊息讀進去」的練習和高階名詞的同義轉換，像是**劍橋雅思 11** 中的 Preface to How the other half thinks: *Adventures in Mathematical Reasoning* 中，第 32 題 a contrast between reading the book and reading **other kinds of publication**，其實很多時候考生並未將讀過的訊息讀進去，**other kinds of publication** 對應到…when reading **a novel or a newspaper**，**a novel or a newspaper** 即是 **other kinds of**

publication），所以某些段落讀了數次仍找不到答案，書中特別根據的這類的答題提供了更多的練習，提升考生一看到某些字就能聯想且更快的答題，例如在本書 Test 2 學歷的價值中，看到 an **establishment** that parents fancy，establishment 就要想到是institution，an **estimation** used by a **department**，department 就要想到可能是 HR 這個部門（考生可能看到文章出現過 HR，但看到題目卻對應不起來，而重複查找，其實這會浪費更多時間），而在 a **standardized examination** and its effectiveness，**standardized examination** 要想到是文章中的SAT。

本書還包含了近年來在考試中有出現過的題型，同篇文章中有**三種類型配對題**的設計，而且文章人物很多，如果是 A 文章出現配對題+摘要題，考生可能覺得還好，但是突然是 B 文章出現三個類型的配對題，在某些程度上很傷 mental resource，因為一直在找訊息，也會讓某些考生的答題痛苦指數上升。若配對題完成句子是你的弱項，多練習這類試題能迅速強化找尋訊息的速度。

在備考過程中，有些考生會覺得漫長，除了固定寫官方試題或有上課外，很重要的是**「心理素質」**。當有個人相信你能做到時，那種信念是很無形的，會漸漸強化一個人的學習動機，所以我想說的是 **I believe in you**！當你拿起這本書時，我相信你能做到。就像在《*An Attitude of Excellence*》中，作者在一個 convention 中受到一位攝影師的邀約，希望他能一起走到另一間大廳替他和一些講者拍張照，他答應了。途中，攝影師說到另兩位講者和他都是對於他事業有很大影響力的講者，以致他感到非常興奮。當他來到另一間大廳時，才驚覺要跟他合照的其他兩位都是大咖講者。要合照時，他向攝影師說到 "Those are the great ones. I don't belong in that picture"。一陣對談後，攝影師說道Yes, you do! I believe in you. Please get in the picture!"。照片拍攝後，攝影師又說道 "I'm so excited because I have a dream come true. I have a picture of three great motivators!."。最後這張照片甚至出現在畫廊、其他書籍和人們家中，標題著「**three great motivators**」。幾年過後，作者還被命名為 "One of the Five Top Speakers in the World"。So whatever you do, just don't give up too early⋯because I believe in you.

　　最後要說的是，因為這本書，我詢問了周遭很多的高材生、求學時期就考取雅思平均 8 分和獲取國外英語教學博士的友人們，許多人都覺得出題很新穎，對於三國演義等題材的入題感到新奇，對於

PREFACE 作者序

我寫完雅思閱讀書感到驚訝和讚許，也有表達距離雅思考試其實有點久遠或是沒什麼精力再跟雅思閱讀試題鬥智鬥力了。一直以來，都希望學習是有趣的、吸引讀者學習的（有些雅思閱讀文章蠻枯燥的，像我如果寫到像是 ancient Chinese chariots 等閱讀文章，就會覺得怎麼是這類的，然後出現寫題目模式，迅速答完，感覺自己超級像個答題機器人了），另一方面，也希望在寫試題之餘，有些文章能引發讀者思考。

很感謝我的兩位友人寫了推薦序：北京的友人思彤（求學時期很早就考取雅思平均 8 分的朋友）和在台灣求學時期就一直名列前茅，近期獲取美國愛荷華大學外語教學博士的 Christine Etzel。（真的很有北京學霸跟台灣高材生合力推薦的 fu）最後還要感謝倍斯特出版社給予本人出書機會，祝所有考生一次就考取理想的雅思成績。

韋爾 敬上

EDITOR

　　雅思閱讀因為文章的長度、題型多樣搭配，需在時限內完成 40 題題目，對大多數考生造成很大的壓力。有些考生在備考使用了「剪枝」技巧刪除某些字，卻在實際獲取分數仍然無法有顯著的進展。其實「剪枝」是有侷限性的，尤其是難度較高的如：GRE、雅思考試等。有些考生還是**讀不完**或是**讀了但是沒有「讀」進去，每句都看得懂、看得完，但是看不懂題目**，找到對應的段落。

　　而考生更需要加強的是：●**掌握剪枝與跳讀、語法、高階和較隱含的同義字轉換** ●**了解每篇的出題搭配和自己慣有的答題模式** ●**同步閱讀+答題該篇至少兩種試題**（一題題利用關鍵字回頭找太慢了……）。除了掌握速度，也需要綜合這些的技能，才能在拿到試題時立刻能一一拆解並答完題目，耐心等候接下來的寫作測驗。

　　本書在剪枝和跳讀的部分介紹了❶**刪除同位語**以及❷**利用關鍵字跳讀**，這特別在段落標題搭配的題型中大幅省下許多時間。語法強化納入了更多類似於劍橋雅思細節題的設計，協助更快的答題。

　　常常練習越能強化反應速度。《一次就考到雅思閱讀 7⁺》提供給考生許多實用且跨題型閱讀的綜合學習技能。跟著書中的解析學習

EDITOR 編者序

並搭配音檔輔助學習，多寫幾次後馬上就能理出合適自己的答題思路，一次獲取閱讀高分。

倍斯特編輯部 敬上

PREFACE 推薦序

　　雅思閱讀可能是雅思考試中最讓人腎上腺素飆高的部分，非英文母語考生要在時間壓力下閱讀理解長篇複雜文章，並精確作答，是對英文綜合能力和專注力的考驗。本書旨在提升雅思考生的閱讀應試力，即做到速讀的同時精確定位出題點細節並正確作答。本書包含大量有針對性的練習，題目的設計充滿趣味和巧思，拆解雅思出題者常用的套路和陷阱，希望讀者可以用輕鬆的方式達到雅思閱讀能力進階。

　　作者在書中總結出應對不同題目類型的策略，包含官方試題沒有的中譯和解析，且答案解析鉅細靡遺，以使中階至高階的雅思應考者受益。書中涵蓋了長難句分拆、同義轉換、剪枝與跳讀等應試策略，希望讀者通過對題目的練習和理解，提升英文綜合能力，並找到自己應對雅思閱讀的方法和自信。

　　作者韋爾曾出版過備受讀者青睞的應試新多益及新托福的著作，這次拆解雅思閱讀的難點，也融會了作者以往的創作經驗和一貫的對英文學習與研究的熱情。願您在閱讀的同時得到英文能力的提升。

北京 思彤

PREFACE 推薦序

　　與作者韋爾有著幾年的相識，我們認為英文學習應該充滿樂趣，即便過程中難免有所挫折與挑戰，也能從中獲得啟發，英文能力更加精進。此外，我也深切感受到他對英文學習書的熱忱與嚴謹態度。我發現他強大的英文實力來自於多重身份的轉換，既是英語學習者、英語檢定考試佼佼者、又是英語學習用書作者。更重要的是，他擁有一項秘密武器，那就是源源不絕的靈感。他在意的是，該怎樣做既能引發學習者的學習動機，又能達到學習效果。

　　秉著武俠小說中的俠客精神「路見不平拔刀相助」，韋爾已經出版多本英語考試用書，出奇招解救在英語學習過程中遇難的考生。此新作《一次就考取雅思閱讀7+》再次展現他的創意，將貂蟬的美人計、孔明草船借箭和三氣周瑜納入雅思考題，中西合併的另類練習，也只有「韋爾可以超越韋爾」。

　　近年來，外語教學理論與實務重心已從過去的 teacher-centered 轉向 student-centered 的教學方向，本書解析的方向與此不謀而和。韋爾從考生的角度切入去檢驗雅思考題，再透過詳盡的解析與題型安排，幫助考生找出自己弱項，一項項克服，一步步提升雅思英語考試水平。

或許，與其說是俠客，不如說韋爾像是 Spiderman。英文實力如他 "With great power comes great responsibility"，他不負眾望的再次出手寫了《一次就考取雅思閱讀7⁺》，抽絲剝繭幫考生理出雅思考題中的脈絡。這對考生來說實在是一大福音！有了《一次就考取雅思閱讀7⁺》之後，即便準備應試過程有時候會不小心陷入雅思考題的陷阱當中，書中練習必像一張安全網將你接住，讓你放心循著重點解析和引導，再次彈回，終能達到你想要的理想成績。Good luck!

克莉絲汀・愛佐 (Christine Etzel)
美國愛荷華大學外語教學博士
臺灣大學外文所碩士

INSTRUCTIONS

使用說明

* **第 4 題**，雖然文章中沒有比較所提到的三個物種所累積的有害化學物質濃度，可是在其他段落卻有相關訊息表明，❶往前看到上個段落，The pinnacle of the pyramid is the place where apex predators belong. What we can see from the pyramid is more than this. There is a 10% law that applies here. The 10% law is called **Lindeman's Law**. It represents the energy transfer of 10% through each layer, so there is bound to be an energy loss occurring. That is only 10% of the energy is stashed for each level. Apex predators, even though they at the summit of the pyramid, acquire the lowest level of energy. The energy transfer is not that economical. The longer the food chain, the less energy the apex predators acquire. ，由Lindeman's Law，可以了解到能量轉移，隨著食物鏈層級的增加，能量是逐層僅以 10%的量保留下來，所以不是節約的，越是位於食物鏈更高階層者，獲取的能量更少，頂端的頂級掠食者最少。

* **第 4 題**，也因為 **Lindeman's Law**，文章才會接續藉由比較手法寫出**生物累積 (bioaccumulation)** 的論點表示兩者間的差異和接續的文句，The concept that **contrasts** the 10% law is bioaccumulation. **While energy is lost from one layer to the next, harmful substances accumulate. Apex predators are found to amass the most detrimental chemicals.** The intake of several marine creatures, such **tunas**, dolphins, and **whales**, is quite deleterious. ，所以有害物質卻是**逐層累積**的，頂端的掠食者累積最多的有害化學物質。由這些訊息可以推

斷，tuna 位於比 whale 更低階的生物層級，所以 tuna 所累積的有害物質的量是低於 whale 的，但題目卻是說 tuna 所累積的有害物質的量比 whale 更多。，兩者間的訊息是互相矛盾的，所以**第 4 題**答案要選 **False**。

* 大概掃描一下選項，但是可以**先跳過摘要題出題過的段落**，**第 5 題** The **zenith** of the pyramid is，可以定位到 The **pinnacle** of the pyramid is the place where apex predators **belong**，同義轉換的部分要注意到 **zenith = pinnacle**，**belong = stay**，所以**第 5 題**的答案為 **E the location that apex predators stay**。

* **第 6 題**，The **greater number** of creatures is at the apex，可以定位到 The longer the food chain, the less energy the apex predators acquire. It is really detrimental if organisms at the top of the food chain **remain too many**.，同義轉換的部分要注意到 **greater number = remain too many**，所以**第 6 題**的答案為 **G the hinderance for a population is larger**。

* **第 7 題**，The **variety** of the ecosystem is related to，variety 腦海中有想到 diversity 會更好，定位到 It really depends on the diversity of the ecosystem. The more **diversified** an ecosystem, the more **complex** an ecosystem will be.還有 We can tell an ecosystem's **biodiversity** through looking at how **complex** a food web is. The less **intricate** food web is more

36　37

超強獨創三合一

【影子跟讀】和【中英對照】設計且閱讀文章均錄音

* 閱讀文章每篇均錄音，有效輔助仰賴耳朵聽來學習的考生。此外，考生更能同步運用音檔做影子跟讀練習，提升聽力專注力和口説能力。

* 聆聽音檔，藉由精選試題中各篇章的文句大幅強化考生 **Academic Writing** 的實力，一次就考取**寫作 7 分**以上的得分。

* 閱讀文章中英對照，便於基礎學習者藉由中譯輔助學習，自學就能達到理想成績。

究極語法強化，秒答各個題目
● 迅速破解**摘要題**和**選擇式配對題**
等，即使依據關鍵字定位到某句
話後，能須仰賴**語法**來協助答題
的題型，在更短時間內答完更具
精心設計的題目或陷阱題。

對題時，知道答案後，要再看答案選項欄的選項，並選出符合的答案，所以用 blaze 找，可以馬上找到 **D flame**，所以第 **1** 題答案為 **D**。

● 第 **2** 題，He makes a promise with Liu Bei（劉備），whereas Kong Ming remains **2._____**, **saying that Nanjun will be their territory soon**. 對應到 He makes a pact with Liu Bei（劉備）. If he cannot take down Cao Ren, Liu Bei is free to initiate an attack to Nanjun. Kong Ming **dispassionately** analyzes the situation to Liu Bei, **saying that Nanjun will be their territory soon,**，可以先消化訊息，然後理解孔明講話的部分，可以知道孔明面對劉備的急問，是很沉著冷靜的，可以看到 **dispassionately** 這個字，並馬上使用這個字去找，但是找之前，也可以在看一下空格的語法，空格前為 remains 所以後面要加形容詞，所以要找等於 dispassionately 這個字且是形容詞的字，馬上可以看到 **H placid**，第 **2** 題答案為 **H**。

● 第 **3** 題，Zhou Yu's scheme of **taking down a 3._____. important place like Yiling can give him an upper hand**, but Cao Ren（曹仁）possesses a secret weapon. 對應到 Zhou Yu（周瑜）comes up with other plans. That is, to **seize a geographically advantageous** place like Yiling. While taking down Yiling seems to give Zhou Yu an upper hand, Cao Ren（曹仁）possesses a secret weapon, his father's letter. 這題也可以消化一下再答，**plans** 對應到 **scheme**，

take down 對應到 **seize**，空格中的意思對應到 a **geographically advantageous**，空格中的詞性根據語法要選副詞，可以找到 **I strategically**，地理情勢有利的剛好對應具戰略性地重要地方，所以第 **3** 題答案為 **I**。

● 第 **4** 題，**Miscalculating** the situation makes Zhou Yu hooked, and gets harmed by an arrow that contains **4._____**. 對應到 Zhou Yu manages to steal Nanjun, without realizing both sides of Nanjun are armed with arrows, and in the city, there is a trap waiting for them. When Zhou Yu realizes that there is a trap, he is hit by **a poisonous arrow**. It is not until this point that Zhou Yu comes to the realization that he totally **underestimates** Cao Ren's ability，試題中以更濃縮的語句表達這個段落，**Miscalculating** 可以對應到 **underestimates**。試題還改寫成非直接表明重 X 箭，而是重了箭，箭裡含有 X，出題者很愛這樣改，所以理解後可以知道空格對應到的訊息是 a poisonous arrow，**a poisonous arrow = an arrow that.has/contains toxin/venom**，所以要選名詞，馬上可以找到 **J venom**，所以第 **4** 題答案為 **J**。

● 第 **5** 題，Then, Zhou Yu counterplots. **5._____ a deceased body** is the main reason that Cao Ren eventually loses.，以 **a deceased body** 找可以在次段找到，After some deliberation, Cao Ren thinks now is the perfect time to

英文試題

Questions 14-19
Look at the following statements (Questions 14-19) and the list of BOOKS below.

Match each statement with the correct people, A-G

Write the correct letter, A-G, in boxes 14-19 on your answer sheet.
NB You may use any letter more than once.

14 includes the idea that superficiality beguiles people's thinking
15 includes the idea that improvement can be made in something that is deemed meaningless
16 includes the idea about the importance of continued learning
17 includes the idea of a disposition that being phlegmatic helps in a situation
18 includes the idea of a psychological trait that is h... success
19 includes the idea that a vicious cycle is related... habits

List of BOOKS

A Rich Dad Poor Dad
B The Millionaire Next Door
C Millionaire Teacher
D The Richest Man in Babylon
E Millionaire Success Habits
F The Millionaire Fastlane
G Secrets of the Millionaire Mind

同篇章包含三種類型的配對題設計

● 熟悉此類型的答題，並多練習這類型的題目設計，強化不斷搜尋訊息的能力且不頭昏腦脹影響思考和判斷。

魔王題

● 題目設計中加入更隱晦的改寫表達，且出題與官方出題完全一致，強化考生高階同義表達和突破更高分雅思閱讀關卡的必備綜合技能。

Questions 20-23
Look at the following statements (Questions 20-23) and the list of people below.

Match each statement with the correct people, A-E

Write the correct letter, A-E, in boxes 20-23 on your answer sheet.
NB You may use any letter more than once.

20 has a job that provides material comfort
21 knows the importance of reading
22 is the one who will encounter financial constraint in a later life
23 are not having sufficient money in the time of need

List of people

A neighbors
B thirtysomethings
C Star
D Lucy
E Bill Gates

Questions 24-27
Complete each sentence with the correct ending, A-G below.
Write the correct letter, A-G, in boxes 24-27 on your answer sheet.

24 Exorbitant consumption is related to
25 Similar ideas are expressed in bestsellers that inform us
26 A notion put forward by a bestseller tells us that the rich realize
27 A perspicacious concept is used to warn a certain age group so that they can understand

A the importance of stockpiling currency
B the importance of success
C the importance of life-long learning
D the importance of finance
E the importance of earning more money
F the notion of "keep up with the Jones"
G the notion of frugality

解析

Step 1：迅速看題型配置，再定出解題步驟

這篇文章的題型有：❶選擇題、❷判斷題和❸摘要題。

選擇題的考法有時候蠻細節的，有時候好幾個選項改寫到很容易混淆，在劍橋雅思 10 到 13 中，**選擇題的考法**（不論該篇文章搭配選擇題還有其他那些題型）很一致，都會出現「**在文章的幾段時...**」，所以很好定位，也讓的讀蠻順暢的，所以遇到這樣子的選擇題建議可以順著文章讀就好了（**順讀**），不一定需要看題目再以關鍵字回去看文章。

Step 2：腦海中浮現答題策略，開始答題

這篇既然有❶選擇題、❷判斷題和❸摘要題，建議順著文章讀，讀文章前先掃描判斷題和摘要題的關鍵字，順著文章並解答**選擇題**時，還看是否有其他兩個題型問到的資訊，也可以同步答。

◆ **第 28 題**，可以根據題目訊息「**In the first paragraph**」，迅速定位到第一段，（根據出題點，這段文字幾乎不會被出題者使用在其他題型的分配上了，除了該篇文章的搭配還有 **which paragraph contains the following information**，所以看過這段文章後答完這題就差不多了，這篇文章的其他題目幾乎會均分在其餘段落。）

◆ **第 28 題**，題目是問 the writer refers to a saying from

famous author to show，選項 A Under normal circumstances, people have to work to support themselves，文章中確實有出現 people have to work to support themselves，但是沒有回答到作者提到那句俗諺的原因，所以可以刪除。選項 B，Work can be meaningful to someone，雖然段落後也有提到 a job that is so meaningful to his or her life，這選項也不太適合當答案，算是干擾選項，可以刪除。

◆ **第 28 題**，選項 C，work is more important than eating or making love，其實重點不是哪個比較重要，但藉由描述可以表達出工作是比起兩者，能長時間從事的一個行為，而這標值得我們思考，主要還是 you certainly can do the work for consecutive eight hours or longer. Work is so important to us in that it occupies a significant portion of time daily，這段英文其實與**選項 D** the peculiarity of work since it is something that people can successively do for long hours 吻合，所以答案**選項 D** 是最合適的答案。

◆ **第 29 題**，可以根據題目訊息「**In the second paragraph**」，迅速定位到第二段，題目詢問 bestsellers are used to demonstrate，所以可以先思考下，作者為什麼在這個段落中提

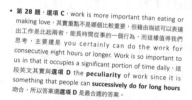

【時間統籌】強化，時間永遠站在你這邊

- 了解各篇章的題目搭配，並根據這些搭配構思出各答題策略，有效協助基礎學習者掌握是否該**順讀**或依據關鍵字**定位**回文章找相關訊息，把消失的時間全找回來，時限內答完所有試題。

- 此外，還包含同步答同篇文章中**兩種**類型或一次攻略**三種**類型題目的設計。

mind of people who read about him. · consolidate 對應到試題的 condolidation，然後兩個套色標示的 arrows 和 wind，其實是借東風和草船借箭，風和箭這兩樣顯示出孔明的智慧，所以第 9 題為 arrows 和 wind。

- 再來看第 10 題，Stratagems are used consecutively. The first one is employed by Zhou Yu 看到這兩句其實對應到 B 段落，蔣幹重了周瑜的計謀，緊接著 Upon viewing the letter, Cao Cao acts merely on impulse, making a regrettable decision. He beheads both Cai Mao（蔡瑁）and Zhang Yun（張允），two major commanders of marine warfare，這兩句對應到第 10 題，其中 acts merely on impulse = sudden thought，beheads...two major commanders = makes him lose two...，所以第 10 題答案為 commanders。

- 再來看第 11 題，Zhou Yu is so pleased to learn the news that two major threats are long gone, but he later realizes the real menace is Kong Ming because Kong Ming is too smart. 對應到題目的 While some stratagems will pose no more harm to Zhou Yu's army, a closer look can reveal that the actual.... · more... · harm = major threats are long gone，

【跳讀】和【關鍵字】定位
- 解析中均附【跳讀】和【關鍵字】定位的設計，比起剪枝閱讀的技巧，節省更多時間，迅速答完各題。

- 緊接著是第 12 題，請運用【跳讀】和【關鍵字定位】，用試題的 only ten days 定位到 C 段落 He sets a deadline, which is only ten days, and under the military law.，對應到 there is a _____，其實是出題者將兩個訊息拆開敘述，思考一下就可以推測出緊接著是要說 10 天期限後，是有 deadline 的，所以第 12 題答案為 deadline。

- 再來是最後一題，答題時間有限請運用【跳讀】和【關鍵字定位】，先用 twenty boats 定位到 Now twenty boats are linked together by a long rope, sailing to the North coast.和 About 3 a.m to 5 a.m twenty boats are approaching the North coast, very close to where Cao Cao's navy force reside.

- 然後迅速接續讀文章，Around ten thousand crossbowmen are responding to the surprise attack, firing as many arrows as others can imagine. Within a few minutes, Kong Ming's boats are peppered with arrows.，試題中 Kong Ming's boats 對應文章，然後 peppered with arrows 為 have gathered enough arrows，答案就在這附近，緊接著看到 discharged by Cao's 13._____，代表由箭所發射出的，discharged by = firing，而執行這個動作的一定是人，所以別誤選其他名詞像是 arrows，所以可以推斷是由 crossbowmen 所執行這個動作的，故題答案為 crossbowmen。

251

- 額外補充的部分是，其實遇到像是引導副詞子句的連接詞像是 if, when, since, unless 等等，可以直接跳讀主要子句（但如果是過於細節性的部分還是建議選擇不要跳讀），其實只看主要子句會快非常多，主要子句描述的一定是重要的訊息，【副詞子句連接詞+S+V....、S+V...】，直接跳讀後面套色部分，可以大幅刪減掉許多訊息，尤其某些文體時可以讀得更快。

- 在這篇文章中還出現蠻多副詞子句連接詞的，❶ 像 A 段落的 As the fiction progresses, several successful predictions and great feats of major events...，其實 As the fiction progresses 可以直接刪除不看也沒有影響句子意思，只是陳述到隨著小說進展。
❷ Upon viewing the letter, Cao Cao acts merely on impulse, making a regrettable decision. 也可以刪除或略不看【介係詞引導的子句】，即前面的 Upon viewing the letter，主要訊息還是在 Cao Cao acts merely on impulse, making a regrettable decision.
❸ He beheads both Cai Mao（蔡瑁）and Zhang Yun（張允），two major commanders of marine warfare，其實也可以刪除【同位語補充說明】的部分，例如 two major commanders of marine warfare，知道這兩個人物夠了，不是可抱著題的挖空有出到關鍵字，其實定位後即使跳讀後還是能找到。

- ❹ If Kong Ming is not able to gather one hundred thousand arrows, he will have to face the execution. ❺ When Kong

252

Ming so _____ _____ _____ _____ thing. ❻ _____ _____ _____ _____ order the entire army to remain impervious to the situation. ❼ Within a few minutes, Kong Ming's boats are peppered with arrows.

- ❽ As the sun is about to rise and the fog is about to be cleared up, Kong Ming orders all twenty boats sail back to the South shore. ❾ As the boat sails south, all soldiers on the boats roar "thanks the prime minister for the arrows". ❿ When Cao Cao realizes it is Kong Ming's stratagem, they have already sailed around twenty miles away from the North coast.等等的。
其實要注意一個大重點，剪枝技巧其實沒有掌握高階同義轉換和時間統籌來得重要，當訊息都剪完後，或也都看懂每句話其實雅思閱讀 7 分以下的考生，所面臨的還是對應不到同義轉換的部分，而沒辦法選出答案或找到答案，可以多掌握書中或官方試題中所有同義轉換對應到的部分。

除了這些之外，還有一些在學術文章中常見的句型，其實也可以只看快速看看主要敘述句例如：❶-❺ 的句型

- ❶ Like/Unlike
❶ 的句型的話，【Like/Unlike+S+V...、S+V...】刪除前面的部分，直接看主要子句的部分即可，重要訊息其實在主要子句。

閱讀【剪枝】技巧
- 收錄主要的閱讀剪枝介紹，優化閱讀速度，閱讀更重要的部份。

253

- Chameleons should really watch out the sting to their body parts or most importantly their eyes; **otherwise 【第 35 題摘要題】**, they might have to pay a heavy price for underestimating the black thick-tailed scorpions that are probably one-thirds of their body.

- Chameleons in the desert are not quite as flexible as chameleons in another ecosystem. In the forest, **for example 【第 28 題段落題題】**, we are amazed by how chameleons catch insects, such as mantises, grasshoppers, and smaller insects, and we are able to witness chameleons swiftly escaping larger predators, **such as 【第 36 題摘要題】** ravens, and their tongues.

- It is **not so much as** a wonderful design of the natural world as the brutality of the natural world. **Although 【第 39 和 40 題摘要題】** the rattlesnake is packaged with powerful venom, the king snake is gifted with complex protein that protects itself from getting harmed by the rattlesnake.

- **In addition to 【第 31 題段落題題】** the lurking danger that endangers creatures in the desert, heat in the desert can cause quite a damage in an instant.

- **In addition**, they are also skillful at conserving water in the body. Exhalation of air will not cause any loss of water from camels' body **because 【第 39 題摘要題】** camels' nostrils help them preserve it.

- **Also 【第 40 題摘要題】**, they have an exceptionally powerful kidneys that help them regulate the use of water.

- **Because of** camel's physiological adaptability, the role of camels has changed over the year. They **are used for 【第33 題段落題題】** multiple purposes that elevate their values to local residents and the government.

1
2
3
4 Reading Passage 3

掌握【承轉詞】和【對等連接詞】

- 【承轉詞】和【對等連接詞】的出現就代表了考點的出現，文章訊息中語氣轉折等是作者寫作的目的，或要凸顯文句差異或襯托出某些特點，而通常出題者也會根據這些訊息點出題，掌握這些關鍵詞幾乎就能找到對應的答案，雅思閱讀獲取高分的考生也都很能掌握這些詞。

目次 CONTENTS

Test 2

Reading ❶

歷史人物文章：三國演義之三氣周瑜

- 摘要配對題：定位後，正確選項要符合空格的語法（兩道程序）
- 摘要題：高階同義字轉換 ❶

Reading ❷

商業類文章：學校沒教你的事，18 歲前就該懂得金錢的知識

- 強化連答三類型配對題、關鍵字搜尋
- 強化答選項中抽象概念和高階名詞的魔王題

Reading ❸

社會議論文：學歷的價值

- 配對細節題：高階同義字轉換 ❷
- 刪除專有名詞和人物等同位語的敘述和跳讀

Test 3

Reading ❶
歷史人物文章：三國演義之貂蟬美人計

Reading ❷
教育類文章：數位世代父母教育小孩的挑戰

Reading ❸
商業類文章：工作滿意度和工作價值

Test 4

Reading ❶

歷史人物文章：三國演義之孔明的智慧「草船借箭」

- ◆ 摘要題：跨較長段落，需掌握跳讀和關鍵字定位
- ◆ 高階同義字轉換 ❹

Reading ❷

心理學個案探討：關於愛情

- ◆ 摘要題：詞性轉換、改寫、亂序出題和-ed/-ing 結尾互換

Reading ❸

生物學探討：沙漠中生物的生存

- ◆ 段落標題題：掌握同義轉換、區分中心主旨和 supporting details、利用關鍵字跳讀
- ◆ 摘要題：高階同義字轉換 ❺

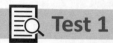

READING PASSAGE 1

You should spend about 20 minutes on **Questions 1-13**, which are based on Reading Passage 1 below.

Biological Concepts:
Food Chain, Food Web, and Bioaccumulation

A. "The mantis stalks the cicada, unaware of the oriole behind." is a saying familiar to any one of us. It is an endless killing game for all species to sustain their lives. Relationships among species are linked and the victory is often transient. In fact, there are multiple relationships worth exploring. The relationships whether it is linear or non-linear make up this ecosystem.

B. On the forest floor, a tarantula soundlessly awaits in its lair, waiting for a meal. The meal ranges from small insects to small snakes. When the tarantula senses there is a trace of the prey, it initiates an attack. At other times, it could be a case that goes like a tarantula anticipates the prey which walks into its burrow and within striking distance, it kills the prey. The injection of venomous fangs can kill prey in an instant. Or the scenario can be more than anyone of us to imagine. A giant centipede crawls towards the lair of the tarantula, right after the tarantula makes a kill. The giant centipede can easily take down prey, such as tarantulas.

C. At other times, you get to witness the fight between a scorpion and a giant centipede. After a few struggles, a scorpion meets its doom and the giant centipede feeds on its flesh. However, giant centipedes cannot always be the ones which eat others. They can sometimes meet their natural enemy on their way to find foods. Bullfrogs are considered one of the centipede's predators. Centipedes can hardly escape when they are in bullfrogs' mouths. Bullfrogs can also encounter their predators, such monkeys, raccoons, and larger birds. They have zero chance of winning.

D. The life in every ecosystem is so intricate that the above-mentioned species are only a part of it. We can easily see a linear line through several prey-predator relationships. The linear line forms a very simple food chain, which consists of producers, consumers, and decomposers. Producers are often ignored, but they are indeed quite indispensable. Consumers are more widely known, since they are the species, we are quite familiar with, such as lions and other carnivores. Consumers are mostly animals. Vegetarian animals are considered the first consumers which feed on producers, such as plants. Small carnivores are classified as secondary consumers and third consumers. Larger carnivores are the fourth consumers and the fifth consumers. There could be six or more advanced consumers. It really depends on the diversity of the ecosystem. The more diversified an ecosystem, the more complex an ecosystem will be. At the very end of the food chain, the last consumers are called apex predators. They have no competitors in the ecosystem. Natural death or natural disasters can be the direct cause of their death.

E. In fact, different animals can feed on the same or similar species, so the complexity of the food chain is actually intertwined. The relations of the complicated networks form a food web. We can tell an ecosystem's biodiversity through looking at how complex a food web is. The less intricate food web is more fragile than the one which has multiple networks.

F. The food chain or the food web can be realized in the pyramid form. The lowest layer at the bottom is producers. The second and the third are the first consumers and the second consumers. The pinnacle of the pyramid is the place where apex predators belong. What we can see from the pyramid is more than this. There is a 10% law that applies here. The 10% law is called Lindeman's Law. It represents the energy transfer of 10% through each layer, so there is bound to be an energy loss occurring. That is only 10% of the energy is stashed for each level. Apex

Test 1

TEST 1
Reading Passage 1

TEST 2

TEST 3

TEST 4

predators, even though they are at the summit of the pyramid, acquire the lowest level of energy. The energy transfer is not that economical. The longer the food chain, the less energy the apex predators acquire. It is really detrimental if organisms at the top of the food chain remain too many.

G. The concept that contrasts the 10% law is bioaccumulation. While energy is lost from one layer to the next, harmful substances accumulate. Apex predators are found to amass the most detrimental chemicals. The intake of several marine creatures, such as tunas, dolphins, and whales, is quite deleterious. High concentration of mercury, cadmium, and lead can sometimes be found in these marine creatures. These harmful chemicals cannot be metabolized. The next time you are seeing certain foods on the dinner plate, you probably need to take a moment to think or have a second thought, not drastically put those in your mouth.

H. The notion of a food chain can be used in so many different ways, quite practical in our daily lives, so I guess that's all for today's lecture.

Questions 1-4

Do the following statements agree with the information given in the Reading Passage ?

In boxes 1-4 on your answer sheet, write

TRUE- if the statement agrees with the information
FALSE- if the statement contradicts the information
NOT GIVEN- if there is no information on this

1. It can be deduced that the mantis is the predator of cicada.

2. The complexity of the food web is related to an ecosystem's stability.

3. According to Lindeman's Law, secondary consumers acquire less energy than apex predators.

4. The intake of tunas accumulates greater harmful substances than that of whales.

Test 1

Reading Passage 1

TEST 1
TEST 2
TEST 3
TEST 4

Questions 5-9

Complete each sentence with the correct ending, A-G below.

Write the correct letter, A-G, in boxes 5-9 on your answer sheet.

5 The zenith of the pyramid is

6 The greater number of creatures is at the apex

7 The variety of the ecosystem is related to

8 The amount of harmful substances in marine creatures is related to

9 Apex predators are bound to get less energy if

A the stability of the ecosystem

B the intricacy of the ecosystem

C the food chain is lengthier

D the rank in the food chain

E the location that apex predators stay

F the amount of the energy loss

G the hinderance for a population is larger

Questions 10-13

Complete the summary below
Choose ONE WORD ONLY from the passage for each other
Write your answers in boxes 10-13 on your answer sheet.

The Concept of Food Chain and Food Web

In an ecosystem, the victory is often fleeting. A tarantula which swiftly initiates an attack by inserting its **10.**_____ _____ fang can instantly be killed by its predator, such as a giant centipede. The giant centipede can be murdered by its predators, such as Bullfrogs, and Bullfrogs can be killed by their predators, **11.**_____, which are known for washing their food before eating.

The food chain is linear, made up of three major components, such as producers, consumers, and **12.**_____. Small and lager carnivores occupy mostly the category from secondary to the fifth consumers. There could be six or more advanced consumers. Since advanced consumers are at the summit of the food chain, they live their life without **13.**_____ _____.

試題中譯

問題 1 到 4

以下敘述是否和閱讀篇章的資訊相同？
在 **1-4** 的答案欄中寫下：

TRUE – 如果敘述與資訊一致
FALSE – 如果敘述與資訊不一致
NOT GIVEN - 如果閱讀篇章中並未提及此敘述

1.能夠推斷出螳螂是蟬的掠食者。

2.食物網的複雜度與生態系統的穩定性有關。

3.根據林德曼定律，次級消費者獲取比頂級消費者少的能量。

4.攝取鮪魚所累積的有害物質比攝取鯨魚所累積的有害物質多。

問題 5 到 9

請將 5-9 與 A-G 做正確的配對

在你的答案紙，5-9 的答案欄中，寫上正確的字母 A-G

5 金字塔頂端是

6 越多數量的生物在頂端時

7 與不同類型的生態系統有關的是

8 與海洋生物所含的有害物質的量

9 頂端掠食者必定會獲取較少的能量，如果

A 生態系統的穩定性

B 生態系統的複雜度

C 食物鏈越冗長的話

D 在食物鏈的位階

E 頂端掠食者所待的位置

F 能量損失的量

G 對族群的阻礙較大

Test 1

TEST
1 Reading Passage 1

TEST
2

TEST
3

TEST
4

問題 10 到 13

完成下列摘要題

段落中的每個答案，請勿超過一個單字

在你的答案紙，10-13 答案欄中，寫上你的答案

食物鏈和食物網的概念

在生態系統中，勝利通常是短暫的。狼珠可以迅速地發動攻擊，注射牠的 10.＿＿＿＿＿＿＿ 牙，也能即刻被牠的掠食者，例如巨型蜈蚣給殺死。巨型蜈蚣也能被牠的掠食者，例如牛蛙謀殺，而牛蛙也能被以吃食物前會洗東西的習慣而聞名的掠食者 11.＿＿＿＿＿＿＿ 殺死。

食物鏈是線性的，由三個主要的物種所組成，生產者、消費者和 12.＿＿＿＿＿＿＿。小型和較大型的肉食性動物佔據了大多數的範疇，通常由次級到第五級消費者組成。也可能有第六級消費者或更高階的消費者。既然頂級消費者位於食物鏈的頂端，牠們的生活中沒有 13.＿＿＿＿＿＿＿.

Step 1：迅速看題型配置，再定出解題步驟

　　這篇文章的題型有：❶判斷題❷配對_完成句子和❸摘要題。

　　別小看**這三個題型**的搭配，其實這樣的搭配，有時候判斷題和完成句子題很分散，不好搜尋到答案，建議邊讀邊寫判斷題和摘要題，有一定了解後，答完成句子題會很快速。

Step 2：腦海中浮現答題策略，開始答題

　　這篇既然有❶判斷題❷配對_完成句子和❸摘要題，先邊閱讀邊寫判斷題和摘要題。

◆ **第 1 題**，It can be deduced that the mantis is the predator of cicada.很幸運地定位到首段第一句"The mantis stalks the cicada, unaware of the oriole behind."，可以知道是螳螂捕蟬，推斷出螳螂是掠食者捕食蟬，所以**第 1 題**的答案為 **True**。

◆ **第 10 題**，接著看到第二段，看到 tarantula，所以可以跳到摘要題，In an ecosystem, the victory is often fleeting. A tarantula which swiftly initiates an attack by **inserting** its 10.＿＿＿＿＿＿ **fang** can instantly be killed by its predator, such as a giant centipede.，試題對應到 When the tarantula senses there is a trace of the prey, it initiates an attack. At other times, it could be a case that goes like a tarantula anticipates the prey which walks into its burrow and within striking distance, it kills the prey. The **injection** of **venomous fangs** can kill prey in an instant.，試題以更濃縮的文句表達，但不難定位，注意 **inserting = injection**，和 fang 的位置，所以**第 10 題**的答案為 **venomous**。

◆ 看到**第 11 題**，The giant centipede can be murdered by its predators, such as Bullfrogs, and **Bullfrogs** can be killed by their predators, 11._____, **which are known for washing their food before eating.**，接續讀到次段中間 Bullfrogs are considered one of the centipede's predators. Centipedes can hardly escape when they are in bullfrogs' mouths. **Bullfrogs** can also encounter their predators, such **monkeys, raccoons, and larger birds**.，要注意提到牛蛙的部分有列舉出**三個**天敵，但是題目**只有一個空格**，還有題目後方多了形容詞子句描述該天敵的特徵（利用語法中，形容詞子句中的補述協助判斷答案），所以從三個中選擇符合該子句描述的即可，所以**第 11 題**的答案為 **raccoons**。

◆ 接著看到第 **12 題**，The food chain is linear, made up of three major components, such as producers, consumers, and 12._____.並於次段找到對應的項目 The linear line forms a very simple food chain, which consists of producers, consumers, and **decomposers**.，答案很明顯對應到，所以**第 12 題**的答案為 **decomposers**。

- 接著**第 13 題**，Small and lager carnivores occupy mostly the category from secondary to the fifth consumers. There could be six or more **advanced consumers**. Since advanced consumers are at the summit of the food chain, they live their life **without** 13._____.，用 **advanced consumers** 定位，定位到 At the very end of the food chain, the last consumers are called **apex predators**. They **have no competitors** in the ecosystem. Natural death or natural disasters can be the direct cause of their death.，同義轉換的部分要注意到 **advanced consumers = apex predators**，**have no = without**，所以**第 13 題**的答案為 **competitors**。這樣摘要題全答完了。

- 接著繼續讀次個段落，看有沒有跟判斷題相對應的敘述，然後看到 The less intricate **food web** is more fragile than the one which has multiple networks.剛好對應到**第 2 題** The complexity of the food web is related to an ecosystem's stability.，如果沒這麼快看出可以多思考下，因為用 **stability** 去定位可能找很久都找不到，但是文章敘述中有比較食物網的複雜度，越不複雜的食物網較脆弱，所以食物網的複雜度其實影響到生態系統的穩定性喔！，所以**第 2 題**的答案為 **True**。

- 接著看判斷題**第 3 題**，According to Lindeman's Law, secondary consumers acquire less energy than apex predators，以 **Lindeman's Law** 定位到 The 10% law is called

Lindeman's Law. It represents the energy transfer of 10% through each layer, so there is bound to be **an energy loss occurring**. That is only 10% of the energy is stashed for each level. Apex predators, even though they are at the summit of the pyramid, acquire the lowest level of energy. The energy transfer is not that economical. **The longer the food chain, the less energy the apex predators acquire.**得知在每個層級均有能量的流失且越上層者獲取的能量越少,所以反向思考後可以推斷出第二級的消費者獲取的能量**多於**頂級掠食者,但試題卻描述成第二級的消費者獲取的能量**少於**頂級掠食者,試題和原段落的描述相矛盾,所以**第 3 題**的答案為 **False**。

◆ **第 4 題**,The **intake** of **tunas** accumulates greater **harmful substances** than that of **whales**.運用關鍵字(粗體字 intake, tunas, harmful, substances, and whales)定位到 The intake of several marine creatures, such as **tunas, dolphins, and whales,** is quite deleterious. High concentration of mercury, cadmium, and lead can sometimes be found in these marine creatures.,文章中列舉了三種海洋生物都有高濃度的有害物質,也提到攝取,但**沒有比較攝取哪類的海洋生物會累積較多的有害物質,(多寫試題後就會發現,這在雅思閱讀中很常見,比較兩個文章中提過但未比較的對象,如果是這樣的話答案就是 Not Given)**但這題跟某些較難的判斷題一樣在其他段落中有其他訊息,所以還要仔細看完才判斷。

◆ **第 4 題**，雖然文章中沒有比較所提到的三個物種所累積的有害化學物質濃度，可是在其他段落卻有相關訊息表明，❶往前看到上個段落，The pinnacle of the pyramid is the place where apex predators belong. What we can see from the pyramid is more than this. There is a 10% law that applies here. The 10% law is called **Lindeman's Law**. It represents the energy transfer of 10% through each layer, so there is bound to be an energy loss occurring. That is only 10% of the energy is stashed for each level. Apex predators, even though they at the summit of the pyramid, acquire the lowest level of energy. The energy transfer is not that economical. The longer the food chain, the less energy the apex predators acquire.，由 Lindeman's Law，可以了解到能量轉移，隨著食物鏈層級的增加，能量是逐層僅以 10%的量保留下來，所以不是節約的，越是位於食物鏈更高階層者，獲取的能量更少，頂端的頂級掠食者最少。

◆ **第 4 題**，也因為 **Lindeman's Law**，文章才會接續藉由**比較手法**寫出**生物累積 (bioaccumulation)** 的論點表示兩者間的差異和接續的文句，The concept that **contrasts** the 10% law is bioaccumulation. **While energy is lost from one layer to the next, harmful substances accumulate. Apex predators are found to amass the most detrimental chemicals.** The intake of several marine creatures, such **tunas**, dolphins, and **whales**, is quite deleterious.，所以有害物質卻是**逐層累積**的，頂端的掠食者累積最多的有害化學物質。由這些訊息可以推

斷，tuna 位於比 whale 更低階的生物層級，所以 tuna 所累積的有害物質的量是**低於** whale 的，但**題目**卻是說 tuna 所累積的有害物質的量比 whale **更多**。，兩者間的訊息是互相矛盾的，所以**第 4 題**答案要選 **False**。

◆ 大概掃描一下選項，但是可以**先跳過摘要題出題過的段落，第 5 題** The **zenith** of the pyramid is，可以定位到 The **pinnacle** of the pyramid is the place where apex predators **belong**，同義轉換的部分要注意到 **zenith = pinnacle**，**belong = stay**，所以**第 5 題**的答案為 **E the location that apex predators stay**。

◆ **第 6 題**，The **greater number** of creatures is at the apex，可以定位到 The longer the food chain, the less energy the apex predators acquire. It is really detrimental if organisms at the top of the food chain **remain too many**.，同義轉換的部分要注意到 **greater number = remain too many**，所以**第 6 題**的答案為 **G the hinderance for a population is larger**。

◆ **第 7 題**，The **variety** of the ecosystem is related to，variety 腦海中有想到 diversity 會更好，定位到 It really depends on the diversity of the ecosystem. The more **diversified** an ecosystem, the more **complex** an ecosystem will be.還有 We can tell an ecosystem's **biodiversity** through looking at how **complex** a food web is. The less **intricate** food web is more fragile than the one which has multiple networks. ，所以**第 7 題**的答案為 **B the intricacy of the ecosystem**。

◆ **第 8 題**，The amount of harmful substances in marine creatures is related to，很明顯可以定位到倒數第 2 段，While energy is lost from one layer to the next, harmful substances accumulate. Apex predators are found to amass the most detrimental chemicals.，很清楚表明了 rank 的影響，食物鏈越往下層累積的更多，所以**第 8 題**的答案為 **D the rank in the food chain**。

◆ **第 9 題**，Apex predators are bound to get **less energy** if，對應到 The energy transfer is not that economical. The **longer** the food chain, the less energy the apex predators acquire.，所以食物鏈越冗長，所獲得的能量越少，所以**第 9 題**的答案為 **C the food chain is lengthier**。結束這篇，盡快讀下一篇。

中譯和影子跟讀　　　　　　　　　　　MP3 001

A. "The mantis stalks the cicada, unaware of the oriole behind." is a saying familiar to any one of us. It is an endless killing game for all species to sustain their lives. Relationships among species are linked and the victory is often transient. In fact, there are multiple relationships worth exploring. The relationships whether it is linear or non-linear make up this ecosystem.

「螳螂捕蟬，黃雀在後」是句對我們來説再熟悉不過的俗諺。無止盡的掠殺對於所有物種而言是在於延續他們的生命。物種的關係是連結在一起的，而勝利通常是短暫的。事實上，有著多樣的關係值得探討。不論是線性或非線性關係均構成了這個生態系統。

B. On the forest floor, a tarantula soundlessly awaits in its lair, waiting for a meal. The meal ranges from small insects to small snakes. When the tarantula senses there is a trace of the prey, it initiates an attack. At other times, it could be a case that goes like a tarantula anticipates the prey which walks into its burrow and within striking distance, it kills the prey. The injection of venomous fangs can kill prey in an instant. Or the scenario can be more than anyone of us to imagine. A giant centipede crawls towards the lair of the tarantula, right after the tarantula makes a kill. The giant centipede can easily take down prey, such as tarantulas.

在樹林地面，狼蛛靜待於自己的巢穴內，等待著餐點上門。餐點的範圍從小型昆蟲到小型蛇類。當狼蛛感受到有獵物的蹤跡時，牠便發動攻擊。在其他時候例子可能會是以這個方式發展，狼蛛期待獵物走進巢穴，在攻擊範圍內，牠殺死獵物。注射的毒牙能即刻殺死獵物。或者是情節的發展超過我們任何一人所能設想的。在狼珠獵殺成功後，巨型蜈蚣爬向狼珠的巢穴。巨型蜈蚣便能輕易拿下像是狼珠這般的獵物。

C. At other times, you get to witness the fight between a scorpion and a giant centipede. After a few struggles, a scorpion meets its doom and the giant centipede feeds on its flesh. However, giant centipedes cannot always be the ones which eat others. They can sometimes meet their natural enemy on their way to find foods. Bullfrogs are considered one of the centipede's predators. Centipedes can hardly escape when they are in bullfrogs' mouths. Bullfrogs can also encounter their predators, such monkeys, raccoons, and larger birds. They have zero chance of winning.

在其他時候，你能目睹到毒蠍和巨型蜈蚣的戰鬥。幾番掙扎後，毒蠍死亡，蜈蚣以其血肉為食物。然而，巨型蜈蚣不可能總是捕食其他生物者。牠們有時候可能在找尋食物的途中遇到牠們的天敵。牛蛙被視為是蜈蚣的天敵。當牠們在牛蛙口中時，蜈蚣幾乎無法逃脫。牛蛙也可能會遇到牠們的天敵，像是猴子、浣熊和較大型的鳥類。牠們戰勝的機會幾乎是零。

D. The life in every ecosystem is so intricate that the above-mentioned species are only a part of it. We can easily see a linear line through several prey-predator relationships. The linear line forms a very simple food chain, which consists of producers, consumers, and decomposers. Producers are often ignored, but they are indeed quite indispensable. Consumers are more widely known, since they are the species, we are quite familiar with, such as lions and other carnivores. Consumers are mostly animals. Vegetarian animals are considered the first consumers which feed on producers, such as plants. Small carnivores are classified as secondary consumers and third consumers. Larger carnivores are the fourth consumers and the fifth consumers. There could be six or more advanced consumers. It really depends on the diversity of the ecosystem. The more diversified an ecosystem, the more complex an ecosystem will be. At the very end of the food chain, the last consumers are called apex predators. They have no competitors in the ecosystem. Natural death or natural disasters can be the direct cause of their death.

每個生態系統中的生命是如此複雜，以至於上述的物種都僅是部分而已。我們能輕易地透過幾個獵物和掠食者關係中看到線性關係。線性關係形成了非常簡單的食物鏈，通常由生產者、消費者和分解者所組成。生產者通常被忽略，但是牠們卻是不可或缺的。消費者更廣為人知，因為牠們是我們相當熟悉的生物，像是獅子和其他肉食性動物。消費者大多是動物。素食動物被視為是初級消費者，因為牠們依靠生產維生，例如植物。小型肉食性動物被歸類在第二級消費者和第三級消費者的範疇。較大型的肉食性動物是第四級消費者和第五級消費者。還可能有第六級或更高階的消費者。這真的要視生態系統中的多樣性而定。一個生態系統越具多樣性，生態系統就會更為複雜。在食物鏈終端，最後一級的消費者被稱為頂端掠食者。牠們在生態系統中沒有競爭者。自然死亡或天然災害可能會是牠們直接死亡的原因。

E. In fact, different animals can feed on the same or similar species, so the complexity of the food chain is actually intertwined. The relations of the complicated networks form a food web. We can tell an ecosystem's biodiversity through looking at how complex a food web is. The less intricate food web is more fragile than the one which has multiple networks.

事實上，不同的動物可能以相同或相似的物種為食，所以一個食物鏈的複雜性確實是緊密相連的。這個複雜的網路關係構成了食物網。我們可以透過觀看食物網複雜度，看出一個生態系統的多樣性。較不複雜的食物網比具備複雜網路關係的食物網更為脆弱。

F. The food chain or the food web can be realized in the pyramid form. The lowest layer at the bottom is producers. The second and the third are the first consumers and the second consumers. The pinnacle of the pyramid is the place where apex predators belong. What we can see from the pyramid is more than this. There is a 10% law that applies here. The 10% law is called Lindeman's Law. It represents the energy transfer of 10% through each layer, so there is bound to be an energy loss occurring. That is only 10% of the energy is stashed for each level. Apex predators, even though they are at the summit of the pyramid, acquire the lowest level of energy. The energy transfer is not that economical. The longer the food chain, the less energy the apex predators acquire. It is really detrimental if organisms at the top of the food chain remain too many.

食物鏈或是食物網也能以金字塔的形式現出。底端最低階層的是生產者。第二和第三層為初階消費者和第二級消費者。金字塔頂端是頂級掠食者所屬的範疇。我們能從金字塔看到的不僅於此。10%定律也適用於此。10%定律稱作林德曼定律。它代表了能量於每個階層以 10%轉移，所以必定會有能量損失的情況發生。在每個階層中，能量僅儲存 10%。頂端掠食者，即使他們在金字塔頂端他們所獲得的能量卻最低。能量轉移不是那麼節約。食物鏈越長，頂級掠食者所能獲得的能量較少。位於食物鏈頂端的有機物保存的數量太多，會是相當具危害性的。

G. The concept that contrasts the 10% law is bioaccumulation. While energy is lost from one layer to the next, harmful substances accumulate. Apex predators are found to amass the most detrimental chemicals. The intake of several marine creatures, such as tunas, dolphins, and whales, is quite deleterious. High concentration of mercury, cadmium, and lead can sometimes be found in these marine creatures. These harmful chemicals cannot be metabolized. The next time you are seeing certain foods on the dinner plate, you probably need to take a moment to think or have a second thought, not drastically put those in your mouth.

10%定律這個觀念與生物累積的觀念是對比的。雖然能量從這個階層到下個階層流失了，有害物質卻是累積的。從頂端掠食者中可以發現累積有害物質的量是最多的。幾個海洋生物的攝取，例如鮪魚、海豚和鯨魚，是相當有害的。高濃度的水銀、鎘和鉛有時候能於這些海洋生物中發掘出來。這些有害化學物質無法被代謝出。下一次當你看到餐桌上特定的食物時，你可能需要片刻思考下或再考慮一下，別太快將那些海洋生物放入你的口中。

H. The notion of a food chain can be used in so many different ways, quite practical in our daily lives, so I guess that's all for today's lecture.

食物鏈的概念能以許多不同的方式運用在其中，對我們的生活相當實用，所以我想今天的課堂就到這邊。

READING PASSAGE 2

You should spend about 20 minutes on **Questions 14-27**, which are based on Reading Passage 2 below.

Job Interviews and Job-seeking Case Studies

A. Preparing for interviews is a very big thing for many college graduates. In the era of underachievement, securing an interview is arduous and daunting. It is more than just having a great resume and preparing typical 100 must-read interview questions. Furthermore, having an interview does not equal as having the offer in hand. There are many ways that college graduates apply. Some even use *Knock'em Dead* as the basis when it comes to preparing interviews, but are still looking for jobs. What seems to go wrong for those college graduates and for those who have had a few jobs before. Let's take a look at our interviews with several candidates.

B. Traditional routes of going to prestigious schools cannot be a panacea in today's job search, letting alone getting a great job. Bestsellers, such as *Rich Dad Poor Dad* and *The Millionaire Fastlane*, all caution millions of readers that having a great education simply is not enough. *The Millionaire Fastlane* even states in the introduction that "go to college, get good grades, get good job, save 10% of your paycheck····." only leads you to walk on the slow lane.

C. While it seems upsetting and most college graduates are still going through an ongoing search for the first job, Cindy has already got a job offer in her senior year. Cindy had such a rare temperament when I saw her. She was good-looking and had a euphonious voice. She got an offer from XXX airline. Looking back, Cindy told us she wasn't a great student, and she wasn't the teacher's pet, either. Every now and then, she skipped a few classes to do what she likes, as long as those skipping won't get her flunked. The whole point was she knew what she really wanted, to be a flight attendant. She didn't want to follow what her parents told her to get good grades in every course and be a straight A student. It wasn't like she didn't like As in transcripts. When she told one of her professors that she couldn't do the final because XXX airline starts the training earlier, every one of her classmates got jealous.

D. Another candidate is Mary. After she graduated from a prestigious university, she really wanted to do the working holiday things. All her classmates told her that it was going to be so much fun. They prepared tons of things and recorded everything whenever they needed so that looking back it would be a perfect memory to them. Viewing how many likes through her Facebook pages can reveal how wonderful her life was. When she came back, the glorious life in Australia did not seem as glorious as it seems. She went through several interviews and got all job offers, but the salary was not as high as she expected.

E. One day, she happened to meet with one of her high school classmates, who did not attend a university as great as she was, but now has an incredible job with a decent salary. She told Mary how rewarding that experience was, half-joking that four years at this job really gave her an edge to the salary part. When she wanted to leave the company, the boss unexpectedly raised her salary, and she seemed satisfied with the salary bump. At last, she informed Mary that her real problem is she has no experience. Like many college graduates who do not know that when they come back from working holiday, they still have to start from scratch. All these comments made Mary somewhat hurt.

F. Our last candidate is Victoria. We recommend her not to badmouth her previous employers during an interview. She instantly laughs. She has had several exchanges for the job, and cannot seem to find the satisfied one. After those exchanges, she now finds how hard it is for her to get a job. She had several jobs that lasted only for a few months. What is done is done, right. Being upsetting and pessimistic won't help.

G. There are still other ways for her to get the offer. Preparing 100 interview questions is like for the person who starts looking for a job. Studying technical aspects of the job you are applying only gets you half-way because you still have to go through interviews. No matter how high you get in the written, if you cannot convince your future employer or HR personnel, you are not getting the job. What Victoria needs is to craft her story. Bestsellers, such as *The Defining Decade*, seem to be the cure for someone like Victoria. "Interviewers want to hear a reasonable story about the past, present, and future." If you can tell a believable story linking what you did to what you would like to do in the future, you are still having a shot. Sensible stories kind of make up for past indiscretions.

Questions 14-18

Reading Passage 2 has seven paragraphs, A-G

Which paragraph contains the following information?

Write the correct letter, A-G, in boxes 14-18 on your answer sheet.

NB You may use any letter more than once.

14 mention of an academic report

15 mention of getting an incredible opportunity before graduation

16 mention of a transient work experience

17 a description of the reason that influences the amount of the salary

18 reference of a behavior that can get someone unhired

Questions 19-24

Look at the following statements (Questions 19-24) and the list of people and books below.

Match each statement with the correct people and books, A-H

Write the correct letter, A-H, in boxes 19-24 on your answer sheet.

NB You may use any letter more than once.

19 can be a remedy for someone who is lost in the job search

20 gets retained by a superior

21 has to make her narrative convincing

22 mentions a traditional route that everyone follows

23 is far ahead of her classmates

24 serves as the foundation for graduates to prepare interview questions

List of people and books

A *Knock'em Dead*

B *Rich Dad Poor Dad*

C *The Millionaire Fastlane*

D *The Defining Decade*

E Cindy

F Mary

G Victoria

H Mary's classmates

Test 1

Reading Passage 2

TEST 1

TEST 2

TEST 3

TEST 4

Questions 25-27

Complete the summary below

Choose NO MORE THAN TWO WORDS from the passage for each answer

Write your answers in boxes 25-27 on your answer sheet.

Some graduates even use *Knock'em Dead* as the foundation when it comes to preparing interviews, but in the era of underachievement, a fantastic **25.**_____ and a thorough study of normally-asked questions are not enough.

Traditional routes of going to prestigious schools cannot be a panacea in today's job search. Cindy represents an unconventional type and had a peculiar **26.**_____ , who did not follow the advice of her parents. She eventually got hired by XXX airline as a **27.**_____.

問題 14 到 18

閱讀文章第一篇有七個段落，A-G

哪個段落包含了下列資訊？

在 14-18 答案欄中寫上正確的字母 A-G

你可能使用任何一個字母超過一次

14 提到了一份學術報告

15 提及在畢業前獲取了極佳的機會

16 提及一份短暫的工作經驗

17 描述影響薪資總額的理由

18 提到讓某人未受聘僱的行為

Test 1

1
TEST
Reading Passage 2

2
TEST

3
TEST

4
TEST

問題 19 到 24

看下列的問題（問題 19-24）和以下列表中的人物和書籍

請將每個敘述與 A-H 選項做正確的配對

在 19-24 答案欄中，寫上正確的字母 A-H
你可能使用任何一個字母超過一次

19 可以是對於在找尋工作中感到迷失者的治療良方
20 受到上司的慰留
21 必須讓她的敘述令人信服
22 提及每個人都遵循的傳統道路
23 遠超越她的同班同學
24 充當畢業生準備面試問題的基礎

人物和書籍列表

A *Knock'em Dead*
B《窮爸爸和富爸爸》
C 百萬富翁快車道
D《關鍵性的十年》
E 辛蒂
F 瑪莉
G 維多利亞
H 瑪莉的同班同學

問題 25 到 27

完成下列摘要題

段落中的每個答案，請勿超過一個單字

在 25-27 答案欄中，寫上你的答案

當提及準備面試時，有些畢業生甚至使用 *Knock'em Dead* 當作基礎，但是在學非所用的時代中，一份很棒的 25.＿＿＿＿＿＿＿＿ 和透徹研讀常會問到的問題是不夠的。

傳統道路的上名校無法成為今日找工作的萬靈丹。辛蒂代表著非傳統的類型，有著獨特的 26.＿＿＿＿＿＿＿＿，且不遵循父母的建議。她最終受雇 XXX 航空公司成為 27.＿＿＿＿＿＿＿.

Test 1

1
TEST
Reading Passage 2

2
TEST

3
TEST

4
TEST

解析

Step 1：迅速看題型配置，再定出解題步驟

　　這篇文章的題型有：❶**配對_段落細節題**（Which paragraph contains the following information）、❷**配對_人物和書籍題**和 ❸**摘要題**。

　　配對_段落細節題敘述開頭常以...an example of/a reference of.../mention of...等等開始，名詞片語或子句有時候拉太長，這樣回推其實太慢，看到這類題目直接理解成，段落中**有提到、描述或列舉中那些資訊**，並且以關鍵字快速定位回文章收詢。

Step 2：腦海中浮現答題策略，開始答題

　　這篇既然有❶**配對_段落細節題**（Which paragraph contains the following information）、❷**配對_人物和書籍題**，建議先答這兩個題型，並一併搜尋這兩個題型的相關關鍵字，**逐題回去尋找資訊太浪費時間，請同步找**，所以掃描第 14 題到第 18 題關鍵字，至少腦海中要浮現 4-5 個關鍵點，例如 an **academic report**, an **incredible opportunity** before **graduation**, a **transient** work experience, reason that influences the amount of the **salary**, a **behavior** that can get someone **unhired**, a **remedy** for someone who is lost in the job search, **retained by a superior**, make **narrative convincing**, a **traditional** route that everyone follows, far ahead of her classmates, **foundation** for graduates to prepare **interview** question，掌握這些資訊後開始讀段落。

◆ 還有另一個閱讀重點是**閱讀框架**，一篇閱讀文章，通常都有固定搭配，例如一個關於演化的文章，可能會有幾個學者（某些學者贊成，而某些反對某些論述，然後試題中就會搭配配對題，其實了解了特定的閱讀框架後就能更容易掌握這些訊息，然後答題），在這篇的話就是要注意**每個人物和書籍，每個人物和書籍均是出題點**。

◆ 從首段開始看，看到 Some even use **Knock'em Dead** as the **basis** when it comes to preparing interviews, but are still looking for jobs.，可以馬上對應到第 24 題 serves as the **foundation** for graduates to prepare interview questions，在同義轉換的部分要注意到 **foundation = basis**，所以**第 24 題**的答案為 **A Knock'em Dead**。

◆ 緊接著在 B 段落 **The Millionaire Fastlane** even states in the introduction that **"go to college, get good grades, get good job, save 10% of your paycheck**...." only leads you to walk on the slow lane.，可以對應到**第 22 題**的 mentions a traditional route that everyone follows，如果沒辦法這麼快意會到，可以思考下，就是因為走在傳統的道路上才會走在慢車道，列舉的**"go to college, get good grades, get good job, save 10% of your paycheck** 都在是走在慢車道/遵循傳統路徑的行為，（但其實，實際上若要獲取更多財富，你要做的其實遠大於這些，在這篇並未探討到），所以**第 22 題**的答案為 **C The Millionaire Fastlane**。

Test 1

1 TEST
Reading Passage 2

2 TEST

3 TEST

4 TEST

◆ 接著在 C 段提到 Cindy 要多注意，因為是其中一個人物，所以出題點會變多的，Cindy had already **got a job offer in her senior year.** She **got an offer from XXX airline**.... When she told one of her professors that she **couldn't do the final** because XXX airline starts the training earlier, every one of her classmates got jealous. ，剛好對應到 **getting an incredible opportunity** before graduation，**got an offer from XXX airline = getting an incredible opportunity before graduation**，**got a job offer in her senior year** 和 **couldn't do the final** 得知是 **before graduation**，所以第 **15** 題的答案為 **C**。

◆ 在 C 段落還有提到 She didn't want to follow what her parents told her to get good grades in every course and be a straight A student. It wasn't like she didn't like As in transcripts.剛好對應到 **an academic report**，所以第 **14** 題的答案為 **C**。

◆ 還有剛提到的 When she told one of her professors that she couldn't do the final because XXX airline starts the training earlier, every one of her classmates got jealous.（畢業前獲得錄取通知和讓同學感到忌妒等）都對應到了 is far ahead of her classmates，所以第 **23** 題的答案為 **E**。

◆ 接續盡快看 D 和 E 段落，在 E 段落可以看到 At last, she

informed Mary that her real problem is she has no experience. Like many college graduates who do not know that when they come back from working holiday, they still have to start from scratch.，對應到 the reason that influences the amount of the salary，且從這兩個段落的描述得知，因為這些因素使得 Mary 起薪無法太高是因為如此，所以**第 17 題**的答案為 **E**。

◆ 除此之外還有一則訊息，When she wanted to leave the company, the boss unexpectedly raised her salary, and she seemed satisfied with the salary bump.，由這些訊息可以推斷（公司因為她離職而加薪留人，而她也很滿意薪資的漲幅）gets retained by a superior，但別誤選成瑪莉，所以**第 20 題**的答案為 **H**。

◆ 接續讀 F 段落，We recommend her not to **badmouth** her previous employers during an interview.，對應到 a behavior that can get someone unhired，這算是在面試的大忌，所以很好猜到，看到 **badmouth** 就要多留神了，所以**第 18 題**的答案為 **F**。

◆ 除此之外還有另一個訊息也對應到了，要注意，After those exchanges, she now finds how hard it is for her to get a job. She had several jobs that lasted only for a few months.，可以對應到 **a transient work experience**，所以**第 16 題**的答案

Test 1

1
TEST
Reading Passage 2

2
TEST

3
TEST

4
TEST

也是 **F**。

♦ 閱讀最後一段，Bestsellers, such as *The Defining Decade*, seem to be the cure for someone like Victoria.剛好對應到第 19 題 can be a remedy for someone who is lost in the job search，所以**第 19 題**的答案是 **D *The Defining Decade***。

♦ 還有其他訊息也對應到了，**What Victoria needs is to craft her story**. Bestsellers, such as *The Defining Decade*, seem to be the cure for someone like Victoria. "Interviewers want to hear a reasonable story about the past, present, and future." If you can tell a **believable** story linking what you did to what you would like to do in the future, you are still having a shot. Sensible stories kind of make up for past indiscretions.，這些訊息都是在說 **has to make her narrative convincing**，**第 21 題**的答案是 **G Victoria**。

♦ 接著看摘要題，Some graduates even use *Knock'em Dead* as the foundation when it comes to preparing interviews, but in the era of underachievement, a fantastic 25. _____ and a thorough study of **normally-asked questions** are not enough.，可以迅速定位到第一段 It is more than just having a great resume and preparing **typical 100 must-read interview questions**. ...There are many ways that college graduates apply. Some even use **Knock'em Dead** as the basis when it comes to preparing interviews, but are still looking for jobs.，只是試題的語序有更改，在同義轉換的部分要注意到 **normally-asked questions = typical 100 must-read interview questions**，所以第 **25** 題答案很明顯是 **resume**。

◆ Traditional routes of going to prestigious schools cannot be a panacea in today's job search. Cindy represents an unconventional type and had a **peculiar** 26.＿＿＿＿＿＿＿，who did not follow the advice of her parents.，試題首句可以馬上定位到第二段，然後看到 Cindy 時馬上跳到下個段落，定位到 Cindy had such a **rare temperament** when I saw her. She is good-looking and has a euphonious voice.，在同義轉換的部分要注意到 **peculiar = rare**，所以第 **26** 題答案很明顯是 **temperament**。

◆ 接著看到第 **27** 題，She eventually got hired by XXX airline as a 27.＿＿＿＿＿＿＿. 對應到 **She got an offer from XXX airline.** Looking back, Cindy told us she wasn't a great student, and she wasn't the teacher's pet, either. Every now and then, she skipped a few classes to do what she likes, as long as those skipping won't get her flunked. The whole point was she knew what she really wanted, to be a **flight attendant**，試題用更濃縮的表達方式，其實接著讀就能看到答案是空服員，所以第 **27** 題答案很明顯是 **flight attendant**。

中譯和影子跟讀 MP3 002

A. Preparing for interviews is a very big thing for many college graduates. In the era of underachievement, securing an interview is arduous and daunting. It is more than just having a great resume and preparing typical 100 must-read interview questions. Furthermore, having an interview does not equal as having the offer in hand. There are many ways that college graduates apply. Some even use Knock'em Dead as the basis when it comes to preparing interviews, but are still looking for jobs. What seems to go wrong for those college graduates and for those who have had a few jobs before. Let's take a look at our interviews with several candidates.

準備面試對於許多大學畢業生來說是非常重要的事情。在低就的時代，獲取面試機會是艱辛且令人感到卻步的。不僅是要有出色的履歷和準備典型的面試 100 個必問的問題。此外，有面試機會不等同於工作機會到手邊。大學畢業生有許多應對的方式。當提及準備面試時，有些甚至使用了 Knock'em Dead 當作基礎，但仍在找工作。對於那些大學畢業生和那些曾有幾份工作的求職者來說到底哪裡出了差錯。我們一起來看一下我們所面試的幾位候選人。

B. Traditional routes of going to prestigious schools

cannot be a panacea in today's job search, letting alone getting a great job. Bestsellers, such as *Rich Dad Poor Dad* and *The Millionaire Fastlane*, all caution millions of readers that having a great education simply is not enough. *The Millionaire Fastlane* even states in the introduction that "go to college, get good grades, get good job, save 10% of your paycheck…." Only leads you to walk on the slow lane.

傳統路徑的上頗具名望的學校無法成為今日求職的萬靈丹，更別說是得到好的工作機會了。暢銷書籍，例如《窮爸爸和富爸爸》以及《百萬富翁快車道》，都告誡著讀者受到出色的教育顯然是不夠的。在《百萬富翁快車道》的引言中甚至述説了「上大學、拿高分、獲取好工作、省下你收入的10%...」都僅能讓你走在慢車道上。

C. While it seems upsetting and most college graduates are still going through an ongoing search for the first job, Cindy has already got a job offer in her senior year. Cindy had such a rare temperament when I saw her. She was good-looking and had a euphonious voice. She got an offer from XXX airline. Looking back, Cindy told us she wasn't a great student, and she wasn't the teacher's pet, either. Every now and then, she skipped a few classes to do what she likes, as long

Test 1

1 TEST
Reading Passage 2

2 TEST

3 TEST

4 TEST

as those skipping won't get her flunked. The whole point was she knew what she really wanted, to be a flight attendant. She didn't want to follow what her parents told her to get good grades in every course and be a straight A student. It wasn't like she didn't like As in transcripts. When she told one of her professors that she couldn't do the final because XXX airline starts the training earlier, every one of her classmates got jealous.

雖然這似乎讓人氣餒，但以找尋第一份工作來説，當大多數的大學畢業生都正經歷著持續不斷地尋找時，辛蒂已經於大四時就拿到了工作機會。當我看到她時，辛蒂有著罕見的氣質。她長得漂亮且有著悦耳的聲音。她得到了 XXX 航空公司的工作機會。回顧起來，辛蒂告訴我們，她並不是個傑出的學生，而且他也不是老師寵兒。偶爾她還會翹幾堂課去做自己想做的事，只要翹課的程度不至於讓她不及格。她一直以來都很清楚她想要什麼，成為一位航空飛行員。她不想要遵從她父母告訴她的那些，在每堂課都拿到高分並當個全 A 的學生。這並不是説她不希望在成績單上出現全 A 的成績。當她告訴其中一位教授她無法參予期末考，因為 XXX 航空公司的訓練提前時，幾乎每一位班上的同班同學都感到忌妒。

D. Another candidate is Mary. After she graduated from a prestigious university, she really wanted to do the working holiday things. All her classmates told her that it was going to be so much fun. They prepared tons of things and recorded everything whenever they needed so that looking back it would be a perfect memory to them. Viewing how many likes through her Facebook pages can reveal how wonderful her life was. When she came back, the glorious life in Australia did not seem as glorious as it seems. She went through several interviews and got all job offers, but the salary was not as high as she expected.

另一位候選人是瑪莉。在她畢業於頗負盛名的大學後，她真的想要去從事打工渡假的事情。所有她的同班同學都告訴她，這會很有趣。他們準備了很多的事情，並記錄了他們需要的每件事情，這樣一來，之後回想起來對她們而言會是很棒的回憶。看著她臉書頁面上所獲得的許多讚就揭露出了她過去生活有多麼精彩。當她回來時，在澳洲榮耀般的生活就沒有想像中那麼光榮。她經歷了幾次面試，都拿到了工作機會，但是薪資卻不是她所預期的。

E. One day, she happened to meet with one of her high school classmates, who did not attend a university as great as she was, but now has an incredible job with a decent salary. She told Mary how rewarding that

Test 1

TEST 1

Reading Passage 2

TEST 2

TEST 3

TEST 4

experience was, half-joking that four years at this job really gave her an edge to the salary part. When she wanted to leave the company, the boss unexpectedly raised her salary, and she seemed satisfied with the salary bump. At last, she informed Mary that her real problem is she has no experience. Like many college graduates who do not know that when they come back from working holiday, they still have to start from scratch. All these comments made Mary somewhat hurt.

有一天，她碰巧遇到了她其中一位高中同學，該同學當初所讀的大學並非她就讀的大學出色，但是現在卻有份極好的工作，薪資也頗佳。她告訴瑪莉這個經驗有多麼值得，半開玩笑地述說著，過去四年在這份工作上給予她在薪資這塊有了更好的談判優勢。當她想要離開公司時，老闆很意外地加了她薪水，而她也很滿意薪資的暴升。最後，她告訴瑪莉，瑪莉真正的問題是她毫無工作經驗。像許多大學畢業生一樣不知道自己從打工渡假回來後，他們仍舊要從頭開始。這些評論讓瑪莉有點受傷。

F. Our last candidate is Victoria. We recommend her not to badmouth her previous employers during an interview. She instantly laughs. She has had several exchanges for the job, and cannot seem to find the satisfied one. After those exchanges, she now finds how hard it is for her to get a job. She had several jobs that lasted only for a few months. What is done is done, right. Being upsetting and pessimistic won't help.

我們最後的一位候選人是維多莉亞。我們建議她在面試時別說前雇主的壞話。她馬上捧腹大笑。她有幾次換工作的經驗，而且似乎無法找到滿意的工作。在轉換跑道後，她發現自己要找到一份工作是有多麼困難。她曾有過幾次工作都持續不到幾個月。該發生的都發生了，對吧。感到難過跟悲觀都毫無助益。

G. There are still other ways for her to get the offer. Preparing 100 interview questions is like for the person who starts looking for a job. Studying technical aspects of the job you are applying only gets you half-way because you still have to go through interviews. No matter how high you get in the written, if you cannot convince your future employer or HR personnel, you are not getting the job. What Victoria needs is to craft her story. Bestsellers, such as *The Defining Decade*, seem to be the cure for someone like Victoria. "Interviewers want to hear a reasonable story about the past, present, and future." If you can tell a believable story linking what you did to what you would like to do in the future, you are still having a shot. Sensible stories kind of make up for past indiscretions.

還有其他方式能幫助她拿到工作機會。準備 100 則面試問題像是對於剛開始找工作的人的建議。研讀你所申請的該工作的技術層面只是完成了一半，因為你仍需要通過面試。不論你在筆試時拿到多高的成績，如果你無法說服你的未來雇主或人事專員，你則無法獲得該工作。維多利亞所需要的是精心編織她自己的故事。暢銷書，例如《關鍵性的十年》似乎是對於像維多莉亞這樣情況者的解藥。「面試官只是要聽到關於過去、現在和未來的合理解釋」。如果你可以述說著令人信服的故事，連結著過去你所做的到你未來想從事的，你能有機會的。合理的故事彌補了過去所犯的錯。

READING PASSAGE 3

You should spend about 20 minutes on **Questions 28-40**, which are based on Reading Passage 3 below.

Psychology Case Study: "Give and Take", a strategy employed by *Harry Potter, The Romance of the Three Kingdoms, and Revenge*

A. Similar writing techniques can be found in thousands of fictions and movies in the world. Sometimes writers and authors use identical and familiar patterns so that they can retain a certain number of viewers and audiences. Sometimes they do this is because it is just a part of our lives and we simply cannot live without it. As a saying goes, drama is life and life is drama. It is through portrayal of the similar patterns of life that we finally grasp the meaning of life. One of the arrangements is "life is all about give and take", as can be seen in many famous works, such as Harry Potter, *The Goblet of Fire*, *The Romance of the Three Kingdoms*, and U.S. famous sitcom, *Revenge*. You certainly cannot underestimate the power of "give and take". Even several bestsellers discuss this phenomenon, such as *Give and Take*, and *Rich Dad Poor Dad*. "Give and you shall receive". Let's take a look at how it is used in both eastern and western fictions.

B. In one of the popular U.S sitcoms, *Revenge*, we can also find the traces of "give and take" in several scenes. The heroine Emily Thornes is actually Amanda Clarke. She comes to the town of the Hamptons to get revenge on those who wronged her father, so she exchanges the name and acts as Emily Thornes. Her first step is to buy the beach house, actually her childhood house. The beach house is belonged to Michael and Lydia. Lydia is cheating on Michael, so according to the prenup, she will get nothing in the divorce. But the point is there are multiple people eyeing on the beach house, according to another heroine, Victoria Grayson.

C. During the bidding war, what Emily does not know is that Victoria outbids her at a cash offering, and Nolan outbids Victoria. Things progress to a surprising end. The deed of the house is already in Emily's name. According to Nolan Ross, he wants to return the favor that Emily's father once did to him. Her father, David was the one who believed in him so that Nolan could start a successful company. However, Nolan gets himself in a very big trouble in the very end of season two. In the opening of season three, Nolan is released out of the jail and gets picked up by Emily, who drives him to a great mansion, saying that the house is his. She feels that it is the right thing to do. She is just returning the favor to Nolan Ross.

D. In Harry Potter, *The Goblet of Fire*, three tasks will be given to those champions. Harry is not qualified to attend the contest, but his name is unusually in the goblet of fire. Harry has already known the first task is dragons. Perhaps due to the fact that Harry has a kind heart or Harry is a giver, he informs the only champion who does not know that the first task is dragons. Givers are the ones who help others without thinking too much or whether they will get something in return.

E. According to the bestseller *Give and Take*, there are three types, takers, givers, and matchers. Matchers are the ones who are in the middle. They value a fair return. Takers are the ones who take the most, and it is assumed that takers should be the ones who win the most. Contrary to what readers might think, givers are actually the ultimate winner, since others are benefited by them before. They are willing to return the favors to givers. As the story progresses, Harry has a hard time figuring out the second task. Cedric says to Harry "I owe you one for telling me about the dragons". He is returning the favor to Harry.

F. In *The Romance of the Three Kingdoms*, the portrayal of give-and-take can also be found in the relationship between Guan Yu and Cao Cao. Guan Yu is such a great warrior that even Cao Cao really appreciates him. Guan Yu even has something that Lu Bu clearly lacks. Guan Yu is a man of integrity and loyalty, whereas Lu Bu is a womanizer who also betrays his godfather Ding Yuan. Because of this, Cao Cao wants him even more. He tries his best to please Guan Yu. He gives him lots of treasures and Red Hare, the kind of horse that every warrior wants. Dong Zhuo once uses Red Hare to woo Lu Bu. Loyalty earns the appreciation and trust from Cao Cao, whereas disloyalty makes Lu Bu beheaded. Guan Yu's loyalty makes him leave the camp of Cao Cao, but he appreciates how Cao Cao once treated him. Guan Yu leaves with all the gifts returned to Cao Cao and is forgiven by Cao Cao even though he slays six generals of Cao Cao en route at five passes.

G. As the story progresses to Huarong where the fate of Cao Cao is doomed, Kong Ming knows beforehand that Guan Yu will eventually set Cao Cao free. Kong Ming and Liu Bei already have an understanding that this is actually the time for Guan Yu to return the favor once given by Cao Cao.

H. All three great works have all been linked to give-and-take. Perhaps as a human being, it is just a part of our life, and sometimes there are reasons for certain arrangements in those works.

Questions 28-35

Look at the following statements (Questions 28-35) and the list of people below.

Match each statement with the correct people, A-L

Write the correct letter, A-L, in boxes 28-35 on your answer sheet.

NB You may use any letter more than once.

28 receives a penalty due to one's infidelity

29 disguises the identity by pretending to be someone

30 informs someone who remains novel about the task

31 had faiths about someone who can be successful

32 has notoriety for sexual affairs with someone

33 offers the highest price during the bidding war

34 possesses qualities that make others want to recruit

35 suffers from great losses and still cannot retain someone

List of people

A Harry Potter

B Emily Thornes

C Michael

D Lydia

E Victoria Grayson

F Nolan Ross

G David

H Cedric

I Dong Zhuo

J Cao Cao

K Guan Yu

L Lu Bu

Questions 36-40

Complete the summary below

Choose ONE WORD ONLY from the passage for each answer

Write your answers in boxes 36-40 on your answer sheet.

The power of "give and take" cannot be undervalued. Three great works have used this technique. According to the bestseller *Give and Take*, there are three types, takers, givers, and matchers. **36.**_____ are not the final winners, to people's surprise.

In *The Romance of the Three Kingdoms*, Ding Yuan is betrayed by his son, who is also a **37.**_____, and eventually cost his life because of **38.**_____, whereas Guan Yu earns the **39.**_____ from Cao Cao. He even gets the **40.**_____ and reliability from Cao Cao despite the fact that he kills six generals of Cao en route at five passes

試題中譯

問題 28 到 35

看下列敘述（問題 **28** 到 **35**）和以下列表中的人物

將每個敘述與正確的人物，**A-L** 進行配對

在你的答案紙，**28-35** 答案欄中，寫上正確的字母 **A-L**

NB 你可能使用任何一個字母超過一次

28 因為不忠貞而受到懲罰

29 藉由假裝成某個人來偽裝身分

30 通知對一項任務為何仍一無所知者

31 對於某個人能成功有信念

32 因與某人的感官上的風流韻事而惡名昭彰

33 在競價戰期間，提供最高的估價

34 擁有著其他人想要招募的特質

35 受到巨大的損失而仍無法留住某人

人物列表

A 哈利波特

B 艾蜜莉・索恩

C 麥克

D 莉底亞

E 維多利亞・葛雷森

F 諾蘭・羅斯

G 大衛

H 西追

I 董卓

J 曹操

K 關羽

L 呂布

問題 36 到 40

完成下列摘要題

段落中的每個答案，請勿超過一個單字

在你的答案紙，**36-40** 答案欄中，寫上你的答案

「給予和接受」的力量是不能被低估的。三項名著都使用到了這個技巧。根據暢銷書籍《給予和接受》，存在三個類型，奪取者、給予者和相配者。36. 出乎大家意料之外的是，＿＿＿＿＿＿ 不是最後的贏家。

在《三國演義》中，丁原受到他兒子的背叛，他的兒子同時也是個 37.＿＿＿＿＿＿，而最終招致死亡是因為他的 38.＿＿＿＿＿＿＿，而關羽從曹操那裡贏得了 39.＿＿＿＿＿。他甚至得到曹操的 40.＿＿＿＿＿ 和信任，儘管他在通往五關的途中殺死了六位將軍。

解析

Step 1：迅速看題型配置，再定出解題步驟

　　這篇文章的題型有：❶配對_人物題段落細節題、❷摘要題。

　　配對_人物題搭**摘要題**，在題型搭配上較簡易不複雜，通常一個篇章超過兩個以上的題型搭配都會造成理解跟解題上的困難度，雖然如此還是要小心細節和避免粗心造成的失分。

Step 2：腦海中浮現答題策略，開始答題

　　這篇既然有❶配對_人物題段落細節題、❷摘要題，先答配對題，主義人物跟事件，最後答摘要題。

◆ **第 29 題**，以人物進行搜尋，可以直接定位到第二段，The heroine Emily Thornes is **actually Amanda Clarke**. She comes to the town of the Hamptons to get revenge on those who wronged her father, so she **exchanges the name and acts as Emily Thornes**.，原本是 **Amanda Clarke**，卻更換名字以 **Emily Thornes** 來到小鎮，其實等於第 29 題的敘述 **disguises the identity by pretending to be someone**，所以第 **29 題**的答案是 **B Emily Thornes**。

◆ 接續閱讀，**第 28 題**，Lydia is **cheating** on Michael, so according to the prenup, she will **get nothing in the divorce**.對應到第 28 題的敘述 **receives a penalty** due to one's infidelity，在同義轉換的部分要注意到 **cheating = infidelity**，**receives a penalty = get nothing in the divorce**，要注意這些字的轉換，所以**第 28 題**的答案是 **D Lydia**。

◆ 接續讀，**第 33 題**，可以定位到 But the point is there are multiple people eyeing on the beach house, according to another heroine, **Victoria Grayson**. During the **bidding war**, what **Emily** does not know is that **Victoria** outbid her at a cash offering, and **Nolan** outbids Victoria. Things progress to a surprising end. The **deed** of the house is already in Emily's name. According to Nolan Ross, he wants to return the favor that Emily's father one did to him. ，要特別注意轉折跟好幾個人物的敘述，deed 指的是房契，在競價戰中，可以得知有三個人都出價，最終 Nolan 的高於 Victoria，且房契轉到 Emily 手上了。且有提到 Nolan 想還人情給 Emily 的父親，所以 offers the highest price during the bidding war 的人是 Nolan，所以**第 33 題**的答案是 **F Nolan Ross**。

◆ 接續讀，**第 31 題**，According to **Nolan Ross**, he wants to return the favor that Emily's father one did to him. Her father, **David** was the one who believed in him so that Nolan could start a **successful** company. ，had **faiths** about someone who can be **successful**，**第 31 題**很明顯答案是 **G David**，但要小心別選成 **Nolan Ross**。是 David 對 Nolan Ross

◆ 接續讀，第 **30** 題，讀到 Harry has already known the first task is dragons. Perhaps due to the fact that Harry has a kind heart or Harry is a giver, **he informs the only champion who does not know that the first task is dragons.**可以對應到試題 informs someone who **remains novel** about the task，**who does not know = remain novel**，所以第 **30** 題的答案是 **A Harry Potter**。

◆ 接續讀，第 **34** 題，Guan Yu is such a great warrior that even Cao Cao really appreciates him. Guan Yu even has something that Lu Bu clearly lacks. Guan Yu is a man of integrity and loyalty…，對應到第 **34** 題的敘述 **possesses qualities that make others want to recruit**，所以第 **34** 題的答案是 **K Guan Yu**。

◆ 接著讀到下句，whereas Lu Bu is a womanizer who also betrays his godfather Ding Yuan.，要懂 womanizer 的意思，has notoriety for sexual affairs with someone 剛好對應到這個字的意思，所以第 **32** 題的答案是 **L Lu Bu**。

◆ 第 **35** 題是，Guan Yu's loyalty makes him leave the camp of

Test 1

1
TEST
Reading Passage 3

2
TEST

3
TEST

4
TEST

Cao Cao, but he appreciates how Cao Cao once treated him. Guan Yu leaves with all the gifts returned to Cao and is forgiven by Cao even though he slays six generals of Cao en route at five passes. ，從這些敘述可以知道，曹操過去的禮遇以及關羽斬了曹操六名大將，曹操都原諒他，這幾句其實都對應到了第 35 題的敘述 suffers from great losses and still cannot retain someone，所以**第 35 題**的答案是 **J Cao Cao**。

◆ **第 36 題**，The power of "give and take" cannot be undervalued. Three great works have used this technique. According to the bestseller *Give and Take*, there are three types, takers, givers, and matchers. 36.＿＿＿＿＿＿ are **not** the final winners, to people's surprise.，由關鍵字可以定位到 it is assumed that takers should be the ones who win the most. Contrary to what readers might think, givers are actually the ultimate winner, since others are benefited by them before.，要特別小心看，題目是問 **not**，所以別寫成 givers，**第 36 題**的答案是 **takers**。

◆ **第 37-39 題**，In *The Romance of the Three Kingdoms*, **Ding Yuan** is betrayed by his son, who is also a 37.＿＿＿＿＿＿, and eventually cost his life because of 38.＿＿＿＿＿＿, whereas Guan Yu earns the 39.＿＿＿＿＿＿ and reliability from Cao Cao.，對應到 Guan Yu is a man of integrity and loyalty, whereas Lu Bu is a **womanizer** who also betrays his godfather Ding Yuan. Because of this, Cao Cao wants him even more. He tries his best to please Guan Yu. He gives him lots of treasures and Red Hare, the kind of horse that every warrior wants. Dong Zhuo once uses Red Hare to woo Lu Bu. Loyalty earns the appreciation and trust from Cao Cao, whereas **disloyalty** makes Lu Bu beheaded.。

◆ **第 37 題**由丁原定位和敘述，可以得知 his son = Lu Bu，所以**第 37 題**的答案是 **womanizer**。

◆ **第 38 題**要看到比較後面，試題有調整描述順序，所以可以得知**第 38 題**的答案是 **disloyalty**，其中 **cost his life = beheaded**。

◆ **第 39 題**很明顯答案是 **appreciation**。

◆ **第 40 題**，He even gets **the** 40._____from Cao Cao despite the fact that he kills six generals of Cao en route at five passes，可以對應到 Guan Yu leaves with all the gifts returned to Cao and **is forgiven** by Cao even though he slays six generals of Cao en route at five passes.，很快可以對應到 is forgiven，但空格應要填入名詞，所以可以得知**第 40 題**的答案是 **forgiveness**。

中譯和影子跟讀 MP3 003

A. Similar writing techniques can be found in thousands of fictions and movies in the world. Sometimes writers and authors use identical and familiar patterns so that they can retain a certain number of viewers and audiences. Sometimes they do this is because it is just a part of our lives and we simply cannot live without it. As a saying goes, drama is life and life is drama. It is through portrayal of the similar patterns of life that we finally grasp the meaning of life. One of the arrangements is "life is all about give and take", as can be seen in many famous works, such as Harry Potter, *The Goblet of Fire*, *The Romance of the Three Kingdoms*, and U.S. famous sitcom, Revenge. You certainly cannot underestimate the power of "give and take". Even several bestsellers discuss this phenomenon, such as *Give and Take*, and *Rich Dad Poor Dad*. "Give and you shall receive". Let's take a look at how it is used in both eastern and western fictions.

在世界上，數以千計的小說和電影中可以發現相似的寫作技巧。有時候作家和作者們使用了相同和熟悉的架構，這樣一來他們就能夠留住特定數量的觀看者和觀眾。有時候他們這樣做的目的是因為這是我們生活中不可少的一部分，我們生活中不能沒有它。有句俗諺說：人生如戲，戲如人生。透過相似框架的生命描述，我們最終掌握了生命的意義。其中一個安排是「人生是給予和接受」，這可以在許多名著中找到，例如哈利波特的《火盃的考驗》、《三國演義》和美國的著名影集《復仇》。你確實無法低估「給予和接受」的力量。即使幾個暢銷著作都討論了這個現象，例如《給予和接受》和《窮爸爸富爸爸》。「給予你才能獲得」。現在讓我們看一下在東方和西方小説中都如何使用到這個部分。

B. In one of the popular U.S sitcoms, *Revenge*, we can also find the traces of "give and take" in several scenes. The heroine Emily Thornes is actually Amanda Clarke. She comes to the town of the Hamptons to get revenge on those who wronged her father, so she exchanges the name and acts as Emily Thornes. Her first step is to buy the beach house, actually her childhood house. The beach house is belonged to Michael and Lydia. Lydia is cheating on Michael, so according to the prenup, she will get nothing in the divorce. But the point is there are multiple people eyeing on the beach house, according to another heroine, Victoria Grayson.

在其中一部流行美國影集《復仇》中，我們可以在幾個場景裡發現「給予和接受」。女主角艾蜜莉・索恩其實是亞曼達・克拉克。她來到漢普頓小鎮，要對那些曾冤枉她父親的人復仇，所以她換了名字，充當起艾蜜莉・索恩。她復仇的第一步是購買海邊小屋，實際上是她孩童時期居住的房子。海灘小屋是屬於麥克和莉底亞的。莉底亞對麥克不忠，所以根據婚前協議，她在離婚時不會拿到任何東西。但根據另一位女主角，維多利亞·葛雷森的說法，這時間點有許多人都著眼於海邊小屋。

C. During the bidding war, what Emily does not know is that Victoria outbid her at a cash offering, and Nolan outbids Victoria. Things progress to a surprising end. The deed of the house is already in Emily's name. According to Nolan Ross, he wants to return the favor that Emily's father once did to him. Her father, David was the one who believed in him so that Nolan could start a successful company. However, Nolan gets himself in a very big trouble in the very end of season two. In the opening of season three, Nolan is released out of the jail and gets picked up by Emily, who drives him to a great mansion, saying that the house is his. She feels that it is the right thing to do. She is just returning the favor to Nolan Ross.

在競價戰過程中，艾蜜莉所不知道的是維多利亞在現金供價時出價高於艾蜜莉，而諾蘭出價高於維多利亞。事情進展到令人出乎意外的結局。根據諾蘭·羅斯，他想要還當初艾蜜莉父親替他所作的一切的人情。她父親，大衛相信諾蘭·羅斯的能力，所以諾蘭·羅斯才能創立一間成功的公司。然而，諾蘭在第二季結尾時身陷很大的困難中。在第三季的開場時，諾蘭被監獄釋放出來，由艾蜜莉開車接走，車子駛向一件大豪宅，艾蜜莉説道，這間房子是他的了。她覺得這是件正確的事。她只是還諾蘭‧羅斯這份人情。

D. In Harry Potter, *The Goblet of Fire*, three tasks will be given to those champions. Harry is not qualified to attend the contest, but his name is unusually in the goblet of fire. Harry has already known the first task is dragons. Perhaps due to the fact that Harry has a kind heart or Harry is a giver, he informs the only champion who does not know that the first task is dragons. Givers are the ones who help others without thinking too much or whether they will get something in return.

在哈利波特的《火盃的考驗》中，那些鬥士們會被交付三項任務。哈利並不符合參賽資格，但是他的名字卻不尋常地進入了火盃中。哈利已經知道第一件任務是龍。或許由於哈利有個善良的心或是哈利是給予者，他告知唯一不知道第一項任務的鬥士。給予者是那些不假思索就幫助其他人者，或不論他們是否能從他人身上拿回什麼相對的報酬。

E. According to the bestseller *Give and Take*, there are three types, takers, givers, and matchers. Matchers

Test 1

TEST 1
Reading Passage 3

TEST 2

TEST 3

TEST 4

are the ones who are in the middle. They value a fair return. Takers are the ones who take the most, and it is assumed that takers should be the ones who win the most. Contrary to what readers might think, givers are actually the ultimate winner, since others are benefited by them before. They are willing to return the favors to givers. As the story progresses, Harry has a hard time figuring out the second task. Cedric says to Harry "I owe you one for telling me about the dragons". He is returning the favor to Harry.

根據暢銷書《給予和接受》，有三個類型的分類，奪取者、給予者和相配者。相配者是介於兩者中間。他們重視對等的回應。奪取者是那些拿走大部分者，而且假設下會是奪取者應該要贏最多。但與讀者所想的正好相反，給予者實際上是最終贏家，因為其他人先前曾受惠於他們的幫助。他們願意將那些人情還給給予者。隨著故事進展，哈利在第二項任務時遇到困難而陷入苦思。西追對哈利說道，「你告訴我關於龍的事情，使我欠了你一個人情」。他只是將人情還給哈利。

F. In *The Romance of the Three Kingdoms*, the portrayal of give-and-take can also be found in the relationship between Guan Yu and Cao Cao. Guan Yu is such a great warrior that even Cao Cao really appreciates him. Guan Yu even has something that Lu Bu clearly lacks. Guan Yu is a man of integrity and loyalty, whereas Lu Bu is a womanizer who also betrays his godfather Ding Yuan. Because of this, Cao Cao wants him even more. He tries his best to please Guan Yu. He gives him lots of treasures and Red Hare, the kind of horse that every warrior wants. Dong Zhuo once uses Red Hare to woo Lu Bu. Loyalty earns the appreciation and trust from Cao Cao, whereas disloyalty makes Lu Bu beheaded. Guan Yu's loyalty makes him leave the camp of Cao Cao, but he appreciates how Cao Cao once treated him. Guan Yu leaves with all the gifts returned to Cao Cao and is forgiven by Cao Cao even though though he slays six generals of Cao Cao en route at five passes.

在《三國演義》中，給予和接受的描繪也能在關羽和曹操之間找到。關羽是如此出色的戰士甚至是曹操都真的很賞識他。關羽甚至有些特質是呂布明顯欠缺的。關羽是正直且忠誠的，而呂布是位沉迷女色者，也曾背叛過自己的義父丁原。因為這樣，曹操更想要得到他。他盡他所能的討好關羽。他給予他許多寶藏和赤兔馬，那種每個戰士都想要的馬匹。董卓曾經使用赤兔馬想要追求呂布。忠誠能得到曹操的欣賞和信任，而不忠誠讓呂布丟了人頭。關羽的忠誠讓他離開曹操的營隊，但是他感謝曹操當初如何對他。關羽將所有禮物歸還給曹操，也受到曹的寬恕，即使他在途經五關時，殺了曹操六位大將。

G. As the story progresses to Huarong where the fate of Cao Cao is doomed, Kong Ming knows beforehand that Guan Yu will eventually set Cao Cao free. Kong Ming and Liu Bei already have an understanding that this is actually the time for Guan Yu to return the favor once given by Cao Cao.

隨著故事的進展至華容道，曹操命運走到了盡頭，孔明事先就知道關羽最終會釋放曹操。孔明和劉備已經有個共識，也就是在那個時候讓關羽將人情還給曹操。

H. All three great works have all been linked to give-and-take. Perhaps as a human being, it is just a part of our life, and sometimes there are reasons for certain arrangements in those works.

所有三個偉大的著作都與給予和接受有關連性。或許身為人類，這僅是我們生活的一部分，而且有時候在那些著作中特定的安排是有原因的。

READING PASSAGE 1

You should spend about 20 minutes on **Questions 1-13**, which are based on Reading Passage 1 below.

The Romance of the Three Kingdoms：
Kong Ming Drives Zhou Yu to Fury Three Times

A. Even though the huge blaze engulfs Cao Cao's fleets at Red Cliff（赤壁）, there is still a long way to go. Cao Cao is still occupying the North. Zhou Yu, while still enjoying a triumphant battle, sets his sight on Nanjun（南郡）. He makes a pact with Liu Bei（劉備）. If he cannot take down Cao Ren, Liu Bei is free to initiate an attack to Nanjun. Kong Ming dispassionately analyzes the situation to Liu Bei, saying that Nanjun will be their territory soon. Cao Ren is not that easy to tackle, but Zhou Yu（周瑜）comes up with other plans. That is, to seize a geographically advantageous place like Yiling. While taking down Yiling seems to give Zhou Yu an upper hand, Cao Ren（曹仁）possesses a secret weapon, his father's letter.

B. The following morning, Cao Ren sets a trap waiting for Zhou Yu's army. Zhou Yu manages to steal Nanjun, without realizing both sides of Nanjun are armed with arrows, and in the city, there is a trap waiting for them. When Zhou Yu realizes that there is a trap, he is hit by a poisonous arrow. It is not until this point that Zhou Yu comes to the realization that he totally underestimates Cao Ren's ability. After Zhou Yu has taken a defeat and is seriously injured, insults and provocation permeate outside Zhou Yu's camp, preventing him from having a sound rest. Northern soldiers' mockery does work in some ways. Zhou Yu eventually vomits fresh blood, but in fact it is a stratagem employed by Zhou. He even fakes his own death.

C. After some deliberation, Cao Ren thinks now is the perfect time to ransack Zhou's army. Plunder of Zhou's corpse leaves Nanjun vulnerable to the attack, since there remain very few soldiers to safeguard the city. Eventually, Cao Ren is defeated by Zhou Yu and manages to flee north, but that does not make Zhou Yu a winner. Kong Ming's army has already taken Nanjun during the time Zhou Yu is fighting with Cao Ren. Upon hearing the news that Kong Ming effortlessly takes down Nanjun, he faints right on the spot. This is the first time Kong Ming drives Zhou Yu to fury.

D. If this is the first, there is bound to be the second. Jingzhou is considered a strategically important place during that time. This place symbolizes scramble between both camps Liu Bei and Sun Quan（孫權）. It also embodies the battle of wits between Kong Ming and Zhou

Yu. Two prodigies engage in an ongoing fight.

E. Upon hearing the news about the death of Liu Bei's wife, lady Gan, Zhou Yu comes up with a plan by using a honey trap, they can eventually use Liu Bei as a hostage. In exchange, Kong Ming has no choice but to return Jingzhou to Wu. He explains the whole thing to Sun Quan. On the surface, they arrange a marriage for Liu Bei and Sun Quan's sister. When Liu Bei comes to Wu to propose, they seize the opportunity to imprison Liu Bei.

F. As clever as this honey trap sounds, it is seen right through by Kong Ming, who asks Liu Bei to marry Sun Quan's sister and counterplot Zhou Yu. It turns out Liu Bei gets along with Sun Quan's sister and gets favored by Sun Quan's mother. Zhou Yu fails to incarcerate Liu Bei, yet he still manages to use other things, such as mansions, to lure Liu Bei. He even alienates Liu Bei from Kong Ming and others. Ultimately, Liu Bei is enchanted by material comfort. Kong Ming knows too well that Liu Bei cannot stand such temptation, so he sends Zhao Zilong（趙雲）to inform Liu Bei that Cao Cao is planning to attack Jinzhou. Lady Sun（孫夫人）is moved by Liu Bei, and they plan to flee the country when they pay the tribute to the ancestor at the river bank. They eventually take the boat arranged by Kong Ming, get rid of pursuing troops, and successfully escape. The triumph of fleeing drives Zhou Yu to fury for the second time.

G. Despite a series of setbacks, to regain Jingzhou（荊州）is still the biggest concern for Zhou Yu. Lu Su（魯肅）makes an attempt to persuade Liu Bei to return Jingzhou, but Kong Ming and Liu Bie have already rehearsed the whole thing to counter with Lu Su's questioning. The act makes Lu Su believe that there is actually a dilemma for Liu Bei. He returns to Wu and Zhou Yu comes up with another plan. On the surface, they are assisting Liu Bei to capture Xi Chuan, but their real motive is to claim Jingzhou. On their way to Xi Chuan（西川）, they will journey through Jingzhou, and it is at this time they demand Liu Bei provide money and provisions. When Liu Bei shows appreciation for the Wu army, they make their move and end the life of Liu Bei. Kong Ming sees through this plot and wants Liu Bei to counterplot. Soon afterwards, Zhou Yu commands the combination of both land and naval force, around fifty thousand soldiers, ready to make an attack. Warships sail exceedingly fast towards Jingzhou, but the surface of the river remains unbelievably quiet, making Zhou Yu quite suspicious of the whole thing.

H. Zhao Zilong（趙子龍）is staying in Jingzhou, informing Zhou Yu that Kong Ming has already known what he is up to. Eventually, Zhou Yu's injuries, caused by arrows in earlier fights, get even worse. He falls to the ground, but is rescued. When they arrive at Ba Qiu, Zhou Yu receives a letter from Kong Ming. This is the third time that Kong Ming provokes Zhou Yu to fury. Zhou Yu sighs with grief and writes a letter to Sun Quan. At the age of only 36, a prodigy, after a few attempts of trying to outwit Kong Ming, dies, marking a tragic end at the end of his journey. It has certainly been a memorable chapter for generations who have read *"The Romance of the Three Kingdoms"*.

英文試題

Questions 1-9

Complete the summary using the list of words and phrases A-Q below. Write the correct letter, A-Q in boxes 1-9 on your answer sheet.

Drive Zhou Yu to fury	EVENTS
The first time	• Although **1.** _____ at Red Cliff has destroyed Cao Cao's fleets, there is still a long way to go. Zhou Yu's next goal is Nanjun（南郡）. He makes a promise with Liu Bei（劉備）, whereas Kong Ming remains **2.** _____ , saying that Nanjun will be their territory soon. • Zhou Yu's scheme of taking down a **3.** _____ important place like Yiling can give him an upper hand, but Cao Ren（曹仁）possesses a secret weapon. • Miscalculating the situation makes Zhou Yu hooked, and he gets harmed by an arrow that contains **4.** _____ . • Then, Zhou Yu counterplots. **5.** _____ a deceased body is the main reason that Cao Ren eventually loses. Eventually, Kong Ming is the one who takes down Nanjun without any effort.

The second time	• Two 6._____ compete for Jingzhou. A honey plot is employed by one side. An arranged matrimony is used to further 7._____ Liu Bei. • Liu Bei eventually succeeds in escaping with his wife, Lady Sun.
The third time	• To recover Jingzhou, Zhou Yu pretends that they are going to provide 8._____ to seize Xi Chuan. • Zhou Yu is armed with lots of warships, travelling at a great speed, but encounter 9._____ at the stream. • Ultimately, the tragedy ends the whole thing.

Boxes

A trap	**B** whizzes
C incarcerate	**D** flame
E looting	**F** geography
G plot	**H** placid
I strategically	**J** venom
K scramble	**L** assistance
M serenity	**N** wits
O battle	**P** territory
Q death	

Questions 10-13

Look at the following statements (Questions 10-13) and the list of people below.

Match each statement with the correct people, A-I

Write the correct letter, A-I, in boxes 10-13 on your answer sheet.

NB You may use any letter more than once.

10 has given his son a note in advance
11 counterfeits the demise of his own
12 is dispatched to thwart someone from the seduction
13 laments his inability to outmaneuver someone

List of people

A Kong Ming
B Zhao Zilong
C Zhou Yu
D Cao Ren
E Lu Su
F Sun Quan
G Lady Sun
H Cao Cao
I Liu Bei

問題 **1** 到 **9**

運用以下列表中 **A-Q** 的字和片語來完成摘要題

在你的答案紙，**1-9** 答案欄中，寫上正確的字母 **A-Q**

迫使周瑜憤怒	
第一次	• 儘管在赤壁的 1.＿＿＿＿＿已經摧毀了曹操的艦隊，仍有很長遠的路要走。周瑜的下個目標是南郡。他允諾劉備，而孔明則保持 2.＿＿＿＿＿，說到南郡即將會是我們的領土。 • 周瑜的計謀是拿下像是彝陵這樣具 3.＿＿＿＿＿重要性的地方，此舉能讓他佔上風，但是曹仁卻有著秘密武器。 • 誤算情勢讓周瑜中計，而且受到由含有 4.＿＿＿＿＿的弓箭所傷。 • 然後，周瑜將計就計。5.＿＿＿＿＿一具死亡的身軀是曹仁最終輸了的主因。最後，孔明不費吹灰之力拿下南郡。
第二次	• 兩位 6.＿＿＿＿＿競逐荊州。其中一方用上了美人計。策畫的婚姻用於進一步 7.＿＿＿＿＿劉備。 • 劉備最終與其妻子孫夫人成功脫逃。

第三次

- 為了收復荊州，周瑜假裝他們在前往該地途中提供 8.＿＿＿＿＿＿＿ 以攻佔西川。.
- 周瑜武裝了許多軍艦，以極快的速度航行，但是卻在溪流處遭遇了 9.＿＿＿＿＿＿＿.
- 最終，一場悲劇終結了整件事。

填空欄

A 陷阱	**B** 奇才們
C 監禁	**D** 火焰
E 搶劫	**F** 地理
G 計謀	**H** 沉著的
I 戰略性地	**J** 毒液
K 爭奪	**L** 協助
M 寧靜	**N** 智慧
O 戰鬥	**P** 領地
Q 死亡	

問題 **10** 到 **13**

看下列敘述（問題 **10** 到 **13**）和以下列表中的人物

將每個敘述與正確的人物，**A-I** 進行配對

在你的答案紙，**10-13** 答案欄中，寫上正確的字母 **A-I**

NB 你可能使用任何一個字母超過一次

10 已經事先給予他兒子筆記

11 偽造自己的死亡

12 受派遣前往阻饒一個人受到誘惑

13 悲嘆自己無法運用策略擊敗某人

List of people

A 孔明

B 趙子龍

C 周瑜

D 曹仁

E 魯肅

F 孫權

G 孫夫人

H 曹操

I 劉備

解析

Step 1：迅速看題型配置，再定出解題步驟

這篇文章的題型有：❶配對式摘要題 ❷配對_人物題。

配對式摘要題要特別注意，不太像是一般的摘要題對應到後找某些字就可以了，而是需要根據欄位中的選項，選出空格中合適的答案，有時候題目雖然不多（**劍橋雅思 10-13**），但卻不太好答或花考生太多時間了，有時候考得比較是隱含的意思（**劍橋雅思官方指南**），所以不是對應到該字就可以了，有時候其實可以用**語法協助篩選掉一些選項**，常見的題型搭配有「選擇題」+「摘要配對題」+「判斷題」，這篇的題型是「摘要配對題」+「配對題」，趕快一起來看看。

Step 2：腦海中浮現答題策略，開始答題

這篇既然有❶**配對式摘要題**、❷**配對_人物題**，建議順著文章讀邊讀邊找資訊，對閱讀掌握更好者，可以掃描人物題的敘述後，兩個題型同步進行答題會更快，解析部分還是以先答完摘要題後再答人物題。

◆ **第 1 題**，Although **1.** _____ at Red Cliff has destroyed Cao Cao's fleets, there is **still a long way to go**. Zhou Yu's next goal is Nanjun（南郡）.對應到 Even though the huge **blaze** engulfs Cao Cao's fleets at Red Cliff（赤壁），there **is still a long way to go.**，可以知道答案是 **blaze**，如果是傳統摘要題可以直接填這個答案，可是題目是**選擇式的摘要配**

對題時，知道答案後，要再看答案選項欄的選項，並選出符合的答案，所以用 **blaze** 找，可以馬上找到 **D flame**，所以第 **1** 題答案為 **D**。

◆ 第 **2** 題，He makes a promise with Liu Bei（劉備），whereas Kong Ming remains **2.＿＿＿＿＿＿**, **saying that Nanjun will be their territory soon**. 對應到 He makes a pact with Liu Bei（劉備）. If he cannot take down Cao Ren, Liu Bei is free to initiate an attack to Nanjun. Kong Ming **dispassionately** analyzes the situation to Liu Bei, **saying that Nanjun will be their territory soon.**，可以先消化訊息，然後理解孔明講話的部分，可以知道孔明面對劉備的急問，是很沉著冷靜的，可以看到 **dispassionately** 這個字，並馬上使用這個字去找，但是找之前，也可以在看一下空格的語法，空格前為 **remains** 所以後面要加形容詞，所以要找等同於 **dispassionately** 這個字且是形容詞的字，馬上可以看到 **H placid**，第 **2** 題答案為 **H**。

◆ 第 **3** 題，Zhou Yu's scheme of **taking down a 3.＿＿＿＿ important place like Yiling can give him an upper hand**, but Cao Ren（曹仁）possesses a secret weapon. 對應到 Zhou Yu（周瑜）comes up with other plans. That is, to **seize a geographically advantageous** place like Yiling. While taking down Yiling seems to give Zhou Yu an upper hand, Cao Ren（曹仁）possesses a secret weapon, his father's letter.，這題也可以消化一下再答，**plans** 對應到 **scheme**，

take down 對應到 **seize**，空格中的意思對應到 **a geographically advantageous**，空格中的詞性根據語法要選**副詞**，可以找到 **I strategically**，**地理情勢有利的**剛好對應**具戰略性地重要**地方，所以**第 3 題**答案為 **I**。

◆ **第 4 題**，**Miscalculating** the situation makes Zhou Yu hooked, and gets harmed by an arrow that contains **4.___ _____**. 對應到 Zhou Yu manages to steal Nanjun, without realizing both sides of Nanjun are armed with arrows, and in the city, there is a trap waiting for them. When Zhou Yu realizes that there is a trap, he is hit by **a poisonous arrow**. It is not until this point that Zhou Yu comes to the realization that he totally **underestimates** Cao Ren's ability.，試題中以更濃縮的語句表達這個段落，**Miscalculating** 可以對應到 **underestimates**。試題還改寫成非直接表明重 X 箭，而是重了箭，箭裡含有 X，出題者很愛這樣改，所以理解後可以知道空格對應到的訊息是 a poisonous arrow，**a poisonous arrow = an arrow that.has/contains toxin/venom**，所以要選名詞，馬上可以找到 **J venom**，所以**第 4 題**答案為 **J**。

◆ **第 5 題**，Then, Zhou Yu counterplots. **5._____ a deceased body** is the main reason that Cao Ren eventually loses.，以 **a deceased body** 找可以在次段找到，After some deliberation, Cao Ren thinks now is the perfect time to ransack Zhou's army. **Plunder** of Zhou's **corpse** leaves Nanjun vulnerable to the attack, since there remain very few soldiers to safeguard the city.，在同義轉換的部分要注意到 **corpse** 對應到 **a deceased body**。經由理解文意後，得知曹仁是想要搶奪屍體，所以要找 **plunder** 的同義字，可以找到 **E looting**，所以**第 5 題**答案為 **E**。

◆ **第 6 題**，Two 6.＿＿＿＿＿＿ compete for Jingzhou. A honey plot is employed by one side.，要注意干擾選項，可以馬上找到 It also embodies the battle of wits between **Kong Ming** and **Zhou Yu**. Two **prodigies** engage in an ongoing fight.，經消化訊息後可以得知是兩大奇才爭奪荊州的概念，所以可以用**奇才**去找（也是要知道 **prodigies= whizzes**，還有別誤選成 wits，其實根據語法空格是要選**複數**，不懂 whizzes 的考生可能會選成 wits），馬上找到了 **B whizzes**，所以**第 6 題**答案為 **B**。

◆ **第 7 題**，**An arranged matrimony** is used to further 7.＿＿＿＿＿ Liu Bei.由 **An arranged matrimony** 為關鍵字，迅速定位到 On the surface, they **arrange a marriage** for **Liu Bei** and Sun Quan's sister. When Liu Bei comes to Wu to propose, they seize the opportunity to **imprison** Liu Bei.，根據句意和文法，要選**監禁的動詞**，**imprison = incarcerate**，**C incarcerate**，考生也必須知道這個字，如果不知道則要多背其他同反義字，所以**第 7 題**答案為 **C**。

◆ 第 8 題，To **recover Jingzhou**, Zhou Yu pretends that they are going to provide **8.＿＿＿＿＿＿to seize Xi Chuan**.，運用 **recover Jingzhou** 為關鍵字，迅速定位到 Despite a series of setbacks, to **regain Jingzhou**（荊州）is still the biggest concern for Zhou Yu.首句，**順便標記跳過的段落，配對題的出題考點可能在該段落**，等等看配對題可以先看該段落，來找配對的人物。繼續在這個段落讀，要消化這個事件的來龍去脈。

◆ On the surface, they are **assisting** Liu Bei **to capture Xi Chuan**, but their real motive is to claim Jingzhou. On their way to Xi Chuan（西川）, they will journey through Jingzhou, and it is at this time they demand Liu Bei provide money and provisions.理解後可以看到，可以知道關鍵字是 **assisting**，依據語法**要選名詞**，所以盡快找同義字，可以找到 **L assistance**，所以**第 8 題**答案為 **L**。

◆ 第 9 題，Zhou Yu is armed with lots of **warships,** travelling at a great **speed**, but encounter **9.＿＿＿＿＿＿** at the **stream**.，運用 **warships, speed, stream** 盡快定位到，**Warships** sail exceedingly **fast** towards Jingzhou, but the surface of the **river** remains unbelievably **quiet**, making Zhou Yu quite suspicious of the whole thing.，如果沒這麼快理解可以多想一下，其實是異常的**寧靜**讓周瑜起疑，所以要找與寧靜的同義字，而根據語法要選**名詞**，**M serenity**，所以**第 9 題**答案為 **M**。

◆ 第 **10** 題，has given his son **a note** in advance，在前面其實曹仁的部分就可以知道，信件是曹仁的父親提前給的，而這裡的 note 換成了 letter，題目在 father 和 son 的表達作轉換，所以給信的人是曹操，由此可知**第 10 題**答案為 **H Cao Cao**。

◆ 第 **11** 題，**counterfeits** the **demise** of his own，一氣周瑜的部分可以得知，周瑜中計後也將計就計，所以假死，可以盡快定位回該段 in fact it is a stratagem employed by Zhou. He even **fakes** his own **death**.，**fake = counterfeit**，**demise = death**，所以第 **11** 題答案為 **C Zhou Yu**。

◆ 第 **12** 題，is **dispatched** to **thwart** someone from the **seduction**，可以先找剛才跳過的段落，用 **dispatched, thwart, seduction** 盡快定位到，Kong Ming knows too well that Liu Bei cannot stand such **temptation**, so he **sends** Zhao Zilong（趙雲）to inform Liu Bei that Cao Cao is planning to attack Jinzhou.，在同義轉換的部分要理解到 **is dispatched = sends**，**seduction = temptation**，所以第 **12** 題答案為 **B Zhao Zilong**。

◆ 第 **13** 題，**laments** his inability to **outmaneuver** someone，可以定位到最後一段 Zhou Yu **sighs with grief** and writes a letter to Sun Quan. At the age of only 36, a prodigy, after a few attempts of trying to **outwit** Kong Ming, dies, marking a tragic end at the end of his journey.，在同義轉換的部分要理解到，**laments = sighs with grief**，**outmaneuver = outwit**，所以**第 13 題**答案為 **C Zhou Yu**。要注意選項有 **A-I**，但其實好幾個雅思閱讀題型，確實有可能一個答案出現兩次的情況，像這題**周瑜就出現兩次**，要注意就是了。

A. Even though the huge blaze engulfs Cao Cao's fleets at Red Cliff（赤壁）, there is still a long way to go. Cao Cao is still occupying the North. Zhou Yu, while still enjoying a triumphant battle, sets his sight on Nanjun（南郡）. He makes a pact with Liu Bei（劉備）. If he cannot take down Cao Ren, Liu Bei is free to initiate an attack to Nanjun. Kong Ming dispassionately analyzes the situation to Liu Bei, saying that Nanjun will be their territory soon. Cao Ren is not that easy to tackle, but Zhou Yu（周瑜）comes up with other plans. That is, to seize a geographically advantageous place like Yiling. While taking down Yiling seems to give Zhou Yu an upper hand, Cao Ren（曹仁）possesses a secret weapon, his father's letter.

即使巨大的烈焰吞沒了曹操位於赤壁的軍艦，仍有很長的一段路要走。曹操仍占據著北方。周瑜雖然正享受著勝利之役帶來的喜悅感，卻也將目標放在奪取南郡。他與劉備訂了契約。如果他無法拿下曹仁的話，劉備可以隨時對南郡發起攻勢。孔明冷靜地向劉備分析著情勢，說道南郡即將會是他們的領地。曹仁並不是那麼容易對付的，但是周瑜想了其他的計畫。也就是佔領像是彝陵這樣享有地理位置優勢的地方。雖然佔據彝陵似乎讓周瑜占了上風，曹仁仍持有著秘密武器，他父親的信。

B. The following morning, Cao Ren sets a trap waiting for Zhou Yu's army. Zhou Yu manages to steal Nanjun, without realizing both sides of Nanjun are armed with arrows, and in the city, there is a trap waiting for them. When Zhou Yu realizes that there is a trap, he is hit by a poisonous arrow. It is not until this point that Zhou Yu comes to the realization that he totally underestimates Cao Ren's ability. After Zhou Yu has taken a defeat and is seriously injured, insults and provocation permeate outside Zhou Yu's camp, preventing him from having a sound rest. Northern soldiers' mockery does work in some ways. Zhou Yu eventually vomits fresh blood, but in fact it is a stratagem employed by Zhou. He even fakes his own death.

次日早晨，曹仁為了應對周瑜的軍隊，設置了陷阱等待著。周瑜設法偷南郡，卻沒有意識到南郡雙邊都已武裝了弓箭，而且在城裡頭，有陷阱等著他們。當周瑜意識到有陷阱時，他被毒箭擊中。直到此時此刻，周瑜才意識到他全然低估了曹仁的能力。在周瑜吞了敗仗且重傷後，侮辱和挑釁在周瑜營外蔓延著，阻礙他安然休養。北方軍隊的嘲諷在某些程度上發揮了作用。周瑜最終吐了鮮血，但實際上卻是周瑜採用的一則詭計。周瑜甚至假死。

C. After some deliberation, Cao Ren thinks now is the perfect time to ransack Zhou's army. Plunder of Zhou's corpse leaves Nanjun vulnerable to the attack, since there remain very few soldiers to safeguard the city. Eventually, Cao Ren is defeated by Zhou Yu and manages to flee north, but that does not make Zhou Yu a winner. Kong Ming's army has already taken Nanjun during the time Zhou Yu is fighting with Cao Ren. Upon hearing the news that Kong Ming effortlessly takes down Nanjun, he faints right on the spot. This is the first time Kong Ming drives Zhou Yu to fury.

在一些深思熟慮後，曹仁認為現在是洗劫周瑜軍隊的最佳時機。掠奪周瑜的屍體讓南郡易受到攻擊，因為守衛南郡城的士兵相當少。最終，曹仁被周瑜所打敗，而設法逃往北方，但是這並未讓周瑜成為贏家。在周瑜與曹仁對戰時，孔明的軍隊早已經拿下南郡。在聽到孔明不費吹灰之力拿下南郡時，他當場暈倒。這是「孔明一氣周瑜」。

D. If this is the first, there is bound to be the second. Jingzhou is considered a strategically important place during that time. This place symbolizes scramble between both camps Liu Bei and Sun Quan（孫權）. It also embodies the battle of wits between Kong Ming and Zhou Yu. Two prodigies engage in an ongoing fight.

如果這是第一次的話，那一定就會有第二次。荊州被視為是當時戰略重要的地點。這個地方象徵著兩個陣營劉備和孫權的爭奪。這也體現了孔明和周瑜之間的鬥智。兩個奇才進行了一場持續性的爭鬥。

E. Upon hearing the news about the death of Liu Bei's wife, lady Gan, Zhou Yu comes up with a plan by using a honey trap, they can eventually use Liu Bei as a hostage. In exchange, Kong Ming has no choice but to return Jingzhou to Wu. He explains the whole thing to Sun Quan. On the surface, they arrange a marriage for Liu Bei and Sun Quan's sister. When Liu Bei comes to Wu to propose, they seize the opportunity to imprison Liu Bei.

在聽到劉備的夫人，甘夫人過世的消息後，周瑜想了一個計畫，藉由美人計他們最終可以利用劉備當作人質。如此一來，孔明就不得不將荊州歸還給吳國以此作交換。他向孫權解釋到這件事。表面上，他們替劉備和孫權的妹妹配婚。當劉備到吳國提親時，他們抓住機會趁此時幽禁劉備。

F. As clever as this honey trap sounds, it is seen right through by Kong Ming, who asks Liu Bei to marry Sun Quan's sister and counterplot Zhou Yu. It turns out Liu Bei gets along with Sun Quan's sister and gets favored by Sun Quan's mother. Zhou Yu fails to incarcerate Liu Bei, yet he still manages to use other things, such as mansions, to lure Liu Bei. He even alienates Liu Bei from Kong Ming and others. Ultimately, Liu Bei is enchanted by material comfort. Kong Ming knows too well that Liu Bei cannot stand such temptation, so he sends Zhao Zilong（趙雲）to inform Liu Bei that Cao Cao is planning to attack Jinzhou. Lady Sun（孫夫人）is moved by Liu Bei, and they plan to flee the country when they pay the tribute to the ancestor at the river bank. They eventually take the boat arranged by Kong Ming, get rid of pursuing troops, and successfully escape. The triumph of fleeing drives Zhou Yu to fury for the second time.

儘管這則美人計聽起來很聰明，卻為孔明所識破，因此孔明要求劉備將計就計的去迎娶孫權的妹妹。結果，劉備與孫權的妹妹相處良好，而且受到孫權母親的青睞。周瑜未能幽禁劉備，可是他仍使用其他事物，例如豪宅，來引誘劉備。他甚至讓劉備與孔明和其他人疏遠。最後，劉備沉迷於物質的享受。孔明很了解劉備，深知他無法抵抗那樣的誘惑，所以他派了趙雲去告知劉備曹操正計畫要攻打荊州。孫夫人為劉備所打動，而他們計畫當前往河邊祭祖時，逃離吳國。他們最終乘著孔明所安排的船隻，擺脫追逐的軍隊，而且成功逃脫。成功逃離視為是二氣周瑜。

G. Despite a series of setbacks, to regain Jingzhou（荊州）is still the biggest concern for Zhou Yu. Lu Su（魯肅）makes an attempt to persuade Liu Bei to return Jingzhou, but Kong Ming and Liu Bie have already rehearsed the whole thing to counter with Lu Su's questioning. The act makes Lu Su believe that there is actually a dilemma for Liu Bei. He returns to Wu and Zhou Yu comes up with another plan. On the surface, they are assisting Liu Bei to capture Xi Chuan, but their real motive is to claim Jingzhou. On their way to Xi Chuan（西川）, they will journey through Jingzhou, and it is at this time they demand Liu Bei provide money and provisions. When Liu Bei shows appreciation for the Wu army, they make their move and end the life of Liu Bei. Kong Ming sees through this plot and wants Liu Bei to counterplot. Soon afterwards, Zhou Yu commands the combination of both land and naval force, around fifty thousand soldiers, ready to make an attack. Warships sail exceedingly fast towards Jingzhou, but the surface of the river remains unbelievably quiet, making Zhou Yu quite suspicious of the whole thing.

儘管一系列的挫折，收復荊州仍是周瑜最大的考量。魯肅試圖說服劉備歸還荊州，但是孔明和劉備已經演練過整件事的說法，以應對魯肅的質問。此舉讓魯肅相信劉備真的有困難之處。他回到吳國，和周瑜想了另一個計策。在表面上，他們協助劉備奪得西川，但是他們真正的目的是奪取荊州。在他們前往西川的途中，他們會途經荊州，就在這個時候，他們要求劉備提供金錢和供應物。當劉備表現出對於吳國軍隊的感激時，他們採取行動，終結劉備的生命。孔明看穿了這個伎倆，想要劉備將計就計。隨後不久，周瑜命令水陸結合的軍隊，大約五萬大軍，準備發動攻擊。戰船以極快的速度行駛朝往荊州，但是河面仍舊維持著異常的寧靜，這整件事讓周瑜相當起疑。

H. Zhao Zilong（趙子龍） is staying in Jingzhou, informing Zhou Yu that Kong Ming has already known what he is up to. Eventually, Zhou Yu's injuries, caused by arrows in earlier fights, get even worse. He falls to the ground, but is rescued. When they arrive at Ba Qiu, Zhou Yu receives a letter from Kong Ming. This is the third time that Kong Ming provokes Zhou Yu to fury. Zhou Yu sighs with grief and writes a letter to Sun Quan. At the age of only 36, a prodigy, after a few attempts of trying to outwit Kong Ming, dies, marking a tragic end at the end of his journey. It has certainly been a memorable chapter for generations who have read "*The Romance of the Three Kingdoms*".

趙雲待在荊州，告知周瑜，孔明已經知道他的計謀。最終，周瑜因先前戰鬥時受到的箭傷，傷勢因而更加嚴重。他跌落地面，但被救了起來。當他們抵達巴丘時，周瑜收到了一封來自孔明的信件。這是三氣周瑜。周瑜悲痛的長嘆，並寫了封信給孫權。僅僅 36 歲的一位奇才，在幾次嘗試性的要智勝孔明後與世長辭了，畫下的他旅程中悲劇性的結尾。這確實是後人讀三國演義時，令人難忘的篇章。

You should spend about 20 minutes on **Questions 14-27**, which are based on Reading Passage 2 below.

Things That You Won't Learn in School: things such as money

A. Being wealthy is probably one of the goals made by everyone, since wealth brings material comfort to us. People are striving to get rich, climbing the social ladder in the huge corporations in the hope that one day it will be a dream come true. As more and more books related to richness and wealth are getting published, people nowadays are having the opportunity to move towards the goal of getting rich with the right mindset. Being wealthy or rich is not as simple as you imagine. "More money certainly cannot solve more problems", a famous saying from one of the bestselling books, *Rich Dad Poor Dad*. Often habits and one's thinking play a huge role in how one gets wealthy. It is just something people are often ignored or they are reluctant to admit. Let's take a look at the following books that discuss wealth.

B. In *The Millionaire Next Door*, it overturns conventional views that people who drive luxury cars and people living in fancy mansions are the wealthy ones. It also challenges the idea that living in a luxurious residentiary area reflects a person's wealth. Sometimes it is something invisible or relatively marginal that shapes our wealth or helps us retain our wealth. As people are more familiar with American cultures, the phrase "keep up with the Jones" is often heard. People are so easily influenced by those who live close to them. The idea of "keep up with the Jones" aggravates the phenomenon of excessive spending, since you want to keep up with your neighbors. Whether it is the new sports car they are parking in their garage or the expensive schools they send their kids into, those trivial, petty, and unnecessary comparisons are causing superfluous spending. For the long term, this behavior is the invisible hand that takes away the wealth from you.

C. Furthermore, people nowadays are falling into the trap of having to earn more. How people spend their paycheck determines how wealthy they are. The idea of living-the-life-to-the-fullest is dragging todays' people down the poverty, since more money cannot solve the problem. In *The Millionaire Next Door*, it also cautions "one earns to spend. When you need to spend more, you need to earn more". If you really care about your wealth, then quit having the mindset of "work hard and play hard". It really is the reasons why multiple thirtysomethings are not having an adequate amount of savings nowadays.

D. In another book, *Millionaire Teacher*, it explores other areas that can be quite insightful for today's twentysomethings, since the earlier you start, the better your retirement life is. It discusses a story of a girl named Star and her girlfriend Lucy. How is the person like Lucy, who has a fantastic job and lives a luxurious life, will be having a financial problem in the long term, and for a person like Star, who earns much less than Lucy, is the one who informs Lucy that "she is the one in financial trouble". It is worth people's time rethinking about their finance.

E. In addition to topics these above-mentioned two books explore, many books all mention the importance of saving money. In *The Richest Man in Babylon*, it talks about "money comes from those who save it". Another book, *Rich Dad Poor Dad* also mentions a similar concept. It is really essential for anyone to save the money. Books have informed us of the importance of saving money, and in *Millionaire Success Habits*, it states something different, "the success hack, however isn't as much about money as it is about confidence." Confidence and success are correlated. The extra cash does work in the time of need and is the invisible hand that shapes one's confidence on the inside. When you are not desperate for money, you seem quite poised. This is especially helpful when it comes to finding a job. You won't seem reckless and you won't have to settle for a job that is less than you deserve. Trust me, stashing money is not an old concept. It is always perennially in vogue.

F. Education is also the key to getting wealthy. Going to a prestigious university is not that important. The point is that you really need to have a life-long learning mindset. In *The Millionaire Fastlane*, it certainly sets people straight. "The rich understand that education doesn't end with a graduation ceremony; it starts. The world is in constant flux, and as it evolves your education must evolve". That is why you can find many celebrities, such Bill Gates and many others all have reading habits. This might dull many people, but it really is the key. The suggestion in *Secrets of the Millionaire Mind* at the very end of the book is not nothing. "Each month read at least one book" actually helps. Thus, with the right mindset, correct habits, and continued education, all people can gain the wealth they need and thrive in this age of turmoil and economic downturn.

Questions 14-19

Look at the following statements (Questions 14-19) and the list of BOOKS below.

Match each statement with the correct people, A-G

Write the correct letter, A-G, in boxes 14-19 on your answer sheet.

NB You may use any letter more than once.

14 includes the idea that superficiality beguiles people's thinking

15 includes the idea that improvement can be made in something that is deemed meaningless

16 includes the idea about the importance of continued learning

17 includes the idea of a disposition that being phlegmatic helps in a situation

18 includes the idea of a psychological trait that is helpful to success

19 includes the idea that a vicious cycle is related to one's habits

List of BOOKS

A *Rich Dad Poor Dad*

B *The Millionaire Next Door*

C *Millionaire Teacher*

D *The Richest Man in Babylon*

E *Millionaire Success Habits*

F *The Millionaire Fastlane*

G *Secrets of the Millionaire Mind*

Questions 20-23

Look at the following statements (Questions 20-23) and the list of people below.

Match each statement with the correct people, A-E

Write the correct letter, A-E, in boxes 20-23 on your answer sheet.

NB You may use any letter more than once.

20 has a job that provides material comfort

21 knows the importance of reading

22 is the one who will encounter financial constraint in a later life

23 are not having sufficient money in the time of need

List of people
A neighbors
B thirtysomethings
C Star
D Lucy
E Bill Gates

Questions 24-27

Complete each sentence with the correct ending, A-G below. Write the correct letter, A-G, in boxes 24-27 on your answer sheet.

24 Exorbitant consumption is related to

25 Similar ideas are expressed in bestsellers that inform us

26 A notion put forward by a bestseller tells us that the rich realize

27 A perspicacious concept is used to warn a certain age group so that they can understand

A the importance of stockpiling currency
B the importance of success
C the importance of life-long learning
D the importance of finance
E the importance of earning more money
F the notion of "keep up with the Jones"
G the notion of frugality

問題 14 到 19

看下列敘述（問題 14 到 19）和以下列表中的人物

將每個敘述與正確的人物，**A-G** 進行配對

在你的答案紙，**14-19** 答案欄中，寫上正確的字母 **A-G**

NB 你可能使用任何一個字母超過一次

14 包括了表面的事物蒙蔽了人們的思考

15 包括了被視為是無意義的事情卻反而能增進的想法

16 包括了關於持續學習的重要性的想法

17 包括了在情境下，冷靜的性情能有所助益的想法

18 包括了一個心理學特徵，有助於成功的想法

19 包括了惡性循環與一個人的習慣有關的想法

書籍列表

A 《窮爸爸富爸爸》

B 《原來有錢人都這麼做》

C 《我用死薪水輕鬆理財賺千萬》

D 《巴比倫最富有的人》

E 《百萬成功習慣》

F 《財富快車道》

G 《有錢人跟你想的不一樣》

Test 2

1
TEST

2
TEST
Reading Passage 2

3
TEST

4
TEST

問題 **20** 到 **23**

看下列敘述（問題 **20** 到 **23**）和以下列表中的人物

將每個敘述與正確的人物，**A-G** 進行配對

在你的答案紙，**20-23** 答案欄中，寫上正確的字母 **A-G**

NB 你可能使用任何一個字母超過一次

20 有份工作提供了物質的舒適

21 知道閱讀的重要性

22 在稍後的人生中會遭遇到財務困境

23 在急需要時，沒有足夠的金錢

人物列表

A 鄰居

B 30 多歲的人

C 星星

D 露西

E 比爾 · 蓋茲

問題 24 到 27

看下列敘述（問題 24 到 27）和以下列表中的人物

將每個敘述與正確的敘述，**A-G** 進行配對

在你的答案紙，**24-27** 答案欄中，寫上正確的字母 **A-G**

NB 你可能使用任何一個字母超過一次

24 與過度消費有關聯的是

25 相似的想法藉由暢銷書之手來告知我們

26 由暢銷書所提出的概念告訴我們富人了解到

27 一個具洞察力的概念用於警告特定的年齡層，如此他們才能了解
到

A 儲藏貨幣的重要性

B 成功的重要性

C 終身學習的重要性

D 財政的重要性

E 賺更多錢的重要性

F 與鄰居或朋友家比排場、比闊氣的概念

G 節儉的概念

解析

Step 1：迅速看題型配置，再定出解題步驟

這篇文章的題型有：❶配對_書籍❷配對_人物題和❸配對_完成句子。

別小看**這三個題型**的搭配，其實某種程度上來說**很消耗腦力**，如果其中一篇文章要用到 30 分鐘來答題就不好了，有時候真的別小看配對題，選項太抽象或改寫到你找不到部分，就是俗稱的魔王題，有些考生會有遇到就認了的想法，就像劍橋雅思 4 中的 play is a serious business 一樣，而這篇建議考生可以多寫幾次，可以練習搜尋「**閱讀文意**」的能力。

Step 2：腦海中浮現答題策略，開始答題

這篇既然有❶**配對_書籍**❷**配對_人物題**和❸**配對_完成句子**，建議先掃描試題，發現書籍的配對題都時由「**include the idea...**」開頭，然後完成句子的開頭也都類似「**the importance of...**」和「**the notion of...**」，其實蠻抽象的概念，要特別小心，然後還要邊讀邊注意提到的相關**人物和書籍**。

◆ 邊閱讀邊答前兩個類型的配對題，直接很快掃描到第一段的 *Rich Dad Poor Dad*，發現試題中的敘述 14-19 題均沒有符合的，快速跳到下個關鍵點。

◆ 第二段開頭 In *The Millionaire Next Door*, it **overturns**

conventional views that people who drive luxury cars and people living in fancy mansions are the wealthy ones. It also challenges the idea that living in a luxurious residentiary area reflects a person's wealth. Sometimes it is something invisible or relatively marginal that shapes our wealth or help us retain our wealth.，注意 overturns 和相關描述，**出題者未將考點直接改寫成一個相對應的敘述**，然後考生可以直接查找進行配對，可是仔細想下，這些奢華的物品等，其實就是 superficial，表面上外人所看到的光鮮亮麗，這些光鮮亮麗並不完全反映出很多事實，如同開名車的人，不代表這個人有錢等等的。所以第 14 題的 **superficiality beguiles people's thinking** 其實是這本書所傳達的意思，所以**第 14 題**的答案為 **B**。

◆ 接續讀，其實也需要一些時間體會，Furthermore, people nowadays **are falling into the trap of having to earn more**. …The idea of living-the-life to-the-fullest is dragging todays' people down the poverty, since more money cannot solve the problem. In ***The Millionaire Next Door***, it also cautions **"one earns to spend. When you need to spend more, you need to earn more".** If you really care about your wealth, then quit having the mindset of **"work hard and play hard"**.，falling into the trap 其實就等同於 **a vicious cycle**，這也與一個人的習慣有關的，活在當下的人就是這樣的體現，而努力花錢和努力賺錢的人，其行為和習慣就是如此，所以會需要賺更多的錢才能維持相對應的生活方式，所以**第 19 題**的答案也是 **B**。（如果想不出來可以多思考一下）

◆ 接續讀下段，注意關鍵字 **Millionaire Teacher**，且段落有提到人名，很明顯是出題考點，How is the person like Lucy, who **has a fantastic job and lives a luxurious life**, will be having a financial problem in the long term，**has a fantastic job and lives a luxurious life** 對應到第 **20** 題的 **has a job that provides material comfort**，所以第 **20** 題的答案也是 **D**。

◆ 接續讀，the person like Lucy, who has a fantastic job and lives a luxurious life, will be having **a financial problem in the long term**, and for a person like Star, who earns much less than Lucy, is the one who informs Lucy that **she is the one in financial trouble**，這些敘述都表明了題目的 is the one who will encounter financial constraint in a later life，所以第 **20** 題的答案也是 **D**。注意 Lucy 出現兩次，還有要小心句子較複雜別粗心對到錯的答案。

◆ 接續讀下一段，馬上定位到 **The Richest Man in Babylon** 和 **Rich Dad Poor Dad**，但是都沒有對應到的相關訊息，所以盡快往下找，找到 **Millionaire Success Habits**，提到了 "the success hack, however isn't as much about money as it is about **confidence**." **Confidence** and **success** are correlated. The extra cash does work in the time of need and is the invisible hand that shapes one's confidence on the inside.，要特別注意別只是讀過去了，讀到 confidence 時就要有些警覺在，剛好對應到第 **18** 題的敘述 a psychological trait that is helpful to success，其中 **confidence = a psychological trait**，所以**第 18 題**的答案是 **E**。

◆ 除了答完看也要多注意有沒有其他訊息也對應到這本書的內容，緊接著看到 When you are not desperate for money, you seem quite poised. This is especially helpful when it comes to finding a job. ，要**注意 poised**，所以不只是自信，存錢的另一個好處是讓你冷靜／沉著，剛好對應到另一個敘述 **a disposition that being phlegmatic helps in a situation**，冷靜是種 disposition，還要看懂 **phlegmatic** 這個字，所以**第 17 題**的答案也是 **E**。

◆ 又解決了一題，盡快往下看，剩最後一段了，定位到 *the Millionaire Fastlane*，"The rich understand that education doesn't end with a graduation ceremony; it starts. The world is in constant flux, and **as it evolves your education must evolve**"，這邊的敘述都跟**持續學習和進步**有關，剛好對應到第 16 題的敘述 the idea about the importance of continued learning，**第 16 題**的答案也是 **F**。

◆ 接著，That is why you can find many celebrities, such **Bill Gates** and many others all have **reading habits**. ，剛好對應到 knows the importance of **reading**，所以**第 21 題**的答案也是 **E Bill Gates**。

◆ 接著定位到 ***Secrets of the Millionaire Mind***，The suggestion in *Secrets of the Millionaire Mind* at the very end of the book is not **nothing**. "Each month read **at least one book**" actually helps.對應到第 15 題的敘述 the idea that **improvement** can be made in something that is deemed **meaningless**，每個月看一本書被視為是 NOTHING，但是卻是有幫助的，是具有 improvement 的，所以**第 15 題**的答案也是 **G**。

◆ 配對題前兩大題僅剩**第 23 題**，可以邊回去讀其他段落邊找，順便把最後一大題的配對題敘述快速掃描過，**Exorbitant consumption**，可以快速定義到 People are so easily influenced by those who live close to them. The idea of **"keep up with the Jones"** aggravates the phenomenon of **excessive spending**, since you want to keep up with your neighbors.，**Exorbitant consumption = excessive spending**，所以與**"keep up with the Jones"**有關所以**第 24 題**的答案是 **F**。

◆ 然後，**Similar** ideas are expressed in **bestsellers** that inform us，可以對應到剛才其實有看到的一個重點，有兩本暢銷書有提到存錢的重要性，***The Richest Man in Babylon*** 和 ***Rich Dad and Poor Dad***，**saving money = stockpiling currency**，所以**第 25 題**的很明顯是答案 **A**。

◆ 第 **26** 題利用題目敘述中的 **the rich** 定位到剛才看過的一個重點，In *the Millionaire Fastlane*, it certainly sets people straight. "**The rich** understand that education doesn't end with a graduation ceremony，所以可以得知富人知道 the importance of life-long learning，所以**第 26 題**的很明顯是答案 **C**。

◆ 第 **27** 題利用題目敘述中的 **perspicacious** 和 **a certain age group**，這題有點難，剛好掃描到 It really is the reasons why multiple **thirtysomethings** are not having an adequate amount of savings nowadays.，不是這題問的，可是是剛才其中一題配對題，第 23 題的答案，**not having an adequate amount of savings = are not having sufficient money**，所以**第 23 題**的很明顯是答案 **B**。

◆ 繼續掃描**第 27 題**的相關訊息，其實很不好找，In another book, *Millionaire Teacher*, it explores other areas that can be quite **insightful** for today's **twentysomethings**, since the earlier you start, the better your retirement life is，其中 **insightful = perspicacious**，. **Twentysomethings = a certain age group**，找到後可以快點想下這題的配對選項，其實對於 20 多歲的人是可以多了解財務，**the importance of finance**，所以**第 27 題**的很明顯是答案 **D**。

中譯和影子跟讀　　　　　　　　　　　🔘 MP3 005

A. Being wealthy is probably one of the goals made by everyone, since wealth brings material comfort to us. People are striving to get rich, climbing the social ladder in the huge corporations in the hope that one day it will be a dream come true. As more and more books related to richness and wealth are getting published, people nowadays are having the opportunity to move towards the goal of getting rich with the right mindset. Being wealthy or rich is not as simple as you imagine. More money certainly cannot solve more problems, a famous saying from one of the bestselling books, *Rich Dad Poor Dad*. Often habits and one's thinking play a huge role in how one gets wealthy. It is just something people are often ignored or they are reluctant to admit. Let's take a look at the following books that discuss wealth.

既然財富帶給我們物質上的舒適感，想當然的成為富有的人可能是每個人的目標之一。人們試圖著要變有錢，在大型公司裡攀爬上社會階梯，希望有天能夢想成真。當越來越多關於富有和財富的書籍出版，人們現在擁有機會變富有，並朝向該目標邁進，只要有對的心態。變富有或有錢不是你所想像的那樣簡單。暢銷書之一的《窮爸爸富爸爸》中的一句名言：更多的金錢確實無法解決更多的問題。通常習慣和一個人的思維在一個人如何變富有，扮演著巨大的角色。這點不僅常常被人們忽略，也常常是不願意被承認的。讓我們來看看下列書籍中所討論到關於財富的部分。

B. In *The Millionaire Next Door*, it overturns conventional views that people who drive luxury cars and people living in fancy mansions are the wealthy ones. It also challenges the idea that living in a luxurious residentiary area reflects a person's wealth. Sometimes it is something invisible or relatively marginal that shapes our wealth or helps us retain our wealth. As people are more familiar with American cultures, the phrase "keep up with the Jones" is often heard. People are so easily influenced by those who live close to them. The idea of "keep up with the Jones" aggravates the phenomenon of excessive spending, since you want to keep up with your neighbors. Whether it is the new sports car they are parking in their garage or the expensive schools they send their kids into, those trivial, petty, and unnecessary comparisons are causing superfluous spending. For the long term, this behavior is the invisible hand that takes away the wealth from you.

在《原來有錢人都這麼做》中，它推翻了傳統的觀點，開豪華車和居住在奢華豪宅的人們是具有財富者。它也挑戰了居住在豪華住宅區是反映出一個人對財富的想法。有時候這些

Test 2

1
TEST
2 Reading Passage 2
TEST

3
TEST

4
TEST

隱形的或相對微不足道的想法形塑著我們的財富和協助我們留住財富。隨著人們更熟悉美國文化，「與鄰居或朋友家比排場、比闊氣」是常聽到的俗諺。人們很容易受到居住在他們附近的人的影響。「與鄰居或朋友家比排場、比闊氣」加劇了過度消費的現象，因為你想要趕上你的鄰居們。不論是鄰居們停靠在車庫的新跑車或是他們將小孩送進的昂貴學校，那些微不足道、瑣碎且不需要的比較，正導致過度消費。長遠來看，這個行為是把你將財富推離你的隱形推手。

C. Furthermore, people nowadays are falling into the trap of having to earn more. How people spend their paycheck determines how wealthy they are. The idea of living-the-life to-the-fullest is dragging todays' people down the poverty, since more money cannot solve the problem. In *The Millionaire Next Door*, it also cautions "one earns to spend. When you need to spend more, you need to earn more". If you really care about your wealth, then quit having the mindset of "work hard and play hard". It really is the reasons why multiple thirtysomethings are not having an adequate amount of savings nowadays.

此外，人們現今正陷入必須要賺取更多的陷阱。人們如何花費及他們的收入決定著他們會多富有。充分運用生命值的想法正將現代人拉往貧窮，因為更多的金錢無法解決問題。在《原來有錢人都這麼做》中，它告誡著「人為了花費而賺取更多。當你需要花費更多時，你需要賺取更多。」如果你真在乎你的財富，那麼就戒除「努力工作和努力花錢」的心態。這真的是現今許多三十多歲的人沒有足夠的存款的原因。

D. In another book, *Millionaire Teacher*, it explores other areas that can be quite insightful for today's twentysomethings, since the earlier you start, the better your retirement life is. It discusses a story of a girl named Star and her girlfriend Lucy. How is the person like Lucy, who has a fantastic job and lives a luxurious life, will be having a financial problem in the long term, and for a person like Star, who earns much less than Lucy, is the one who informs Lucy that "she is the one in financial trouble". It is worth people's time rethinking about their finance.

在另一本書《我用死薪水輕鬆理財賺千萬》中，它探討了其他的領域，對於現今二十多歲的人來說是相當具有洞察力的，因為你越早開始的話，你就能越早退休。它討論著一個叫做星的女孩和她的女性朋友露西。一位像露西這樣有著很棒的工作且過著奢華生活的人，長遠來看會有財務問題，而一位像星這樣，比露西賺相對少的人，卻是由她來告訴露西說「她才是那位會有財務困境者」。這很值得人們花時間去重新思考關於他們的財務。

Test 2

1
TEST

2
TEST
Reading Passage 2

3
TEST

4
TEST

E. In addition to topics these above-mentioned two books explore, many books all mention the importance of saving money. In *The Richest Man in Babylon*, it talks about "money comes from those who save it". Another book, *Rich Dad and Poor Dad* also mentions a similar concept. It is really essential for anyone to save the money. Books have informed us of the importance of saving money, and in *Millionaire Success Habits*, it states something different, "the success hack, however isn't as much about money as it is about confidence." Confidence and success are correlated. The extra cash does work in the time of need and is the invisible hand that shapes one's confidence on the inside. When you are not desperate for money, you seem quite poised. This is especially helpful when it comes to finding a job. You won't seem reckless and you won't have to settle for a job that is less than you deserve. Trust me, stashing money is not an old concept. It is always perennially in vogue.

除了上述這兩本書籍所討論到的主題,許多書籍都有提到存錢的重要性。在《巴比倫最富有的人》中,他談論到「錢來自於那些將它存下的人」。另一本書,《窮爸爸富爸爸》也提到的相似的概念。這對於任何將金錢存下的人來說相當重要。書籍已經告知我們存錢的重要性,而在《百萬成功習慣》中，它陳述了一些不太一樣的部分，「成功，不是關於金錢，而是關於自信」。自信和成功是相互關聯的。額外的現金在需要的時候就能發揮作用，而且這是塑造一個人內在自信的隱形之手。當你不是那麼迫切需要金錢時，你似乎相當鎮定。當提到找工作時，這是相當有幫助的。你不會看起來輕率，而且你不用遷就於低於符合你能力的工作。相信我，存錢不是舊觀念。它是永久流行的。

F. Education is also the key to getting wealthy. Going to a prestigious university is not that important. The point is that you really need to have a life-long learning mindset. In *the Millionaire Fastlane*, it certainly sets people straight. "The rich understand that education doesn't end with a graduation ceremony; it starts. The world is in constant flux, and as it evolves your education must evolve". That is why you can find many celebrities, such Bill Gates and many others all have reading habits. This might dull many people, but it really is the key. The suggestion in *Secrets of the Millionaire Mind* at the very end of the book is not nothing. "Each month read at least one book" actually helps. Thus, with the right mindset, correct habits, and continued education, all people can gain the wealth they need and thrive in this age of turmoil and economic downturn.

教育也是獲得財富的關鍵。進入頗負盛名的大學不是那樣重要。重點是你真的需要有終身學習的心態。在《財富快車道》中，它確實導正了人們的觀念。「有錢人了解到教育並不止於畢業典禮，它是開始。這個世界是不斷的在變動，而當它演進時你的教育也必須演進」。這也是為什麼你能發現許多名人，像是比爾‧蓋茲和許多其他人都有閱讀的習慣。這可能會讓許多人感到沉悶，但是這真的是關鍵。在《有錢人跟你想的不一樣》書籍最尾端的建議不是沒什麼。「每個月至少閱讀一本書」是真的有幫助。因此，有著對的心態、正確習慣和持續教育，所有人都能獲得他們所需的財富，並且能在這個混亂且經濟蕭條的時代繁盛著。

You should spend about 20 minutes on **Questions 28-40**, which are based on Reading Passage 3 below.

The Value of a Diploma

A. The value of a college diploma has been an ongoing debate for generations after generations. People with different educational backgrounds can have quite different viewpoints. Sometimes values have been distorted through our upbringing and sometimes the media is guiding millions of twentysomethings into the wrong path, letting them know the value of a college diploma is valued less. It seems that different parties can hardly reach the consensus. Luckily, several bestsellers have brought us to the right path. Let's take a look.

B. *The Third Door* is very similar to *Lean In : for Graduate* in that it explores several issues really suitable for high school students and college graduates to read. The author of *The Third Door* also has the question when it comes to the value of a college diploma. Most twentysomethings deem celebrities, such as Bill Gates and Mark Zuckerberg as college dropouts, but are still very successful. Certainly, a college degree is superfluous and being entrepreneurs is as easy as it seems. The viewpoint is aggravated by news headlines which claim that you don't have to possess a fancy degree to be successful. You can be like Bill Gates and Mark Zuckerberg, tossing prestigious degrees aside, but is this like what the media tells us or are they just telling a simplified version of how things go between those entrepreneurs.

C. The author of *The Third Door* goes even further to search for the answer. What he finds out is totally different from what the media portrays. When asked by venture capitalists, Zuckerberg answers that he plans to continue his junior education. Later, he only states the fact the he wants to take a semester off, not being a reckless dropout. When it comes to Bill Gates, "Gates didn't impulsively drop out of college either". If things do not go well or successful, entrepreneurs are still going back to continue their education. They are still valuing the importance of having a college degree. College degrees are not worthless. In fact, they are still essential and quite valuable. It is the foundation for anyone of us.

D. It is quite true that the importance of the college education can never be underestimated. You cannot get through the screening process by company HR, if you do not possess a college degree, and without work experiences, the evaluations can mostly be based on your college degree.

E. After you graduate, a fancy diploma can sometimes be the golden ticket for college graduates, opening certain doors for many twentysomethings. They get to have the experiences others may have never had in their lifetime. Because of this, parents are so eager to send their kids to the Ivies, deeming this is the only way for their kids to be successful. This has led to a mania, a phenomenon elucidated and explored further by bestselling books, such as *Where You Go Is Not Who You Will Be*. Parents are going to the extreme, trying their best to send their kids to elite kindergartens. According to the author, "if you don't have perfect scores on every standardized test since the second grade, your visions of Stanford would be termed hallucinations".

F. In addition to grades, there are other criteria and it is quite impossible for ones to excel at everything. The important point is for parents to dial back. Possessing a fancy degree is just a good start, but it is not a guarantee. There are multiple difficult life lessons that simply possessing high SAT scores won't be the cure. Even professors, such as Michael J. Mauboussin, a Columbia Business professor and a bestselling author of *The Success Equation: Untangling Skill and Luck in Business, Sports, and Investing*, admit that they speculate the validity of the SAT. It is great to have a fancy diploma but life is long and arduous and the most important thing for us to do is to have a life-long learning mindset.

G. Life is like the survival of the fittest. Every year, millions of college graduates are looking for a job. The society certainly eliminates the ones who do not keep improving themselves. Like what is described in *The Millionaire Fastlane*, "The world is in constant flux, and as it evolves your education must move with it or you will drift to mediocrity." It is also important to know that "careers aren't built on the names of colleges" because "it is built on carefully honed skills, ferocious work ethics, and good attitudes."

H. So for millions of parents and college graduates, it is quite essential for us to really know the true value of a college diploma, and uses it to our advantage, not against us. In the era of great turmoil and underachievement, all of us should be truly well-prepared, looking at what's beyond the name of prestigious university and climbing out of the mess so that we can thrive on what life is about to test us.

Questions 28-34

Reading Passage 3 has six paragraphs, A-F

Which paragraph contains the following information?

Write the correct letter, A-F, in boxes 28-34 on your answer sheet.

NB You may use any letter more than once.

28 mention of an establishment that parents fancy

29 a description of an estimation used by a department

30 mention of a common ground that is unlikely to arrive at

31 mention of a standardized examination and its effectiveness

32 mention of three characteristics that careers are constructed

33 a description of unlikelihood to be omnipotent

34 a description of two bestsellers ideal for certain age groups to read

Questions 35-36
Complete the sentences below
Choose ONE WORD ONLY from the passage for each answer.
Write your answers in boxes 35-36 on your answer sheet.

35. Most twentysomethings think they can be like _____ without the need to have a fancy degree to be successful.

36. For college graduates who do not have many work experiences, companies can chiefly do the _____ on the basis of their educational backgrounds.

Do the following statements agree with the information given in the Reading Passage 3?

In boxes 37-40 on your answer sheet, write

TRUE- if the statement agrees with the information
FALSE- if the statement contradicts the information
NOT GIVEN- if there is no information on this

37. The media is the main culprit that leads twentysomething to believe college degrees are not valuable.

38. What the author of *The Third Door* finds is very similar to what the media describes.

39. Venture capitalists convince Zuckerberg to keep on his junior education.

40. Kids sending to elite kindergartens are bound to get higher SAT scores.

試題中譯

問題 **28** 到 **34**

閱讀文章第一篇有六個段落，**A-F**

哪個段落包含了下列資訊？

在你的答案紙，**28-34** 答案欄中，寫上正確的字母 **A-F**

NB 你可能使用任何一個字母超過一次

28 提及父母們都偏好的一個學校機構

29 描述由一個部門所使用的評估

30 提及一個共同的立場，卻難以達到

31 提及一個標準化的考試和其效率

32 提及三個建構職涯的的特徵

33 描述無所不能的不可能性

34 描述兩本暢銷書籍非常適合特定的年齡族群閱讀

問題 35-36

完成下列句子

從這篇閱讀文章中，每題選擇不超過一個字的答案

在你的答案紙，**35-36** 題答案欄中寫下你的答案

35. 20 幾歲的人認為他們可能像是 ＿＿＿＿＿＿＿＿ 不需要有花俏的
    學歷就能成功。

36. 對沒有許多工作經驗的大學畢業生來說，公司主要做的 ＿＿＿＿＿＿
    ＿＿＿＿ 是基於他們的教育背景。

問題 **37** 到 **40**

以下敘述是否和閱讀篇章的資訊相同？

在你的答案紙，**37-40** 答案欄中，寫下：

TRUE – 如果敘述與資訊一致

FALSE – 如果敘述與資訊不一致

NOT GIVEN - 如果閱讀篇章沒提到以下敘述

37. 媒體是導致 20 幾歲的人相信大學學歷是沒有價值的罪魁禍首。
38. 《第三道門》的作者所發現的跟媒體所描述的非常相似。
39. 風險資本家們說服 Zuckerberg 持續他的大三教育。
40. 被送至菁英幼稚園的小孩們必定能獲取較高的 SAT 成績。

解析

Step 1：迅速看題型配置，再定出解題步驟

　　這篇文章的題型有：❶配對_段落細節題（Which paragraph contains the following information）、❷單句填空題和❸判斷題。

　　配對_段落細節題敘述開頭常以...an example of/a reference of.../mention of...等等開始，名詞片語或子句有時候拉太長，這樣回推其實太慢，看到這類題目直接理解成，段落中**有提到、描述或列舉中那些資訊**，並且以關鍵字快速定位回文章搜尋，單句填空題有的難，過於細節性的要特別注意，判斷題的話就照常答就好了。

Step 2：腦海中浮現答題策略，開始答題

　　這篇既然有❶配對_段落細節題（Which paragraph contains the following information）、❷單句填空題和❸判斷題，可以先答**配對_段落細節題**，並一併搜尋這兩個題型的相關關鍵字，**逐題回去尋找資訊太浪費時間，請同步找**，所以掃描第 1 題到第 8 題關鍵字，至少腦海中要浮現 4-5 個關鍵點，例如 an **establishment** that parents fancy, an estimation used by **a department**, a **common** ground that is unlikely to arrive at, a **standardized examination** and its **effectiveness**, three characteristics that careers are constructed, **unlikelihood to be omnipotent**, two bestsellers ideal for certain age groups to read，掌握這些資訊後開始讀段落，除了這些資訊也注意每個人物，每個人物均可能是出題點。

◆ 要注意**高階名詞**的使用，高階名詞的使用是初階到中高階閱讀者仍有時候找不到對應訊息的主因，可以多熟悉，然後先邊讀邊答這類型的題目。

◆ 先看第一段，在 Sometimes values have been distorted through our upbringing and sometimes the media is guiding millions of twentysomethings into the wrong path, letting them know the value of a college diploma is valued less. It seems that different parties **can hardly reach the consensus**. 在同義轉換的部分要注意到 **can hardly reach the consensus.** 可以對應到第 30 題的 **a common ground that is unlikely to arrive at** ，所以**第 30 題**答案是 **A**。

◆ 緊接著看 B 段落，***The Third Door*** is very similar to ***Lean In：for Graduate*** in that it explores several issues **really suitable for** high school students and college graduates to read. ***The Third Door*** 和 ***Lean In：for Graduate*** = **two bestsellers**，在同義轉換的部分要注意到 **really suitable for = ideal for**，high school students and college graduates = certain age groups，所以**第 34 題**答案是 **B**。

◆ 接著很快看到 D 段落，It is quite true that the importance of the college education can never be underestimated. You cannot get through the screening process by **company HR**, if you do not possess a college degree, and without work experiences, the evaluations can mostly be based on your college degree. ，**a department = HR**，an estimation 是人事部門的評估（這種類型的轉換在劍橋雅思試題中也很常見），所以**第 29 題**答案為 **D**。

◆ 很快到了 E 段落，This has led to a mania, a phenomenon elucidated and explored further by bestselling books, such as *Where You Go Is Not Who You Will Be*. Parents are going to the extreme, trying their best to send their kids to **elite kindergartens**.，這題比較難，可是 **kindergartens** 其實是 **establishment**，可以利用 parents fancy 協助定位並找到這題的答案，所以**第 28 題**的答案是 **E**。

◆ 馬上看到 F 段落，首句 In addition to grades, there are other criteria and it is **quite impossible for ones to excel at everything**.，要能聯想到 **unlikelihood to be omnipotent**，在同義轉換的部分要注意到 **unlikelihood = impossible**，**excel at everything = omnipotent**，所以**第 33 題**的答案是 **F**。

◆ 接著，Even professors, such as Michael J. Mauboussin, a Columbia Business professor and a bestselling author of *The Success Equation: Untangling Skill and Luck in Business, Sports, and Investing*, admit that they speculate the **validity** of the **SAT**.，看到 **SAT** 和 **validity**，要馬上能聯想到對應的字，分別是 **a standardized examination** 和 **effectiveness**，這樣就能很快答好這題，所以第 **31** 題的答案是 **F**。

◆ 然後是 G 段落，It is also important to know that "careers aren't built on the names of colleges" because "it is built on carefully **honed skills, ferocious work ethics, and good attitudes**."，看到這裡要能聯想到三個特徵，**three characteristics** that careers are constructed 指的就是這三個，所以第 **32** 題的答案是 **G**。

◆ 接著看兩題單句填空題，第 **35** 題 Most **twentysomethings** think they can be like _____ without the need to have a fancy degree to be **successful**.，使用 twentysomethings 和 successful 定位到 Most twentysomethings deem celebrities, such as Bill Gates and Mark Zuckerberg as college dropouts, but are still very successful.，答案很明顯是 **celebrities**，所以第 **35** 題的答案是 **celebrities**。

◆ 第 **36** 題，For college graduates who **do not have many work experiences**, companies can **chiefly** do the _____ __ on the basis of their educational backgrounds.，使用 **do not have many work experiences** 定位到 It is quite true that the importance of the college education can never be underestimated. You cannot get through the screening process by company HR, if you do not possess a college degree, and **without work experiences**, the **evaluations** can **mostly** be **based on your college degree**.，在同義轉換的部分要注意到 **without work experiences = do not have many work experiences**，**mostly = chiefly**，**based on your college degree = on the basis of their educational backgrounds**，所以第 **36** 題的答案是 **evaluations**。

◆ 第 **37** 題，The **media** is the main **culprit** that leads **twentysomething** to believe **college degrees** are not valuable.運用關鍵字定位到首段 Sometimes values have been distorted through our upbringing and sometimes the media is guiding millions of twentysomethings into the wrong path, letting them know the value of a college diploma is **valued less**.。在同義轉換的部分要注意到 **not valuable = valued less** 所以第 **37** 題的答案是 **True**。

◆ 第 **38** 題，What **the author of _The Third Door_** finds is **very similar** to what the media describes.，運用 **the author _of The Third Door_** 定位到 **The author of _The Third Door_** goes even further to search for the answer. What he finds out is **totally different** from what the media portrays.，所以兩者是不同的，題目和文章**語意相斥**，所以第 **38** 題的答案是 **False**。

◆ 第 **39** 題，**Venture capitalists** convince **Zuckerberg** to keep on his junior education. ，運用 **Venture capitalists** 和 **Zuckerberg** 定位並跳讀，When asked by **venture capitalists**, **Zuckerberg** answers that he plans to continue his junior education. Later, he only states the fact the he wants to take a semester off, not being a reckless dropout. ，所以仔細一看後可以知道並沒有 convince，所以**第 39 題**的答案是 **False**。

◆ 第 **40** 題，Kids sending to **elite kindergartens** are bound to get higher **SAT** scores. ，運用 **elite kindergartens** 和 **SAT** 很快就能定位到 Parents are going to the extreme, trying their best to send their kids to elite kindergartens. According to the author, "if you don't have perfect scores on every standardized test since the second grade, your visions of Stanford would be termed hallucinations"。

◆ 繼續閱讀到有題到 **SAT** 的段落也沒有關於 are bound to get higher **SAT** scores 的相關訊息，而且要注意 are bound to 這個**過於絕對**的片語，其實並沒有這樣的關聯性，所以**第 40 題**的答案是 **Not Given**。

中譯和影子跟讀

A. The value of a college diploma has been an ongoing debate for generations after generations. People with different educational backgrounds can have quite different viewpoints. Sometimes values have been distorted through our upbringing and sometimes the media is guiding millions of twentysomethings into the wrong path, letting them know the value of a college diploma is valued less. It seems that different parties can hardly reach the consensus. Luckily several bestsellers have brought us to the right path. Let's take a look.

大學文憑的價值一直在世代間持續的辯論著。有著不同教育背景的人能有相當不同的觀點。透過我們成長過程的不同和有媒體的存在，有時價值一直受到扭曲，將數百萬二十多歲的人導向了錯誤的道路上，讓他們認為大學文憑是相對不具價值的。似乎不同方幾乎不能達成共識。幸運地是，幾個暢銷作家將我們導回了正途。讓我們看一看。

B. *The Third Door* is very similar to *Lean In：for Graduate* in that it explores several issues really suitable for high school students and college graduates to read. The author of *The Third Door* also has the question when it comes to the value of a college diploma. Most twentysomethings deem celebrities such as Bill Gates and Mark Zuckerberg as college dropouts, but are still very successful. Certainly, a college degree is superfluous and being entrepreneurs is as easy as it seems. The viewpoint is aggravated by news headlines which claim that you don't have to possess a fancy degree to be successful. You can be like Bill Gates and Mark Zuckerberg, tossing prestigious degrees aside, but is this like what the media tells us or are they just telling a simplified version of how things go between those entrepreneurs.

《第三道門》與《挺身而進：致畢業生》有非常多的相似之處，因為他們都探討了幾個議題，相當適合高中生和大學畢業生閱讀。當提到大學文憑的價值時，第三道門的作者也有著疑惑。大多數二十多歲的人認為名人像是比爾‧蓋茲和馬克‧佐克伯是大學輟學生，但是仍非常成功。無疑地，大學學歷是不必要的，而且成為創業家就像是表面上那樣看起來很簡單。這個觀點更因為新聞標題而加劇，宣稱你不需要有花俏的學歷就能夠成功。你可以像是比爾‧蓋茲和馬克‧佐克伯，將頗具盛名的學歷丟在一旁，但是真的就像是媒體所告訴我們的這樣或是他們只是告訴了我們關於那些創業家，過於簡化版的事情經過。

C. The author of *The Third Door* goes even further to

search for the answer. What he finds out is totally different from what the media portrays. When asked by venture capitalists, Zuckerberg answers that he plans to continue his junior education. Later, he only states the fact the he wants to take a semester off, not being a reckless dropout. When it comes to Bill Gates, "Gates didn't impulsively drop out of college either". If things do not go well or successful, entrepreneurs are still going back to continue their education. They are still valuing the importance of having a college degree. College degrees are not worthless. In fact, they are still essential and quite valuable. It is the foundation for anyone of us.

《第三道門》的作者更進一步去找尋這個答案。他所找到的答案卻截然不同於媒體所描繪的。當被風險資本家問到時，佐克伯僅述說他想要休學一學期，而非輕率地輟學。當提到比爾蓋茲時，「比爾蓋茲也是，並非衝動地輟學」。如果事情沒有進展順利或成功，創業家仍舊回到校園繼續他們的教育。他們仍舊重視大學學歷的重要性。大學學歷並非無價值。事實上，他們仍舊是重要的，且相當有價值。這是我們任何一人的基礎。

D. It is quite true that the importance of the college education can never be underestimated. You cannot get through the screening process by company HR, if you do not possess a college degree, and without work experiences, the evaluations can mostly be based on your college degree.

相當真實的是，大學學歷的重要性是不能被低估的。如果你不具備大學學歷，而且不具有工作經驗時，你不可能通過公司人事專員的篩選過程。公司對於你的評估真的大多數時候僅能仰賴你的大學學歷。

E. After you graduate, a fancy diploma can sometimes be the golden ticket for college graduates, opening certain doors for many twentysomethings. They get to have the experiences others may have never had in their lifetime. Because of this, parents are so eager to send their kids to the Ivies, deeming this is the only way for their kids to be successful. This has led to a mania, a phenomenon elucidated and explored further by bestselling books, such as *Where You Go Is Not Who You Will Be*. Parents are going to the extreme, trying their best to send their kids to elite kindergartens. According to the author, "if you don't have perfect scores on every standardized test since the second grade, your visions of Stanford would be termed hallucinations".

在你畢業後，花俏的文憑可能有時候是大學畢業生的鍍金門票，為許多二十多歲的人開起特定的機會之門。他們可以有著其他人這輩子都無法經歷過的經驗。也因為這樣，父母非常渴望將他們的小孩子送進常春藤盟校，認為這是他們的小孩子成功的唯一機會。這導致了一個狂熱，這個現象進一步由暢銷書，像是《念哪所學校不代表你未來的成就》解釋和探討著。父母正走向極端，盡他們所能地將他們的小孩送進菁英幼稚園。根據作者，「如果你自從二年級，在每個標準化考試中不具備有完美的分數，你要上史丹佛的願景就會被認為是幻想」。

F. In addition to grades, there are other criteria and it is quite impossible for ones to excel at everything. The important point is for parents to dial back. Possessing a fancy degree is just a good start, but it is not a guarantee. There are multiple difficult life lessons that simply possessing high SAT scores won't be the cure. Even professors, such as Michael J. Mauboussin, a Columbia Business professor and a bestselling author of *The Success Equation: Untangling Skill and Luck in Business, Sports, and Investing*, admit that they speculate the validity of the SAT. It is great to have a fancy diploma but life is long and arduous and the most important thing for us to do is to have a life-long learning mindset.

除了分數之外，還有其他標準，而且不太可能要一個人在每個項目上都擅長。重點是將父母導回正途。擁有花俏的文憑僅是好的開端，但是這並非是保證。有許多人生的難題其實是 SAT 高分所無法解答的。甚至像是麥克‧莫布新，哥倫比亞商學院教授和《成功與運氣：解構商業、運動與投資，預測成功的決策智慧》的暢銷書作者，坦承他質疑 SAT 的有效性。有著花俏的文憑是很棒的，但是人生很長且艱苦，而對我們來說最重要的是有著終身學習的心態。

G. Life is like the survival of the fittest. Every year, millions of college graduates are looking for a job. The society certainly eliminates the ones who do not keep improving themselves. Like what is described in *The Millionaire Fastlane*, "The world is in constant flux, and as it evolves your education must move with it or you will drift to mediocrity." It is also important to know that "careers aren't built on the names of colleges" because "it is built on carefully honed skills, ferocious work ethics, and good attitudes."

人生像是適者生存。每年，數百萬的大學畢業生正找著工作。社會確實淘汰了那些自己本身不持續努力者。像是在《百萬財富快車道》中所描述的，「這個世界不斷地演進，而你的教育必須要跟著成長，否則你就會落入平庸之中」。了解「職涯並不是建立在學校的名字上」這點是很重要的，因為「職涯是建立在幾經磨練的技術、驚人的工作道德和良好的態度上」。

H. So for millions of parents and college graduates, it is quite essential for us to really know the true value of a college diploma, and uses it to our advantage, not against us. In the era of great turmoil and underachievement, all of us should be truly well-prepared, looking at what's beyond the name of prestigious university and climbing out of the mess so that we can thrive on what life is about to test us.

所以對於數百萬父母和大學畢業生來說，相當重要的是真的了解大學文憑的價值，而且利用這點使之成為我們的優勢，而非劣勢。在巨大混亂和學非所用的時代，我們所有人都應該要充分準備，目光要超越有名聲的大學名字之上和從雜亂中爬出，這樣一來我們才能在生命要考驗我們的時候成長茁壯。

READING PASSAGE 1

You should spend about 20 minutes on **Questions 1-13**, which are based on Reading Passage 1 below.

The Romance of the Three Kingdoms:
A honey plot employed by Diao Chan

A. Through thousands of years of evolution, our mind is still not invincible enough to resist any temptation. That is, our decision can still be easily swayed by things we desire or things we care about the most. In *"The Romance of the Three Kingdoms"*, we can clearly see multiple maneuvers employed by different masters to get things to work out the way they have been envisioning or expecting. A pure heart can be the cure for the scheming, but not everyone can be as innocent and unavaricious; therefore, numerous characters in *"The Romance of the Three Kingdoms"* are susceptible to getting used by someone. Most of the time, they are just unaware of how things evolve, but they are just like prey falling onto the sticky and gigantic spider web. There are certain fates that await. Even though some characters possess certain levels of protective mechanisms, it is true that almost everyone has his or her own achiilies' heel. Some weaknesses are more apparent than the others. It is just sooner or later for masters of maneuvers to find out.

B. In *"The Romance of the Three Kingdoms"*, Lu Bu（呂布）is a great warrior. In fact, he is so great that several lords would like to recruit him for different reasons. In the earlier scenes, Lu Bu works for his godfather Ding Yuan（丁原）, and he has no intention to betray Ding Yuan. Deep down, Lu Bu is a very shortsighted guy who puts immediate interests and treasures much ahead of everything else, even the relationship with his godfather. At the time, Dong Zhuo（董卓）is trying to get rid of Ding Yuan, so he adopts his army officer Li Su's idea using plenty of money and Red Hare to sway Lu Bu's fidelity towards Ding Yuan. At the moment Lu Bu sees Red Hare, he instantly loves this incredible horse. His loyalty wanes eventually leading him to fall into the trap set by Li Su and end the life of Ding Yuan.

C. Of course, Dong Zhuo is not the only person who knows plotting and scheming. In a later episode, ministers of Han Dynasty are upsetting about Dong Zhuo, as Dong Zhuo has become increasingly ruthless and powerful. With Lu Bu on his side, several attempts by united allies are dissuaded. A later incident at the feast triggers Wang Yun's plot of overthrowing Dong Zhuo. (everyone at the feast is appalled by how Dong Zhuo murders a minister). Upon reflecting what happened at the banquet, Wang Yun could not sleep. He walked to a garden. There he saw a stunningly beautiful girl, Diao Chan（貂蟬）, who is his serving girl. He had an epiphany, using Diao Chan to drive a wedge between Lu Bu and Dong Zhuo. Since Lu Bu is a womanizer, using Diao Chan as a temptation will work.

D. The following day Lu Bu is invited to Wang Yun's house and is served by Diao Chan. The beauty of Diao Chan moves Lu Bu to a certain degree. The effect is what Wang Yun is going for. He promises Lu Bu that he agrees Diao Chan to be married with him as his concubine. This exhilarates Lu Bu, but what Lu Bu does not know is that the same trick employed by Wang Yun is used the next day when Wang Yun arranges Diao Chan to meet with Dong Zhuo. As predicted, Dong Zhuo is head over hills in love with Diao Chan. Wang Yun wants to send Diao Chan to Dong Zhuo's house in person. Deception furies Lu Bu, but Wang Yun comes up with a different explanation, saying that the prime minister knows that Diao Chan is betrothed to him. Dong Zhuo is simply asking me to send Diao Chan to his house so that he can preside over the wedding for you.

E. Lu Bu assumes that Dong Zhuo will preside over the wedding for him, only to find that Dong Zhuo is the one who sleeps with Diao Chan. There seems to be a contraction between Dong Zhuo and Lu Bu. The seed of anger seems to sow in the heart of Lu Bu. His rebel against Dong Zhuo has become increasingly apparent. Diao Chan, on the other hand, plays both men. She manages to be a perfect concubine for Dong, but in front of Lu Bu, she exhibits the fragile side of herself, beguiling Lu Bu into believing that she has no control over the situation, which makes Lu Bu heartache. Dong Zhuo senses that there seems to be something unusual about Lu Bu's behavior towards Diao Chan. Lu Bu might have feelings toward Diao Chan. The conjecture increases Dong's vigilance and doubts.

F. A later incident in Dong's garden proves that Dong Zhuo is right about them all along. He witnesses Diao Chan is embraced in the arm of Lu Bu. Dong cannot seem to tolerate his view of seeing them. He throws a weapon towards Lu Bu, but the attack is blocked. Dong's military adviser suggests the idea of giving away Diao Chan. This makes Dong hesitant and Dong's negotiation with Diao Chan leads to a getaway for both of them to Mei Wu. Wang Yun makes another move, trying to persuade Lu Bu to kill Dong Zhuo. He even comes up with a sound saying so that Lu Bu does not have to worry about how he is perceived by citizens of his time or people of the later generation. The success of killing Dong Zhuo results from Wang Yuan's plot, but the contribution is mostly the honey trap set by Diao Chan. Even Cao Cao（曹操）and Yuan Shao（袁紹）fail to kill Dong Zhuo.

英文試題

Questions 1-4

Reading Passage 1 has six paragraphs, A-F

Which paragraph contains the following information?

Write the correct letter, A-F, in boxes 1-4 on your answer sheet.

NB You may use any letter more than once.

1 mention of a stratagem that can split two people apart

2 a description of a scene that is unbearable for someone to watch

3 mention of an event that engenders the honey pot

4 mention of a human trait that can be the panacea for the plot

Questions 5-9

Look at the following statements (Questions 5-9) and the list of people below.

Match each statement with the correct people, A-F

Write the correct letter, A-F, in boxes 5-9 on your answer sheet.

NB You may use any letter more than once.

5 whose mood is driven by duplicity

6 whose advice to enlist a great champion works

7 whose alertness is enhanced due to something happening

8 whose affection towards someone pales in comparison with other incentives

9 whose maneuver hoodwinks participants

List of people
A Diao Chan
B Dong Zhuo
C Lu Bu
D Ding Yuan
E Li Su
F Wang Yuan

Questions 10-13

Complete the summary below

Choose ONE WORD ONLY from the passage for each answer

Write your answers in boxes 10-13 on your answer sheet.

Despite thousands of years of developments, our mind has yet to develop invulnerability to withstand any **10.** _____ . Our decisions are readily rocked by things we crave. In "*The Romance of the Three Kingdoms*", numerous **11.**_____ have been used to achieve certain results. Many characters have suffered due to a lack of **12.**_____ on how things will go. An **13.**_____ of a spider web is used to describe the phenomenon. Protection cannot seem to be the cure because almost everyone has his or her own weaknesses.

問題 **1** 到 **4**

閱讀文章第一篇有七個段落，**A-F**

哪個段落包含了下列資訊？

在你的答案紙，**1-4** 答案欄中，寫上正確的字母 **A-F**

NB 你可能使用任何一個字母超過一次

1 提到一個詭計，能拆散兩個人

2 描述一個場景，對於有些人來說難以目睹

3 提及一個事件產生美人計

4 提及人類的特徵，可能成為計謀的萬靈丹

問題 **5** 到 **9**

下列敘述（問題 5 到 9）和以下列表中的人物

將每個敘述與正確的人物，**A-F** 進行配對

在你的答案紙，**5-9** 答案欄中，寫上正確的字母 **A-F**

NB 你可能使用任何一個字母超過一次

5 某人的心情因受欺騙而驅動

6 某人招募優秀鬥士的建議發揮功效

7 某人由於某些事的發生使得警覺性提高

8 某人對於有些人的情感，因為其他誘因而相形見絀

9 某人巧妙地操控其他參與者

人物列表

A 貂蟬

B 董卓

C 呂布

D 丁原

E 李肅

F 王允

問題 10 到 13

完成下列摘要題

段落中的每個答案，請勿超過兩個單字

在你的答案紙，**10-13** 答案欄中，寫上你的答案

儘管數千年的進展，我們的心智尚未發展出無堅不摧的能力來抵擋任何的 10.＿＿＿＿＿＿。我們的決定輕易地受到我們所渴望的事物搖擺。在《三國演義》中，無數的 11.＿＿＿＿＿＿ 已用於達成特定的結果。許多角色因為缺乏 12.＿＿＿＿＿＿ 體認到事情是如何演進，而因此受苦。一個蜘蛛網的 13.＿＿＿＿＿＿ 用於描述這個現象。保護幾乎無法成為救治的良藥，因為幾乎每個人都有他或她的缺點在。

Test 3

1
TEST

2
TEST

3
TEST
Reading Passage 1

4
TEST

解析

Step 1：迅速看題型配置，再定出解題步驟

　　這篇文章的題型有：❶**配對_段落細節題**（Which paragraph contains the following information）、❷**配對_人物題**和❸**摘要題**。

　　配對_段落細節題敘述開頭常以...an example of/a reference of.../mention of...等等開始，名詞片語或子句有時候拉太長，這樣回推其實太慢，看到這類題目直接理解成，段落中**有提到、描述或列舉中那些資訊，並且以關鍵字快速定位回文章搜尋。**

Step 2：腦海中浮現答題策略，開始答題

　　這篇既然有❶**配對_段落細節題**（Which paragraph contains the following information）、❷**配對_人物題**，建議先答這兩個題型，並一併搜尋這兩個題型的相關關鍵字，<u>逐題回去尋找資訊太浪費時間，請同步找。</u>

◆ 所以掃描第 1 題到第 8 題關鍵字，至少腦海中要浮現 4-5 個關鍵點，例如 a **stratagem** that can split two people apart, a **scene** that is unbearable for someone to watch, an **event** that engenders the honey pot, a human **trait** that can be the panacea for the plot, **mood** is driven by **duplicity**, **advice** to enlist a great **champion** works, **alertness** is enhanced due to something happening, **affection** towards someone pales in comparison with **other incentives**, **maneuver hoodwinks** participants，掌握這些資訊後開始讀段落，除了這些資訊也注意每個人物，每個人物均可能是出題點。

◆ 接著開始讀，很快閱讀 A 段落的鋪陳來到 **A pure heart** can be the **cure** for the scheming, but not everyone can be as innocent and unavaricious，要盡快聯想到是 a human trait（如果一看到無法馬上想到，可以多做這個題目的練習，有時候突然想不到，要馬上快點看別題，時間一閃即過，可能之後馬上就想到答案了，到時再回過頭看這題），剛好對應第 4 題，在同義轉換的部分要注意到 **cure = panacea**，所以**第 4 題**很快可以知道答案為 **A**。

◆ 續讀 B 段落，In the earlier scenes, Lu Bu works for his godfather Ding Yuan（丁原），and he has **no intention to betray** Ding Yuan. Deep down, Lu Bu is a very **shortsighted guy who puts immediate interests and treasures much ahead of everything else, even the relationship with his godfather.** 粗體字表明了呂布的為人，而在同義轉換的部分要注意到 **other incentives** 對應到 **immediate interests and treasures**，affection 代表親情，親情比不上其他誘因/**godfather**，所以很快可以知道**第 8 題**答案為 **D Ding Yuan**。

◆ 繼續讀 B 段落 At that time, Dong Zhuo（董卓）is trying to get

rid of Ding Yuan, so he **adopts his army officer Li Su's idea** using plenty of **money and Red Hare** to sway Lu Bu's **fidelity** towards Ding Yuan. At the moment, Lu Bu sees Red Hare, he instantly loves this incredible horse. His loyalty wanes eventually leading him to fall into the trap set by Li Su and end the life of Ding Yuan.，接下來的文句其實都在描述第 6 題的敘述 advice to enlist a great champion works，其中 **enlist** 和 **recruit** 同義轉換，championg 是出類拔萃的人。所以第 6 題的答案為 **E Li Su**。

◆ 續讀 C 段落，A later incident at the feast triggers Wang Yun's plot of overthrowing Dong Zhuo. (everyone at the feast is appalled by how Dong Zhuo murders a minister).，**注意括號部分其實也是常考考點**，別讀太快或是覺得不重要而跳過了，**at the feast** 對應到 **incident**，等同第 3 題的敘述 an event that engenders the honey pot，也是因為這個事件促成了美人計的策劃，所以**第 3 題**答案為 **C**。

◆ 續讀 C 段落 He had an epiphany, using Diao Chan to **drive a wedge between Lu Bu and Dong Zhuo.** Since Lu Bu is a womanizer, using Diao Chan as a temptation will work.，其中 **drive a wedge between Lu Bu and Dong Zhuo** 等同第 1 題的敘述 a stratagem that can split two people apart，故**第 1 題**答案為 **C**。

◆ 接續閱讀 D 段落，要注意人名不斷重複，注意相關細節，在 **Deception furies Lu Bu**, but Wang Yun comes up with a different explanation...，這裡馬上可以聯想到題目第 5 題 **duplicity** 和 **deception** 同義轉換，而 **mood** 和 **furies** 有關，等同題目敘述 mood is driven by duplicity，故**第 5 題**答案為 **C**。

◆ 接續讀 E 段落，定位到 Diao Chan, on the other hand, **plays both men**. She manages to be a perfect concubine for Dong, but in front of Lu Bu, she exhibits the fragile side of herself, beguiling Lu Bu into believing that she has no control over the situation, which makes Lu Bu heartache.，這些敘述馬上可以對應到**第 9 題**的 maneuver hoodwinks participants，participants 廣義上指董卓和呂布，hoodwink 表示哄騙，participants 表示參與者和當局者，故**第 9 題**答案為 **A**。

◆ 接續讀此段落，Dong Zhuo senses that there seems to be something unusual about Lu Bu's behavior towards Diao Chan. Lu Bu might have feelings toward Diao Chan. The conjecture increases Dong's **vigilance** and doubts.，可以馬上對應到題目的 **alertness**，而敘述也相符，alertness is enhanced due to something happening，something happening 指的是呂布和貂蟬間不尋常的行為，故**第 7 題**答案為 **B** 董卓。

◆ 來到最後一段，A later incident in Dong's garden proves that Dong Zhuo is right about them all along. He witnesses Diao Chan is embraced in the arm of Lu Bu. **Dong cannot seem to tolerate his view of seeing them.** 這部分等同於 **a scene that is unbearable for someone to watch**，故**第 2 題**答案為 **F**。

◆ **第 10 題**，Despite thousands of years of **developments**, our mind has yet to develop invulnerability to withstand any 10. _____.對應到 A 段落首句 Through thousands of years of **evolution**, our mind is still not invincible enough to resist any **temptation**.，**developments** 換成 **evolution**，has yet to... = is not...，**develop invulnerability to withstand any** 對應 **invincible enough to resist any**，故**第 10 題**答案很明顯是 **temptation**。

◆ **第 11 題**，Our decisions are readily **rocked** by things we crave. In "*The Romance of the Three Kingdoms*", **numerous** 11. _____ **have** been used to achieve certain results.，以關鍵字 *The Romance of the Three Kingdoms* 定位，可以很清楚對應到 multiple **maneuvers** employed by different masters to get things to work out the way they have been envisioning or expecting，試題以另一個方式改寫成更簡化的描述，上句的 **rocked = swayed**，**numerous** 對應 **multiple**，從 have 得知空格為複數名詞，**第 11 題**答案很明確是

maneuvers。

- 第 **12** 題，Many characters have suffered due to a lack of 12._____ on **how things will go**.對應文章中的 numerous characters in *"The Romance of the Three Kingdoms"* are susceptible to getting used by someone. Most of the time, they are just unaware of **how things evolve**，**how things will go** 對應 **how things evolve**，而空格前方為介係詞，故後面依**語法**來說僅可能是**名詞**或**動名詞**，但描述是 **a lack of** 缺乏，所以要轉換成 **awareness**，而非 **unawareness**，這題要小心點，故第 **12** 題答案為 **awareness**。

- 第 **13** 題，**An** 13._____ of **a spider web** is used to describe the phenomenon. 對應到 they are just like prey falling onto the sticky and gigantic **spider web**.，文章下句的 protective mechanisms 對應到試題下句的 protection，後面敘述也跟答案無關了，這時候要構思出空格中的名詞是什麼，這用於描述這個現象，腦筋轉換一下，**很可能是用蜘蛛網作為類比來描述，而非直述，類比的名詞 analogy 也符合，且開頭為 an，an+analogy 符合語法**，故第 **13** 題答案為 **analogy**，這題要多費神些。

中譯和影子跟讀

A. Through thousands of years of evolution, our mind is still not invincible enough to resist any temptation. That is, our decision can still be easily swayed by things we desire or things we care about the most. In *"The Romance of the Three Kingdoms"*, we can clearly see multiple maneuvers employed by different masters to get things to work out the way they have been envisioning or expecting. A pure heart can be the cure for the scheming, but not everyone can be as innocent and unavaricious; therefore, numerous characters in *"The Romance of the Three Kingdoms"* are susceptible to getting used by someone. Most of the time, they are just unaware of how things evolve, but they are just like prey falling onto the sticky and gigantic spider web. There are certain fates that await. Even though some characters possess certain levels of protective mechanisms, it is true that almost everyone has his or her own achiilies' heel. Some weaknesses are more apparent than the others. It is just sooner or later for masters of maneuvers to find out.

透過幾千年的演化，我們的心智仍沒有演化至無堅不摧般，足以抵抗任何誘惑。也就是，我們渴望的事物或是我們最關切的事物仍輕易地擺動我們的決定。在《三國演義》中，我們可以清楚地看到不同的掌權者所使用的眾多謀略，讓事情以他們一直以來的願景或期待的方式發展。純潔的心是算計的解藥，但不是每個人都可以同樣地天真無邪以及不貪得無厭。因此，在《三國演義》中為數眾多的角色易受到某些人的利用。大多時候，他們沒有察覺到事情是如何演進，但是他們就像是陷入巨大且具黏性的蜘蛛網上的獵物般。特定的命運等待著他們。即使有些角色擁有特定程度的保護機制，幾乎每個人都有他或她本身的弱點卻是千真萬確的。有些弱點比其他的弱點更顯而易見。算計的掌權者遲早會察覺出。

B. In *"The Romance of the Three Kingdoms"*, Lu Bu（呂布）is a great warrior. In fact, he is so great that several lords would like to recruit him for different reasons. In the earlier scenes, Lu Bu works for his godfather Ding Yuan（丁原）, and he has no intention to betray Ding Yuan. Deep down, Lu Bu is a very shortsighted guy who puts immediate interests and treasures much ahead of everything else, even the relationship with his godfather. At the time, Dong Zhuo（董卓）is trying to get rid of Ding Yuan, so he adopts his army officer Li Su's idea using plenty of money and Red Hare to sway Lu Bu's fidelity towards Ding Yuan. At the moment Lu Bu sees Red Hare, he instantly loves this incredible horse. His loyalty wanes eventually leading him to fall into the trap set by Li Su and end the life of Ding Yuan.

在《三國演義》中，呂布是優秀的戰士。事實上，他是如此優秀以至於幾位領主因為不同的理由都想要招募他。在更早前的場景中，呂布替自己的義父工作，而他沒有想背叛丁原的意圖。在內心深處，呂布是非常短視近利的人，會將眼前利益和寶物，放得比任何其他事都還要重要，即使是與自己義父的親屬關係。在當時，董卓正嘗試要除掉丁原，所以他採用的是自己的將士李肅的想法，使用大量金錢和赤兔馬來動搖呂布對丁原的忠誠度。當呂布目睹赤兔馬時，他即刻愛上這匹驚人的馬。他的忠誠度最終消失殆盡，導致他落入了李肅的陷阱，而終結了丁原的生命。

C. Of course, Dong Zhuo is not the only person who knows plotting and scheming. In a later episode, ministers of Han Dynasty are upsetting about Dong Zhuo, as Dong Zhuo has become increasingly ruthless and powerful. With Lu Bu on his side, several attempts by united allies are dissuaded. A later incident at the feast triggers Wang Yun's plot of overthrowing Dong Zhuo. (everyone at the feast is appalled by how Dong Zhuo murders a minister). Upon reflecting what happened at the banquet, Wang Yun could not sleep. He walked to a garden. There he saw a stunningly beautiful girl, Diao Chan（貂蟬）, who is his serving girl. He had an epiphany, using Diao Chan to drive a wedge between Lu Bu and Dong Zhuo. Since Lu Bu is a womanizer, using Diao Chan as a temptation will work.

當然，董卓不是唯一一位懂得策劃和密謀的人。在更後面的集數中，漢朝大臣們對於董卓感到苦惱，當董卓已變得日益殘酷和強大時。隨著呂布在他身旁，聯盟的行動受阻。更後面於宴會中發生的事件觸發了王允密謀要推翻董卓。（每位在宴會者都因董卓如何謀殺大臣的事感到吃驚。）回想起在宴會中發生的一切，王允無法入睡。他走到花園處。在那裡他看見容貌驚為天人的美麗女子貂蟬，貂蟬是位女侍從。他有了一個頓悟，利用貂蟬來分化呂布和董卓。既然呂布是沉迷女色的人，利用貂蟬當作誘惑終能成事。

D. The following day Lu Bu is invited to Wang Yun's house and is served by Diao Chan. The beauty of Diao Chan moves Lu Bu to a certain degree. The effect is what Wang Yun is going for. He promises Lu Bu that he agrees Diao Chan to be married with him as his concubine. This exhilarates Lu Bu, but what Lu Bu does not know is that the same trick employed by Wang Yun is used the next day when Wang Yun arranges Diao Chan to meet with Dong Zhuo. As predicted, Dong Zhuo is head over hills in love with Diao Chan. Wang Yun wants to send Diao Chan to Dong Zhuo's house in person. Deception furies Lu Bu, but Wang Yun comes up with a different explanation, saying that the prime minister knows that Diao Chan is betrothed to him. Dong Zhuo is simply asking me to send Diao Chan to his house so that he can preside over the wedding for you.

次日，呂布受邀至王允的房內，由貂蟬侍奉他。貂蟬的美貌於某些程度上打動了呂布。這個效果就是王允所要的。他承諾呂布，同意貂蟬與他成婚，成為他的妾。此舉令呂布感到興奮，但是呂布所不知道的是，王允隔日也採用了相同的策略，安排貂蟬與董卓見面。如所預測的，董卓對貂蟬為之傾倒。王允想要將貂蟬親自送至董卓住所。欺騙令呂布感到憤怒，但是王允想出了不同的解釋，述説丞相知道貂蟬將許配給他。董卓僅是要求我將貂蟬送至他的房子，這樣一來他就能替你主持婚禮了。

E. Lu Bu assumes that Dong Zhuo will preside over the wedding for him, only to find that Dong Zhuo is the one who sleeps with Diao Chan. There seems to be a contraction between Dong Zhuo and Lu Bu. The seed of anger seems to sow in the heart of Lu Bu. His rebel against Dong Zhuo has become increasingly apparent. Diao Chan, on the other hand, plays both men. She manages to be a perfect concubine for Dong, but in front of Lu Bu, she exhibits the fragile side of herself, beguiling Lu Bu into believing that she has no control over the situation, which makes Lu Bu heartache. Dong Zhuo senses that there seems to be something unusual about Lu Bu's behavior towards Diao Chan. Lu Bu might have feelings toward Diao Chan. The conjecture increases Dong's vigilance and doubts.

呂布假定董卓會主持婚禮，卻發現董卓與貂蟬睡在一塊。在董卓和呂布間似乎有著矛盾存在著。憤怒的種子似乎就這樣於呂布心中播種了。他對董卓的反叛已經日益明顯。貂蟬，另一方面則玩弄著兩個男人。她設法成為董的完美侍妾，但是在呂布面前，她展現出她脆弱的一面，欺騙呂布使他相信，貂蟬對於情勢發展是身不由己，這讓呂布更為頭疼。董卓感受到呂布對於貂蟬似乎有著不尋常的行為。呂布可能對於貂蟬有情愫。這個猜測增加了董卓的戒心和存疑。

F. A later incident in Dong's garden proves that Dong Zhuo is right about them all along. He witnesses Diao Chan is embraced in the arm of Lu Bu. Dong cannot seem to tolerate his view of seeing them. He throws a weapon towards Lu Bu, but the attack is blocked. Dong's military adviser suggests the idea of giving away Diao Chan. This makes Dong hesitant and Dong's negotiation with Diao Chan leads to a getaway for both of them to Mei Wu. Wang Yuan makes another move, trying to persuade Lu Bu to kill Dong Zhuo. He even comes up with a sound saying so that Lu Bu does not have to worry about how he is perceived by citizens of his time or people of the later generation. The success of killing Dong Zhuo results from Wang Yun's plot, but the contribution is mostly the honey trap set by Diao Chan. Even Cao Cao（曹操）and Yuan Shao（袁紹）fail to kill Dong Zhuo.

後來在董卓花園中的事件證實了董卓的猜測無誤。他目睹了貂蟬被呂布擁抱著。董卓無法忍受他所目睹到他們擁抱的景象。他朝呂布擲了一件武器，但是攻擊被呂布阻擋下來。董卓的軍師建議將貂蟬贈與的想法。此舉讓董卓感到躊躇不前，而董卓與貂蟬的協商導致他們倆人雙宿至郿屋。王允使用了另一行動，試著說服呂布殺董卓。他甚至想出了合理的說法，這樣一來呂布就不用擔心他會如何被當時的市民或後代的人們所評價。成功獵殺董卓其實源於王允的密謀，但貢獻其實主要是貂蟬的美人計。即使像是曹操和袁紹都未能殺死董卓。

READING PASSAGE 2

You should spend about 20 minutes on **Questions 14-27**, which are based on Reading Passage 2 below.

Smartphones and Their Ramification to Kids

A. Nowadays, digital devices are an indispensable part of our lives, making today's parents more wearisome to raise kids. Since digital devices are linked to social-networking sites, on-line games or app games and many others, the ramification that the digital devices have brought is severer and broader than anyone can imagine. Some dangers are apparent, while others are hidden behind those digital devices.

B. Smartphones are one of those digital devices. Although the invention of the smartphones has brought a great deal of convenience, the disadvantages outweigh the advantages. One of the features of smartphones is to take photos, and using smartphones to take pictures are more convenient and lightweight than other cameras, which are heavy and inconvenient. Taking selfies and gourmets is a common scene nowadays. However, smartphones are misused by some guys to take a photo of strangers without asking them in person, take obscene pictures in a lady's room, film pornographic videos for individual purposes, and so on. Those photos and videos can be easily spread through the Internet, and sometimes do quite a lot of damage to people who have been recorded or taken photos to.

C. The second feature of the smartphone is related to social networking sites. People with a smartphone can download several apps with multiple purposes. One of them frequently used by people is to download apps of social networking sites. Social networking sites have two parts. The first one is considered somewhat safe and even parents use them. The first one includes Facebook, IG, and so on. Kids can view their profiles and add classmates and some friends. They get to know what their classmates and friends are doing every time they see there is a new message that someone has uploaded a new photo, sent them a private message, and so on.

D. The seemingly reasonable daily update actually does quite some harm for kids. Their values have been shaped by what they see through those pages, but sometimes the virtual world is different from what is happening in the real world. Since social-networking sites are used to bragging and gathering more likes, some behaviors are exaggerated and some fancy watches and bags on those pages crumble what kids used to believe.

E. Kids are not aware of what social networking sites do to their brain, but they are starting to do things towards the bad side. Some are admitting that they are willing to do things that they are not proud of just to get the cool stuff. Some are doing this because they want to brag, too. They want to increase the so-called likes, created by some programmers. Others are doing something bold so that others can perceive them in a certain way. Still others think extravagant lifestyles are important, and they really envy what their friends are having. They have been brainwashed, doing certain things in exchange for something they can brag about. These are what today's parents should really watch out for. Furthermore, there are instances, like half-joking a certain thing that kids deem unharmful, but they eventually get prosecuted by the prosecutor. Kids interpret those kinds of things as being really cool, but in fact they are not, and it is parents' responsibility to correct them before they are doing something regrettable.

F. The second part of the social networking sites is those sites that are used for random hook-ups and other purposes. There are potential dangers lurking beneath. There is no transparency when it comes to those sites, since parents cannot fully grasp what their kids are doing every second of the day, whom they are texting to, and whom they are going to meet. Children who mistakenly or consciously use those sites can be dangerous. Some are not aware of the purpose of those sites as something different from that of Facebook. Children are lured by some strangers. Some are sending naked pictures to please strangers, mistakenly thinking those strangers as good-looking as their profiles present, but are in fact fake ones. Others do meet with some strangers during the midnight when their parents are asleep. Still others get molested, but are afraid of telling their parents the truth. All these make today's educators worried and parents tiresome.

G. Social issues brought by smartphones are more than what we have discussed so far, and lurking dangers are everywhere. Perhaps this is now the time for today's parents to be more vigilant about what their kids are doing, instilling the right messages, telling them to distinguish from right and wrong, and making them less easily influenced by peers. With the right use of smartphones, all kids can benefit from the advantages of using digital devices, grow up safe and sound, and have a happy childhood.

Questions 14-18

Answer the questions below

Choose NO MORE THAN TWO WORDS from the passage for each other

Write your answers in boxes 14-18 on your answer sheet.

14. What are two items that can be easily seen in our lives by people using smartphones to take pictures?

15. What are two items mentioned as frequently used sites and even elder people use them?

16. What are two items mentioned as something that disintegrates kid's values?

17. Who institutes legal proceedings against children?

18. What is the intention of the second part of the social networking sites?

Questions 19-27

Complete the summary below

Choose ONE WORD ONLY from the passage for each other

Write your answers in boxes 19-27 on your answer sheet.

Digital devices are an indispensable, but they pose dangers for users. Dangers can be both obvious and **19.**_____. Compared with cameras, smartphones have their vantage by being handy and **20.**_____. There are three reasons of misusing smartphones, and one of them involves strangers taking **21.**_____ photos in a lavatory.

The **22.** _____ of children have been influenced without even knowing. **23.**_____ are to be blamed because they have made kids want to gather more likes.

Three reasons have been mentioned to explain why parents have encountered difficulties because those sites do not have any **24.**_____.

Kids have been misled into believing **25.**_____ photos of strangers as attractive as their **26.**_____. Today's parents have to be more watchful because children are more likely to be swayed by **27.**_____.

問題 14 到 18

回答下列試題

從段落中的每個答案選擇，請勿超過兩個單字

在你的答案紙，**14-18** 答案欄中，寫上你的答案

14. 在我們生活中很容易看見下列哪兩個項目，並使用智慧型手機來拍攝它們？

15. 下列哪兩個項目是很頻繁使用的網站而且甚至年長者都使用它們呢？

16. 下列哪兩個提及的項目瓦解了小孩的價值呢？

17. 誰會起訴小孩呢？

18. 第二個部分的社交網站的意圖是什麼呢？

Test 3

TEST 1

TEST 2

TEST 3
Reading Passage 2

TEST 4

問題 19 到 27

完成下列摘要題

段落中的每個答案，請勿超過兩個單字

在你的答案紙，**19-27** 答案欄中，寫上你的答案

數位裝置是不可或缺的，但是它們對使用者來說造成了危險。危險可以是明顯的且 19.＿＿＿＿＿＿。與相機相較下，智慧型手機藉由便利性和 20.＿＿＿＿＿＿ 而佔有優勢。有三個誤用智慧型手機的理由，而它們其中之一牽涉到了陌生人在化妝間拍攝 21.＿＿＿＿＿＿＿＿ 照片。

小孩的 22.＿＿＿＿＿＿ 已經受到影響而不自覺。該歸咎於 23.＿＿＿＿＿＿ 因為他們已經讓小孩想要收集更多的讚。

三個已提及的理由去解釋為什麼父母遇到了困難，因為那些網址沒有任何的 24.＿＿＿＿＿＿。

小孩已經被誤導而相信 25.＿＿＿＿＿＿ 陌生人的相片跟他們 26.＿＿＿＿＿＿ 一樣有吸引力。今日的父母必須要更留意因為小孩更易受到 27.＿＿＿＿＿＿ 的牽動。

Step 1：迅速看題型配置，再定出解題步驟

　　這篇文章的題型有：❶簡答題（Which paragraph contains the following information）、❷ 摘要題。這兩個類型都是填單字，要特別注意答題規範，不能超過幾個字，這非常重要，別多寫了。

Step 2：腦海中浮現答題策略，開始答題

　　這篇既然有❶簡答題（**Answer the questions below**）、❷ **摘要題**，簡答題其實不常見，建議邊閱讀邊答這兩題，因為一定要找到該對應的單字，這樣做也比較保險，有時候簡答題因為看不懂或看錯題目敘述而花很多時間在找答案，而影響了其他答題。

◆ 先掃描簡答題，可以看到前三個問題都出現了 **two items**，所以可以掌握這個要點。然後也掃描下摘要題後開始看文章，

◆ 先看第一段，首句 Nowadays, digital devices are an indispensable part of our lives, making today's parents more wearisome to raise kids.對應到試題第一句 Digital devices are an indispensable, but they pose dangers for users.，**緊接著跳讀到** Some dangers are apparent, while others are hidden behind those digital devices.可以得知不是 **apparent** 就是 **hidden**，試題中以 both and 的形式改寫 Dangers can be both

obvious and 19._____. , obvious 對應到 apparent 所以**第 19 題**答案為 **hidden**。

◆ 緊接的快速看第二段，One of the features of smartphones is to take photos, and using smartphones to take pictures are more **convenient** and **lightweight** than other cameras, which are heavy and inconvenient. 對應試題中的 Compared with cameras, smartphones have their vantage by **being handy** and 20._____. , being handy = convenient，所以另一項特徵為 lightweight，故**第 20 題**答案為 **lightweight**。

◆ 下句看到 Taking **selfies** and **gourmets** is a common scene nowadays. 對應到簡答題第 14 題 two items that can be easily seen in our lives by people using smartphones to take pictures?，所以答案是 **selfies** 和 **gourmets**，用智慧型手機來自拍和拍攝美食，故**第 14 題**答案為 **selfies** 和 **gourmets**。

◆ 緊接著看下句 However, smartphones are misused by some guys to take a photo of strangers without asking them in person, take obscene pictures **in a lady's room**, film pornographic videos for individual purposes, and so on. 並別提到了智慧型手機被誤用的三個原因，對應試題 There are three reasons of misusing smartphones, and one of them involves strangers taking 21._____ photos in **a lavatory**.，而空格選項僅對應了其中一個原因，其中 **lavatory** 對應 **a lady's room**，**pictures** 對應 **photos**，所以答案很明顯是 obscene，故**第 21 題**答案為 **obscene**。

- 接著看第三段，The first one is considered somewhat safe and even **parents** use them. The first one includes **Facebook**, **IG**, and so on. 對應簡答題**第 15 題**，two items mentioned as frequently used sites and even elder people use them?，其中 parents 換成 elder people，所以**第 15 題**答案為 **Facebook** 和 **IG**。

- 緊接著第四段末，some behaviors are exaggerated and some fancy **watches** and **bags** on those pages **crumble** what kids used to believe.對應到簡答題**第 16 題** two items mentioned as something that **disintegrates** kid's values?，其中 **disintegrates** 跟 **crumble** 為同義轉換，所以答案為 **watches** 和 **bags**。

- 第五段首句 Kids **are not aware of** what social networking sites do to their **brain**, but they are starting to do things towards the bad side.對應試題的 The 22._____ of children have been influenced **without even knowing**.，**are not aware of** 換成了 **without even knowing**，所以**第 22 題**答

案為 **brain**。

◆ 跳幾句後可以看到 They want to increase the so-called likes, created by some **programmers**.，可以對應到**第 23 題** 23._____ are to be blamed because they have made kids want to gather more likes.，所以**第 23 題**答案為 **Programmers**。

◆ 緊接著可以看到 Furthermore, there are instances, like half-joking a certain thing that kids deem unharmful, but they eventually get prosecuted by the **prosecutor**.對應到簡答題第 17 題 **who** institutes legal proceedings against children?，答案為人，很明顯是 prosecutor，看清楚疑問詞可以更精確找答案，故**第 17 題**答案為 **prosecutor**。

◆ 再來第六段首句 The second part of the social networking sites is those sites that are used for **random hook-ups** and other purposes.可以對應到簡答題第 18 題 is the intention of the second part of the social networking sites?，所以**第 18 題**答案很明顯是 **random hook-ups**。

◆ 下兩句 There is no **transparency** when it comes to those sites, since parents cannot fully grasp what their kids are doing every second of the day, whom they are texting to, and whom they are going to meet. ，對應到 three reasons have been mentioned to explain why parents have encountered difficulties because those sites do not have any 24.＿＿＿＿＿＿. ，**no = do not have any**，所以第 **24** 題答案為 **transparency**。

- 接著 Some are sending naked pictures to please strangers, **mistakenly thinking** those strangers as **good-looking** as their **profiles** present, but are in fact **fake** ones.對應 Kids **have been misled into believing** 25.＿＿＿＿＿＿ photos of strangers as **attractive** as their 26.＿＿＿＿＿＿. ，**mistakenly thinking = have been misled into believing**，**good-looking = attractive**，所以第 **25** 和 **26** 題答案為 **fake** 和 **profiles**。

- 再來是最後一題 Today's parents have to be more **watchful** because children **are more likely to be swayed by** 27.＿＿＿＿＿＿. ，對應到最後一段 Perhaps this is now the time for today's parents to be more **vigilant** about what their kids are doing, instilling the right messages, telling them to distinguish from right and wrong, and **making them less easily influenced by peers**. ，**swayed = influenced**，**watchful = vigilant**，所以第 **27** 題答案為 **peers**。

中譯和影子跟讀 　　　　　　　　　　🔘 MP3 008

A. Nowadays, digital devices are an indispensable part of our lives, making today's parents more wearisome to raise kids. Since digital devices are linked to social-networking sites, on-line games or app games and many others, the ramification that the digital devices have brought is severer and broader than anyone can imagine. Some dangers are apparent, while others are hidden behind those digital devices.

現今，數位裝置是我們生活中不可或缺的一部分，使得今日的父母養育小孩更疲於奔命。數位裝置與社交網站、線上遊戲和 app 遊戲以及許多其他的東西，數位裝置所帶來的影響竟然比起任何人所預想的更嚴重且更廣泛。有些危險很顯然易見，而有的卻潛藏在那些數位裝置中。

B. Smartphones are one of those digital devices. Although the invention of the smartphones has brought a great deal of convenience, the disadvantages outweigh the advantages. One of the features of smartphones is to take photos, and using smartphones to take pictures are more convenient and lightweight than other cameras, which are heavy and inconvenient. Taking selfies and gourmets is a common scene nowadays. However, smartphones are misused by some guys to take a photo of strangers without asking them in person, take obscene pictures in a lady's room, film pornographic videos for individual purposes, and so on. Those photos and videos can be easily spread through the Internet, and sometimes do quite a lot of damage to people who have been recorded or taken photos to.

智慧型手機就是數位裝置的其中一種。儘管智慧型手機的發明已經帶來了大量的便利性,其缺點勝於優點。智慧型手機其中一項特徵就是拍照,而使用智慧型手機拍照比起使用其他相機更方便且攜帶起來輕便,相機顯得笨重且不方便。現今拍自拍照和美食是普遍的場景。然而,智慧型手機被有些男性誤用於未徵詢過他人同意就拍攝陌生人相片、在女性化妝間拍攝猥褻照片以及攝影情色影片供其個人觀看等等的。那些照片和影片都能很輕易地經由網路傳播,且有時候對於被錄製影片或拍攝相片的當事人造成相當大的傷害。

C. The second feature of the smartphone is related to social networking sites. People with a smartphone can download several apps with multiple purposes. One of them frequently used by people is to download apps of social networking sites. Social networking sites have two parts. The first one is considered somewhat safe and even parents use them. The first one includes Facebook, IG, and so on. Kids can view their profiles and add classmates and some friends. They get to know what their classmates and friends are doing every time they see there is a new message that someone has uploaded a new photo, sent them a private message, and so on.

智慧型手機的第二個特徵與社群網站有關。有智慧型手機的人可以由幾個附有眾多用途的 app 進行下載。其中一個被人們頻繁使用的是下載社群網站的 app。社群網站有兩個部分。第一種是包含臉書和 IG 等等的。小孩能瀏覽他們的檔案和加同班同學和有些朋友。每當他們看到有關於有些人上傳了新的相片、傳私人訊息給他們等等的新訊息時，他們能進一步知道他們同班同學和朋友正在做些什麼。

D. The seemingly reasonable daily update actually does quite some harm for kids. Their values have been shaped by what they see through those pages, but sometimes the virtual world is different from what is happening in the real world. Since social-networking sites are used to bragging and gathering more likes, some behaviors are exaggerated and some fancy watches and bags on those pages crumble what kids used to believe.

這些看似合理的每日更新實際上對於小孩來說造成了些許傷害。小孩們的價值觀已經被那些他們所瀏覽的頁面形塑著，但是有時候虛擬世界不同於現實世界。既然社交網站正用於炫耀和收集更多的讚，有些行為受到誇大，而且在那些網頁上瀏覽到的有些豪華手錶和包包瓦解了小孩過去相信的價值觀。

E. Kids are not aware of what social networking sites do to their brain, but they are starting to do things towards the bad side. Some are admitting that they are willing to do things that they are not proud of just to get the cool stuff. Some are doing this because they want to brag, too. Some want to increase the so-called likes, created by some programmers. Others are doing something bold so that others can perceive them in a certain way. Still others think extravagant lifestyles are important, and they really envy what their friends are having. They have been brainwashed, doing certain things in exchange for something they can brag about. These are what today's parents should really watch out for. Furthermore, there are instances, like half-joking a certain thing that kids deem unharmful, but they eventually get prosecuted by the prosecutor. Kids interpret those kinds of things as being really cool, but in fact they are not, and it is parents' responsibility to correct them before they are doing something regrettable.

小孩們並未察覺到社交網站對於他們大腦動了什麼手腳，但是他們的所作所為開始導向壞的方面去發展。有些坦承他們願意從事他們不引以為傲的事情以獲得那些酷的東西。他們之所以這樣做是因為他們想要炫耀。他們想要增加所謂的工程師所設計出的讚的數量。其他人正做些大膽的事，如此一來他們就會受到特定的評價。還有些人認為奢侈的生活方式是重要的，而且他們真的羨慕他們朋友所擁有的。他們已經受到洗腦，做著特定的事情以換取他們能炫耀的東西。這些都是現今父母應該要注意的。此外，有實例，像是小孩子半開玩笑一些他們認為無傷大雅的事情，但是那樣的事情最終讓他們受到檢察官的起訴。小孩將那些事情詮釋成他們認為是真的酷的事，但實際上卻並不然，這是父母的責任，在他們做出一些之後會感到後悔的事之前，先糾正他們。

F. The second part of the social networking sites is those sites that are used for random hook-ups and other purposes. There are potential dangers lurking beneath. There is no transparency when it comes to those sites, since parents cannot fully grasp what their kids are doing every second of the day, whom they are texting to, and whom they are going to meet. Children who mistakenly or consciously use those sites can be dangerous. Some are not aware of the purpose of those sites as something different from that of Facebook. Children are lured by some strangers. Some are sending naked pictures to please strangers, mistakenly thinking those strangers as good-looking as their profiles present, but are in fact fake ones. Others do meet with some strangers during the midnight when their parents are asleep. Still others get molested, but are afraid of telling their parents the truth. All these make today's educators worried and parents tiresome.

第二部分的社交網站是那些用於隨機性行為和其他用途的。有的具有潛在的危險在其中。當提到那些網站時完全沒有透明度可言，因為父母無法全然掌握他們的小孩一天中每分每秒在做些什麼、他們傳訊息給誰以及他們正要跟誰碰面。小孩誤將或未察覺到那些網站可能是有危險的。有些未察覺到那些網站的目的和臉書這樣的社交網站是不同性質的。小孩受到有些陌生人的引誘。有些將裸露的相片傳給陌生人以討好他們，誤以為那些陌生人像是他們檔案所呈現的那樣外貌姣好，但實際上卻是使用假的相片。其他小孩確實在午夜時分，當父母都入睡時，跟有些陌生人碰面。還有其他小孩受到性騷擾，但是卻懼怕將這些實情告知父母。這些都使得現今的教育學者擔憂、父母們感到疲憊。

G. Social issues brought by smartphones are more than

what we have discussed so far, and lurking dangers are everywhere. Perhaps this is now the time for today's parents to be more vigilant about what their kids are doing, instilling the right messages, telling them to distinguish from right and wrong, and making them less easily influenced by peers. With the right use of smartphones, all kids can benefit from the advantages of using digital devices, grow up safe and sound, and have a happy childhood.

由智慧型手機所引起的社會議題比我們所討論到的部分更加廣泛，而潛藏的危險真的無所不在。或許現在正是現今父母對於他們的孩子正在做些什麼更有所警覺的時候，灌輸正確的訊息、告訴他們分辨是非以及讓小孩們更不易受到同儕的影響。有著正確的智慧型手機的使用習慣，所有小孩都能受益於使用數位裝置所帶來的益處、安穩的成長以及有個快樂的童年。

Job Satisfaction and the Value of Jobs

A. Apart from someone who has inherited a great deal of money or someone who was born with a silver spoon, people have to work to support themselves. As a great author once said, you can neither make love nor eat something for eight hours straight, but you certainly can do the work for consecutive eight hours or longer. Work is so important to us in that it occupies a significant portion of time daily. Since it is so vital to us, one really needs to pick the right job, a job that is so meaningful to his or her life. Despite the fact that most people are working to live, not living to work, there are rare cases that exemplify it is possible to find a job that is meaningful to a person or a job that meets the criteria of work-and-life balance, or a job that is entirely satisfactory.

B. Job satisfaction is a broad concept. It is hard to measure and can have multiple ramifications in employees' health and the length of time an employee stays at a company. A person who earns high income is not necessarily a person who is satisfied with the job. Using high income, status, benefits a company offers to measure is simply wrong. It is true that in most occasions, "money acts as a highly accurate yardstick of success", but it can only satisfy one's vanity. In *Getting There*, Stacey Snider, a previous Chairman of Universal, states the fact that her first-year salaries at law firms were incredibly high, but she wanted to avoid that kind of trap. In *The Millionaire Next Door*, authors, Thomas J. Stanley and William D. Danko also caution "one earns to spend. When you need to spend more, you need to earn more".

C. All these are relevant to job satisfaction. Sometimes you can clearly identify that those people are clearly unhappy, but they are already in the trap and they cannot get out. They live in a great mansion and have an expensive lifestyle, so they need those kinds of jobs to sustain their spending. Deep down they hate the job, but they cannot quit the job. In *How Will You Measure Your Life*, the bestselling author, Clayton M. Christensen, a Harvard Business School professor and leading thinker, further elucidates this kind of phenomenon. He says that "many of my peers had chosen careers using hygiene factors as the primary criteria.", and using hygiene factors to find the job will get the result entirely identical to what the other authors have said.

D. In addition to these factors that influence the degree of job satisfaction, there are other factors, such as the personality of the worker, the type of industry, and dexterity of the job content. Personalities will influence how employees react to a situation and how employees respond to different tasks given to them. College graduates without work experiences can find it hard to fit into a workplace where assistance is confined and when they hardly know themselves. Employees with a vibrant and bubbly personality can find a routine job incredibly boring, and thus, they are having a much lower job satisfaction. For employees who are resistant to change or reluctant to change, monotonous and repetitive jobs are perfect for them.

E. By contrast, they are having a higher job satisfaction in this component. As employees have accumulated more experiences and are good at their jobs, their dexterity of the job increases. They are not only increasing their values to the company, but also enhancing their work efficiency. They are able to do jobs of different kinds and sometimes sandwich several different kinds in between. Some employees at this stage might have a different idea about jobs, and are starting to enjoy a flexible work mode, a work that they used to think too daunting and challenging.

F. So dexterity of the job content really plays a pivotal role in how employees feel about their jobs and certainly influence employees job satisfaction. At last, the type of industry you are in matters. Certain types of jobs are just in a fast-mode, and you cannot expect it to lower the speed. There are bound to be lots of phone calls calling in, and clients are really big. Once you have accustomed to that kind of velocity, it really is nothing. It is highly likely that you are going to have a high job satisfaction and get the higher salary at the same time. Don't be afraid to give it a try.

G. To sum up, when it comes to choosing a job, we all have a different consideration. Sometimes certain factors are not as important as they used to be, and only you know yourself well, so go clear your head and find the job that suits you, and give you the most job satisfaction.

Questions 28-32

Choose the correct letter, A, B, C, or D

Write the correct letter in boxes 28-32 on your answer sheet

28. In the **first** paragraph, the writer refers to a saying from a famous author to show

   A. Under normal circumstances, people have to work to support themselves.
   B. Work can be meaningful to someone.
   C. Work is more important than eating or making love .
   D. The pecularity of work since it is something that people can successively do for long hours.

29. In the **second** paragraph, bestsellers are used to demonstrate

   A. Vanity is a vicious trait that everyone should try to avoid.
   B. A vicious cycle can be led if one is not consciously enough.
   C. The relation between money and success.
   D. Law firms deliberately use the trap to retain employees.

30. In the **third** paragraph, people using "hygiene factors" as evaluations to choose their careers

    A. are bound to be happier
    B. are having extravagent lifestyles that others find envious and jealous
    C. are able to get out of the trap whenever they want
    D. are far more unlikely to quit

31. In the **fifth** paragraph, for people who have gathered enough work experiences and are adept at what they do

    A. their work efficiency decreases
    B. they are still learning how to prioritize routine works and are unlikely to perform jobs that need to sandwich in-between
    C. they might consider taking the job that they thought fearsome in the past
    D. they are having a low job satisfaction even if their dexterity of the job increases

Questions 32-35

Do the following statements agree with the information given in the Reading Passage ?

In boxes 32-35 on your answer sheet, write

TRUE - if the statement agrees with the information
FALSE - if the statement contradicts the information
NOT GIVEN - if there is no information on this

32. College graduates can encounter problems related to suitability in the workplace and their understanding about themselves.

33. Employees of outgoing and bubbly types perform relatively well than introvert types especially in routine works.

34. In a fast-mode work environment, you can sneakily slow down the speed, if the client you encounter is small.

35. Since you cannot have a cake and eat it too, the component of the salary part and job satisfaction portion can never be reached.

Questions 36-40

Complete the summary below

Choose ONE WORD ONLY from the passage for each other

Write your answers in boxes 10-13 on your answer sheet.

In a society, money is still the measurement of **36.**_____
__. Some bestsellers have warned us not to fall into that **37.**__
_____. Still people have suffered due to the fact that
they still use hygiene factors as considerations. Even if their
lives have upgraded, they are evidently **38.**_____.

Different jobs suit different people. There are jobs that are
tedious and **39.**_____, but still have fans who enjoy
doing that. There are other jobs that are in a fast work mode,
but familiarity with the **40.**_____ makes the problem
disappear.

問題 28 到 32

選擇正確的字母，**A, B, C, or D**

在你的答案紙，**28-32** 答案欄中，寫上你的答案

28. 在首段中，作家提及一位名作者講過的俗諺是要表示

   A. 在正常情況下，人們必須要去工作來支撐他們自己

   B. 工作可以對一個人是有意義的

   C. 工作比起吃或做愛更重要

   D. 工作的獨特性，因為這是人們可以長時間接續從事的事

29. 在第二個段落，暢銷書用來展示

   A. 虛榮心是邪惡的特質，每個人都需要避開它

   B. 可能致使惡性循環，如果一個人意識不夠清楚的話

   C. 金錢和成功的關係

   D. 法律事務所故意地使用這個陷阱來留住員工

30. 在第三個段落，人們使用「保健因素」當作選擇他們職涯的評估標準

   A. 必定更快樂

   B. 有著更奢侈的生活型態，讓其他人更羨慕和忌妒

   C. 每當他們想要時，能夠擺脫陷阱

   D. 更不可能辭職

31. 在第五個段落，人們已經收集了足夠的工作經驗且擅長他們所從事的

   A. 他們的工作效率減低
   B. 他們仍學習如何將例行性工作排出優先順序，而且更不可能執行需要夾雜住其中的工作任務
   C. 他們可能考慮從是他們先前感到懼怕的工作
   D. 他們有低工作滿意度，即使他們對工作的熟練度提高

問題 **32** 到 **35**

以下敘述是否和閱讀篇章的資訊相同？
在你的答案紙，**32-35** 答案欄中，寫下：

TRUE – 如果敘述與資訊一致
FALSE – 如果敘述與資訊不一致
NOT GIVEN - 如果閱讀篇章沒提到以下敘述

19. 大學畢業生可能遭遇到與職場適合度和他們了解自我的相關問題。

20. 外向和有活力的員工類型比起內向類型，表現相對較佳，尤其是在例行性事務上。

21. 在快速的工作環境中，你可以狡猾地放慢速度，如果你遇到的是小客戶。

22. 既然你魚和熊掌不可兼得，薪資的組成部分和工作滿意度的部分是無法達成的。

問題 36 到 40

完成下列摘要題
段落中的每個答案，請勿超過兩個單字
在你的答案紙，36-40 答案欄中，寫上你的答案

在社會中，金錢仍是 36.＿＿＿＿＿＿＿ 的評估。有些暢銷書已經警告我們別掉入那樣的 37.＿＿＿＿＿＿＿。仍然有人因此而受苦，因為他們仍在使用保健因素當作考量。即使他們的生活已經升級，他們顯然地 38.＿＿＿＿＿＿＿。

不同的工作適合不同的人。有工作是冗長且 39.＿＿＿＿＿＿＿，但是仍有粉絲享受那樣的方式。還有其他的工作是在快速的工作模式，但是隨著熟悉度的 40.＿＿＿＿＿＿＿ 使得問題消失了。

解析

Step 1：迅速看題型配置，再定出解題步驟

　　這篇文章的題型有：❶選擇題、❷判斷題和❸摘要題。

　　選擇題的考法有時候蠻細節的，有時候好幾個選項改寫到很容易混淆，在劍橋雅思 10 到 13 中，**選擇題的考法**（不論該篇文章搭配選擇題還有其他那些題型）很一致，都會出現「**在文章的幾段時...**」，所以很好定位，也讀的蠻順暢的，所以遇到這樣子的選擇題建議可以順著文章讀就好了（**順讀**），不一定需要看題目再以關鍵字回去看文章。

Step 2：腦海中浮現答題策略，開始答題

　　這篇既然有❶選擇題、❷判斷題和❸摘要題，建議順著文章讀，讀文章前先掃描判斷題和摘要題的關鍵字，順著文章讀並邊解答**選擇題**時，邊看看是否有其他兩個題型問到的資訊，也可以同步答。

◆ **第 28 題**，可以根據題目訊息「**In the first paragraph**」，迅速定位到第一段，（根據出題要點，這段文字幾乎不會被出題者使用在其他題型的分配上了，除了該篇文章的搭配還有 **which paragraph contains the following information**，所以看過這段文章後答完這題就差不多了，這篇文章的其他題目幾乎會**均分**在其餘段落。）

◆ **第 28 題**，題目是問 the writer refers to a saying from a

Test 3

1
TEST

2
TEST

3
TEST

Reading Passage 3

4
TEST

famous author to show，**選項 A** Under normal circumstances, people have to work to support themselves，文章中確實有出現 people have to work to support themselves，但是知名作者說的話在這之後，且沒有回答到作者提到那句俗諺的原因，所以可以刪除。**選項 B**，Work can be meaningful to someone，雖然段落後也有提到 a job that is so meaningful to his or her life，這選項也不太適合當答案，算是干擾選項，可以刪除。

◆ **第 28 題，選項 C**，work is more important than eating or making love，其實重點不是哪個比較重要，但藉由描述可以表達出工作是比起兩者，能長時間從事的一個行為，而這樣值得我們思考，主要還是 you certainly can do the work for consecutive eight hours or longer. Work is so important to us in that it occupies a significant portion of time daily，這段英文其實與**選項 D** the **peculiarity** of work since it is something that people can **successively do for long hours** 吻合，所以答案選**選項 D** 是最合適的答案。

◆ **第 29 題**，可以根據題目訊息「**In the second paragraph**」，迅速定位到第二段，題目詢問 bestsellers are used to demonstrate，所以可以先思考下，作者為什麼在這個段落中提到了這幾本暢銷書的書籍，而段落中主要想傳達出的核心思想是「**don't fall into that kind of trap**」和「**掉入那樣的陷阱後，就是惡性循環的開始**」，所以釐清後很快可以選出這題的答案是

選項 **B**。選項 **A** 提到 vanity，vanity 是這個行為中的其中一部分，但不是題目問的，雖然段落後也有提到 it can only satisfy one's vanity。

◆ **第 29 題**，選項 **C** 提到金錢和成功的關係，可以回文章找，其實很容易混淆，誤選 The relation between **money** and **success**，文章中確實有先提到工作滿意度並聊到 **money** acts as a highly accurate yardstick of **success**，但是也不是題目問的原因，金錢雖然是評量成功與否的指標，但是用了某些因素當作選擇才會陷入這樣的陷阱中。**選項 D**，Law firms deliberately use the trap to retain employees.，文章中確實有提到 law firm，但是是藉由這個例子去說明，不進律師事務所可以避免掉入陷阱，而非要探討 Law firms deliberately use the trap to retain employees，所以可以刪除這個選項。

◆ **第 30 題**，可以根據題目訊息「**In the third paragraph**」，迅速定位到第三段，題目詢問 people using "hygiene factors" as evaluations to choose their careers，可以由段落的前幾句了解到掉入這個陷阱的人的生活變成如何，在看到 hygiene factors 的部分，大概能理解出這題要問的了，所以**選項 A** 的 are bound to be **happier** 是錯誤的，因為是 **unhappier**，文章中也很清楚表明說 Sometimes you can clearly identify that those people are clearly **unhappy**。**選項 B** 也不適合，他們確實有著奢華的生活方式，段落文章也沒進一步說 others find envious and jealous，可以排除這個選項。

◆ **第 30 題，選項 C**，are able to get out of the trap whenever they want 和文章中的 **but** they are already in that trap and they cannot get out.所表達的意思相反，故可以排除。也可以多注意**轉折詞像是 but 等字，通常都伴隨著考點**。選項 D 的 are far more unlikely to quit，對應文章中的 so they need those kinds of jobs to sustain their spending. Deep down they hate the job, but they cannot quit the job，所以答案為**選項 D**。

◆ **第 31 題**，可以根據題目訊息「**In the fifth paragraph**」，迅速定位到第五段，**直接跳讀到第五段**，這時候可以**在文章的第四段作個標記**，因為其他兩個題型會用第四段的文章來出題，較不可能用選擇題這四題，已經提過的段落來在出題，這樣的情形太少了。

◆ **第 31 題**，先看題目 for people who have gathered enough work experiences and are adept at what they do，所以已經有足夠工作經驗且擅長他們所從事的工作者，他們...。看**選項 A** 後定位到 They are not only increasing their values to the company, but also **enhancing their work efficiency** 和選項的 **their work efficiency decreases** 語意相反，可以刪除選項 A。

◆ **第 31 題**，選項 B，they are still learning how to prioritize routine works and are **unlikely** to perform jobs that need to sandwich in-between 和 They **are able to** do jobs of different kinds and sometimes **sandwich several different kinds in between**.的語意相反，也可以排除選項 B。

- 第 31 題，選項 C，they might consider taking the job that they thought fearsome in the past 和文章中的 are starting to enjoy a flexible work mode, a work that they used to think too daunting and challenging.為**同義表達**。所以正確答案為**選項 C**。

- 第 31 題，選項 D，they are having **a low job satisfaction** even if **their dexterity of the job increases** 和文章中的敘述 By contrast, they are having **a higher job satisfaction** in this component. As employees have accumulated more experiences and are good at their jobs, **their dexterity of the job increases**.語意相反，故可以排除。

- 第 32 題，以 **college graduates** 為關鍵字定位，可以先排除選擇題出題過的四個段落，剛好定位到還未看過的文章段落，即第四段。**College graduates** without work experiences can find it hard to **fit into a workplace** where assistance is confined and when they hardly know themselves.，然後再看題目敘述 **College graduates** can encounter problems related to **suitability in the workplace** and **their understanding about**

themselves.其實為**同義表達**，所以**第 32 題**的答案為 **True**。

◆ **第 33 題**，接續看題目敘述，看到描述的員工類型，很順利地 bubbly types 為關鍵字，定位到的四段，Employees with **a vibrant and bubbly personality** can find a routine job incredibly boring, and thus, they are having a much lower job satisfaction.，而題目是敘述 Employees of **outgoing and bubbly types** perform relatively well than **introvert types** especially in routine works.，然後要釐清的是❶文章中沒有提到 **introvert types**。❷題目敘述將這兩個類型作了比較，但文章中卻沒有，所以**第 33 題**答案為 **Not Given**。雅思閱讀中很常出現兩個舉例或項目，但是題目卻將兩者作出了比較，而文章中並沒有，而這個落入了 **Not Given** 的範疇。

◆ 緊接著看**第 34 題**，In **a fast-mode work environment**, you can sneakily slow down the speed, if **the client** you encounter is **small**.，用運**跳讀**和**關鍵字定位**，很快可以定位到第六段中間 Certain types of jobs are just in **a fast-mode**, and you cannot expect it to lower the speed.，然後請接續讀下去，There are bound to be lots of phone calls calling in, and **clients** are really **big**.，文章中僅提到不斷有電話打進來，客戶很大咖，題目卻描述成 if **the client** you encounter is **small**，其實文章中沒有這樣的訊息可以做出判斷，所以**第 34 題**答案為 **Not Given**。

- 緊接著看**第 35 題**，Since you cannot have a cake and eat it too, the **component** of the **salary** part and **job satisfaction** portion can never be reached.，使用 component, salary, job satisfaction 為關鍵字定位很順利定位到了第六段 It is highly likely that you are going to have a high job satisfaction and get the higher salary at the same time.，段落中的敘述表明高工作滿意度和獲取高薪是可以**同時達成**的，但試題中卻表明魚和熊掌不可兼得，這兩樣是無法達成的 can never be reached，語意相反，所以**第 35 題**答案為 **False**。

- 寫完判斷題和選擇題後，盡快來看摘要題，**第 36 題**，In a society, money is still the measurement of 36.＿＿＿＿＿＿.，用 money 可以迅速定位到第二段 It is true that in most occasions, "**money** acts as a highly accurate yardstick of success"，**yardstick** 換成了 **measurement**，很明顯這題答案是講這兩者的關聯性，所以**第 36 題**答案為 **success**。

- **第 37 題**，Some **bestsellers** have warned us not to fall into that 37.＿＿＿＿＿＿＿.，bestsellers，可以直接找段落中的暢銷書籍，也可以馬上聯想到選擇題**第 29 題 bestsellers** are used to demonstrate，所以繼續定位在第二段 states the fact that her first-year salaries at law firms was incredibly high, but she wanted to avoid that kind of **trap**，答案很明顯段落中提到的這兩本暢銷書都是要表明要我們免於掉入 trap 中，在警告和提醒我們，所以**第 37 題**答案為 **trap**。

◆ **第 38 題**，Still people have suffered due to the fact that they still use hygiene factors as considerations. Even if their lives have upgraded, they are evidently 38._____.這題可以定位到第三段，然後 hygiene factors 的文句往回讀，理解訊息後，可以得知他們是 unhappy 的，也對應到文句 Sometimes you can clearly identify that those people are clearly **unhappy**, but they are already in that trap and they cannot get out. 只是試題是以**倒敘**的方式去描述，所以**第 38 題**答案為 **unhappy**。

◆ **第 39 題**，Different jobs suit different people. There are jobs that are **tedious** and 39._____, but still have fans who enjoy doing that. 這題可能看起來比較不好找一點，但是用對的關鍵字找還是會快很多，利用形容詞 tedious 找，可以定位到第四段且剛才寫判斷題也大略看過的段落，For employees who are resistant to change or reluctant to change, **monotonous** and **repetitive** jobs are perfect for them. 要能想到 **monotonous** 就是 **tedious**，如果沒辦法這麼快作出聯想，可能要多背同反義字，所以空格處的形容詞很明顯是 **repetitive**，其他文句只是改寫後的表達，**第 39 題**答案為 **repetitive**。

◆ **第 40 題**，There are other jobs that are in **a fast work mode**, but **familiarity** with the 40._____ makes the problem disappear. 可以運用 familiarity 和 a fast work mode 為關鍵字，定位到倒數第二段，可能要**綜合一下訊息**才能答這題。

◆ **第 40 題**，So **dexterity** of the job content really plays a pivotal role in how employees feel about their jobs and certainly influence employees job satisfaction. At last, the type of industry you are in matters. Certain types of jobs are just in a fast-mode, and you cannot expect it to lower the speed. There are bound to be lots of phone calls calling in, and clients are really big. Once you have accustomed to that kind of **velocity**, **it really is nothing**.，這段在講工作的熟練度，其實要表明的是工作**熟練度**提升後，那些影響工作滿意度的因素都消失了，題目以更濃縮的語句來表達這個段落，可以思考一下，**dexterity** 換成了 **familiarity**，**makes the problem disappear** 換成了 **it really is nothing**，第 **40** 題答案為 **velocity**。

中譯和影子跟讀　　　　　　　　　　　　🔘 MP3 009

A. Apart from someone who has inherited a great deal of money or someone who was born with a silver spoon, people have to work to support themselves. As a great author once said, you can neither make love nor eat something for eight hours straight, but you certainly can do the work for consecutive eight hours or longer. Work is so important to us in that it occupies a significant portion of time daily. Since it is so vital to us, one really needs to pick the right job, a job that is so meaningful to his or her life. Despite the fact that most people are working to live, not living to work, there are rare cases that exemplify it is possible to find a job that is meaningful to a person or a job that meets the criteria of work-and-life balance, or a job that is entirely satisfactory.

除了有些已經接手了大量金錢者或是有些含銀湯匙出生者，人們都必須要工作來維持生計。有位偉大的作家曾說，你不可能持續八小時都在做愛或者是吃東西，但是你卻能花費連續八小時或更長時間工作。工作對我們如此重要，因為它佔據了我們每日一大部分的時間。既然工作對我們來說是如此重要，每個人真的需要選擇對的工作，一份對他或她生活都深具意義的工作。儘管大多數的人都是為了生存而工作，而非因工作而活，有罕見的案例顯示有可能找到對一個人有意義的工作或是能達到工作和生活平衡標準的工作，或是全然令人滿意的工作。

B. Job satisfaction is a broad concept. It is hard to measure and can have multiple ramifications in employees' health and the length of time an employee stays at a company. A person who earns high income is not necessarily a person who is satisfied with the job. Using high income, status, benefits a company offers to measure is simply wrong. It is true that in most occasions, "money acts as a highly accurate yardstick of success", but it can only satisfy one's vanity. In *Getting There*, Stacey Snider, a previous Chairman of Universal, states the fact that her first-year salaries at law firms were incredibly high, but she wanted to avoid that kind of trap. In *The Millionaire Next Door*, authors, Thomas J. Stanley and William D. Danko also caution "one earns to spend. When you need to spend more, you need to earn more".

工作滿意度是廣泛的觀念。這是很難去估量的,而且對於一位員工的健康和一位員工待在一間公司是有很多延伸性的影響的。一位賺取高薪的員工不見得是位對工作感到滿意的人。利用高薪、地位和一間公司所能提供的福利去衡量是不正確的。在大多數情況下「金錢充當了衡量成功高度精準的標準」,但是卻僅滿足了一個人的虛榮心。在《勝利,並非事事順利：30 位典範人物不藏私的人生真心話》中，史黛西・史奈德，前環球影城董事長，述説了她第一年在律師事務所非常高額的薪資，但是她想要避免陷入這樣的陷阱中。在《原來有錢人都這麼做》中，作者湯瑪斯・史丹利和威廉・丹柯也警告著，「一個人若賺錢是為了能花費。當你需要花更多錢時，你需要賺取更多。」

C. All these are relevant to job satisfaction. Sometimes you can clearly identify that those people are clearly unhappy, but they are already in the trap and they cannot get out. They live in a great mansion and have an expensive lifestyle, so they need those kinds of jobs to sustain their spending. Deep down they hate the job, but they cannot quit the job. In *How Will You Measure Your Life*, the bestselling author, Clayton M. Christensen, a Harvard Business School professor and leading thinker, further elucidates this kind of phenomenon. He says that "many of my peers had chosen careers using hygiene factors as the primary criteria.", and using hygiene factors to find the job will get the result entirely identical to what the other authors have said.

這些都與工作滿意度有關聯。有時候你可以清楚地辨識出那些顯然不開心的人，但是他們已經陷入了那樣子的陷阱而且他們無法脫困。他們居住在很棒的豪宅中而且享受著高昂的生活型態，所以他們需要那樣子的工作來維持他們的花費。在內心深處，他們憎恨那份工作，但他們無法辭去工作。在《你如何衡量你的人生》中，暢銷書作者克雷頓‧克里斯汀生，哈佛商學院教授和領導性思想家，進一步闡述這樣的現象。他說「許多我的同儕已經使用了保健因素作為選擇職涯主要的標準」，而且使用保健因素去找工作會得到與其他作者已經提到過的全然相同的結果。

D. In addition to these factors that influence the degree of job satisfaction, there are other factors, such as the personality of the worker, the type of industry, and dexterity of the job content. Personalities will influence how employees react to a situation and how employees respond to different tasks given to them. College graduates without work experiences can find it hard to fit into a workplace where assistance is confined and when they hardly know themselves. Employees with a vibrant and bubbly personality can find a routine job incredibly boring, and thus, they are having a much lower job satisfaction. For employees who are resistant to change or reluctant to change, monotonous and repetitive jobs are perfect for them.

除了這些因素會影響工作滿意度的程度外，還有其他因素例如，工作者的個性、產業的類型和工作內容的熟練度。個性會影響員工對於一個情況是如何反應，以及員工對於所給予的不同類型工作是如何反應。當在有限的協助員工的工作職場上，不具工作經驗的大學畢業生，會發現他們很難去融入一間公司，而且他們會覺得例行事務性的工作相當的無聊，因此，他們有較低的工作滿意度。對於每位抗拒改變或是不情願接受改變的員工來說，單調性和重複性的工作對他們來說是完美的。

E. By contrast, they are having a higher job satisfaction in this component. As employees have accumulated more experiences and are good at their jobs, their dexterity of the job increases. They are not only increasing their values to the company, but also enhancing their work efficiency. They are able to do jobs of different kinds and sometimes sandwich several different kinds in between. Some employees at this stage might have a different idea about jobs, and are starting to enjoy a flexible work mode, a work that they used to think too daunting and challenging.

相對之下，他們在這個項目中有著較高的工作滿意度。當員工已經累積了更多的工作經驗且擅長他們的工作時，他們對於工作的熟練度就會提升。他們不僅是會替公司增加價值，而且增加了他們工作的效率。他們能夠從事不同項目的工作而且有時候是幾項不同的工作夾雜在其中。在這個時期，有些員工可能對於工作有著不同的想法，而開始去享受更具彈性的工作模式，一份他們過去認為是太令人膽戰心驚和具挑戰性的工作。

F. So dexterity of the job content really plays a pivotal role in how employees feel about their jobs and certainly influence employees job satisfaction. At last, the type of industry you are in matters. Certain types of jobs are just in a fast-mode, and you cannot expect it to lower the speed. There are bound to be lots of phone calls calling in, and clients are really big. Once you have accustomed to that kind of velocity, it really is nothing. It is highly likely that you are going to have a high job satisfaction and get the higher salary at the same time. Don't be afraid to give it a try.

所以工作的熟練度真的對於員工對於工作的感受扮演著關鍵性的角色，並確實影響員工的工作滿意度。最後，你所身處的不同類型的產業至關重要。特定類型的工作可能是處於快速的模式，而你可能無法期待工作速度調降。必定會有許多的電話打進來，而且客戶是相當大牌的。一旦你已經適應了那樣的速度時，就會覺得那沒什麼了。很可能你正同時有著高的工作滿意度而且享有較高薪資。不用害怕去嘗試。

G. To sum up, when it comes to choosing a job, we all have a different consideration. Sometimes certain factors are not as important as they used to be, and only you know yourself well, so go clear your head and find the job that suits you and give you the most job satisfaction.

總之，當提到工作時，我們都有著不同的考量。有時候特定的因素沒有它們當初那樣的重要了，而且只有你了解自己，所以理清你的思緒和找到合適你且能給予你最大程度工作滿意度的工作。

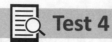

READING PASSAGE 1

You should spend about 20 minutes on **Questions 1-13**, which are based on Reading Passage 1 below.

The Romance of the Three Kingdoms： Wisdom of Kong Ming, a Stratagem That Gathers 100,000 Arrows

A. Kong Ming plays a pivotal role in later successes of the Shu empire. Kong Ming's success relies heavily on his own wisdom, and he has become a legendary figure for later generations. As the fiction progresses, several successful predictions and great feats of major events, such as borrowing arrows from the enemy and praying for an eastern wind at the Altar of the Seven Stars, consolidate his role as a military adviser and most important of all in the mind of people who read about him. In the time of a huge turmoil, every leader is in desperate need of finding great warriors and famous military advisers.

B. Jiang Gan（蔣幹）is fooled by a stratagem used by Zhou Yu（周瑜）, bringing the letter back to Cao Cao（曹操）. Upon viewing the letter, Cao Cao acts merely on impulse, making a regrettable decision. He beheads both Cai Mao（蔡瑁）and Zhang Yun（張允）, two major commanders of marine warfare. Zhou Yu is so pleased to learn the news that two major threats are long gone, but he later realizes the real menace is Kong Ming because Kong Ming is too smart. Zhou Yu sends Lu Su（魯肅）to see whether Kong Ming knows the stratagem he employs.

C. Lu Su does not follow what Kong Ming has asked him. Instead, he tells Zhou Yu that Kong Ming knows everything. This prompts Zhou Yu's later attempts at killing Kong Ming. He puts forward the idea that the army needs one hundred thousand arrows to fight Cao Cao on the Great River. He sets a deadline, which is only ten days, and under the military law. If Kong Ming is not able to gather one hundred thousand arrows, he will have to face the execution. To which, Kong Ming replies that he will only need three days. The trap really makes Zhou Yu ecstatic, knowing that he can finally have an excuse of killing Kong Ming.

D. Zhou Yu is intentionally uncooperative, not giving enough supplies. When Kong Ming sees Lu Su, he makes a complaint about the whole thing. He wants Lu Su to lend him twenty boats, and each with thirty men on it. On each boat, there are thousands of straw bales, covered by black cloth, on both sides of the boat. Two days have passed, and yet Kong Ming does nothing. This makes Lu Su and others more perplexed than ever. It is not until the third day around 1 a.m to 3 a.m that Kong Ming makes the move. Now twenty boats are linked together by a long rope, sailing to the North coast. The heavy fog permeates through the surroundings. On the surface of the river, the fog is even denser, making the boat entirely invisible to the enemy. Kong Ming orders the boat to hasten the speed. About 3 a.m to 5 a.m twenty boats are approaching the North coast, very close to where Cao Cao's navy force resides.

E. To Lu Su's surprise, Kong Ming orders the sailors to beat the drums and make roars, not fearing the attack made by Cao Cao. Cao Cao interprets this attack as an ambush, and since there is a heavy fog, he orders the entire army to remain impervious to the situation. Around ten thousand crossbowmen are responding to the surprise attack, firing as many arrows as others can imagine. Within a few minutes, Kong Ming's boats are peppered with arrows. Kong Ming commands all the boats to turn around, making sure that all the other side of the boat also gathers enough arrows attached on the straw bales. As the sun is about to rise and the fog is about to be cleared up, Kong Ming orders all twenty boats sail back to the South shore.

F. As the boat sails south, all soldiers on the boats roar "thanks the prime minister for the arrows". When Cao Cao realizes it is Kong Ming's stratagem, they have already sailed around twenty miles away from the North coast. On their way back to the south shore, Kong Ming tells Lu Su that three days earlier, he has already predicted that there is going to be a dense fog so that he is dared to promise Zhou Yu three days will be enough to gather all the arrows he needs. Upon hearing this, Lu Su admires Kong Ming even more.

G. When they are back to the South shore, Zhou Yu awaits there with five hundred soldiers there, waiting to check ten thousand arrows. On each boat, there are around five thousand to six thousand arrows, making the total amount more than ten thousand arrows. When Lu Su recounts later to Zhou Yu about the entire incident, Zhou Yu feels astonished by Kong Ming's successful prediction. He then compliments Kong Ming. To which, Kong Ming replies "it's just a small trick and it's nothing", making Zhou Yu extremely unpleasant.

Questions 1-4

Reading Passage 1 has seven paragraphs, A-G

Which paragraph contains the following information?

Write the correct letter, A-G, in boxes 1-4 on your answer sheet.

NB You may use any letter more than once.

1 mention of a realization to a deception but is too late
2 a description of one side's reluctance to collaborate
3 mention of a natural phenomenon that favors one side
4 mention of one's bravery towards a certain thing

Questions 5-8

Look at the following statements (Questions 5-8) and the list of people below.

Match each statement with the correct people, A-E

Write the correct letter, A-E, in boxes 5-8 on your answer sheet.

NB You may use any letter more than once.

5 who at first has no urgency to do things that have to be done within a specific date

6 who is fooled twice

7 who is relieved to see that certain menaces no longer exist

8 who narrates a certain event to someone important

List of people

A Kong Ming

B Jiang Gan

C Zhou Yu

D Cao Cao

E Lu Su

Questions 9-13

Complete the summary below

Choose No More Than Two Words from the passage for each answer

Write your answers in boxes 10-13 on your answer sheet.

Consolidation of Kong Ming's role in later successes of the Shu empire can be traced to his ability to gather two major components, such as **9.**_____ and _____.

Stratagems are used consecutively. The first one is employed by Zhou Yu and Cao Cao's sudden thought makes him lose two **10.**_____. While some threats will pose no more harm to Zhou Yu's army, a closer look can reveal that the actual **11.**_____ remains.

Zhou Yu's attempt to murder Kong Ming leads to an event that requires only ten days to do, and there is a **12.**_____. After Lu Su's help, now twenty boats are ready to sail to the North coast. Eventually, Kong Ming's boats have gathered enough arrows discharged by Cao's **13.**_____. The total amount of gathered arrows is more than ten thousand.

試題中譯

問題 1 到 4

閱讀文章第一篇有七個段落，A-G

哪個段落包含了下列資訊？

在你的答案紙，1-4 答案欄中，寫上正確的字母 A-G

NB 你可能使用任何一個字母超過一次

1 提及意識到受騙但為時已晚
2 描述其中一方在合作上的不情願
3 提及一個自然現象眷顧其中一方
4 提及某個人在做特定事情時的勇敢

問題 5 到 8

看下列敘述（問題 5 到 8）和以下列表中的人物

將每個敘述與正確的人物，**A-E** 進行配對

在你的答案紙，**5-8** 答案欄中，寫上正確的字母 **A-E**

NB 你可能使用任何一個字母超過一次

5 起初對於在特定期限內，必須要完成的事情沒有急迫性

6 受騙兩次

7 對於特定的威脅不存在了感到如釋重負

8 將特定事件敘述給某個重要的人聽

人物列表
A 孔明
B 蔣幹
C 周瑜
D 曹操
E 魯肅

問題 9 到 13

完成下列摘要題

段落中的每個答案，請勿超過兩個單字

在你的答案紙，**9-13** 答案欄中，寫上你的答案

在後期蜀帝國的成功上，孔明地位的鞏固能追溯於他的能力，收集兩個主要的組成物，例如 9.＿＿＿＿＿＿ 和 ＿＿＿＿＿＿。

計謀接連的使出。第一個計謀是由周瑜所運用，而曹操的閃念讓他損失了兩名 10.＿＿＿＿＿＿。有些威脅對於周瑜軍隊不會造成危害，仔細一看能揭露出實際的 11.＿＿＿＿＿＿ 仍存在。

周瑜企圖謀殺孔明導致了一個事件，需要僅 10 日的期限來完成，而有著 12.＿＿＿＿＿＿。在魯肅的幫助下，現在 20 艘船準備好要航向北岸。最終，孔明的船隻收集由曹操軍隊所發射出的 13.＿＿＿＿＿＿ 而有了足夠的箭。收集到的箭的總數超過了十萬隻箭。

Step 1：迅速看題型配置，再定出解題步驟

這篇文章的題型有：❶配對_段落細節題（Which paragraph contains the following information）、❷配對_人物題和❸摘要題。

配對_段落細節題敘述開頭常以⋯an example of/a reference of⋯/mention of⋯等等開始，名詞片語或子句有時候拉太長，這樣回推其實太慢，看到這類題目直接理解成，段落中**有提到、描述或列舉中那些資訊，並且以關鍵字快速定位回文章收詢。**

Step 2：腦海中浮現答題策略，開始答題

這篇既然有❶**配對_段落細節題**（Which paragraph contains the following information）、❷**配對_人物題**，建議先答這兩個題型，並一併收尋這兩個題型的相關關鍵字，**逐題回去尋找資訊太浪費時間，請同步找**，所以掃描第 1 題到第 8 題關鍵字，只少腦海中要浮現 4-5 個關鍵點，例如 deception, reluctance to collaborate, a natural phenomenon, bravery, no urgency, fooled twice, menaces no loner exist, narrate a certain event，掌握這些資訊後開始讀段落，除了這些資訊也注意每個人物，每個人物均可能是出題點。

♦ 很快看到 **B 段**有出現 Jiang Gan（蔣幹） is fooled by a stratagem used by Zhou Yu（周瑜），但是第 6 題提到的是

Test 4

TEST 1

TEST 2

TEST 3

TEST 4

Reading Passage 1

fooled **twice** 所以要小心。下句 Upon viewing the letter, Cao Cao acts merely on impulse, making a regrettable decision. He beheads both Cai Mao（蔡瑁）and Zhang Yun（張允）, two major commanders of marine warfare.，其實就對應到第 1 題，只是表達較隱晦些，但為同義表達，**a realization to a deception but is too late = Cao Cao acts merely on impulse, making a regrettable decision**，曹操因而誤殺了兩名大將，所以**第 1 題**答案為 **B**。並記住曹操和蔣幹各受騙一次，因為這與第 6 題有關。

◆ 次句 Zhou Yu is so pleased to learn the news that two major threats **are long gone**，這對應到第 7 題 is relieved to see that certain menaces no longer exist 為同義轉換，其中 **menaces=threats**，**no longer exist=are long gone**，所以**第 7 題**答案為 **C Zhou Yu**。

◆ 接續閱讀到段落 C，He sets a deadline, which is only ten days, and under the military law.，deadline 其實對應到 within a specific date，但接續讀到 D 段落首句 Zhou Yu is intentionally uncooperative, not giving enough supplies.很明顯對應到**第 2 題**的 one side's reluctance to collaborate，所以答案為 **D**。

◆ 接續閱讀到 Two days have passed, and yet Kong Ming does

nothing. This makes Lu Su and others more perplexed than ever. It is not until the third day around 1 a.m to 3 a.m that Kong Ming makes the move.，讀到這就很明顯知道 at first has no urgency to do things that have to be done within a specific date 指的是孔明，起初不急於行動到第三天才展開行動，為 C 和 D 段落的綜合資訊的濃縮，所以**第 5 題**的答案為 **A Kong Ming**。

- D 段落中後其實看到 the heavy fog 就要馬上聯想到是對應到 natural phenomenon，雖然是用 natural phenomenon 定位回去找，可以多練習這樣的轉換，才不會覺得找不到訊息。The heavy fog permeates through the surroundings. On the surface of the river, the fog is even denser, **making the boat entirely invisible to the enemy**.，後面資訊其實就是表明 a natural phenomenon that favors one side，所以**第 3 題**的答案為 **D**，快速填在答案紙上並繼續作答。

- 緊接著在 E 段落 To Lu Su's surprise, Kong Ming orders the sailors to beat the drums and make roars, **not fearing** the attack made by Cao Cao.，這句對應了第 4 題 one's bravery towards a certain thing，**not fearing = bravery，a certain thing = attack made by Cao Cao**，所以**第 4 題**答案為 **E**。

- 讀到 F 段落，When **Cao Cao realizes it is Kong Ming's**

stratagem, they have already sailed around twenty miles away from the North coast.，可以推測出曹操中了孔明的計，被騙了，這是曹操第二次上當，所以可以馬上答第 6 題受騙兩次，故**第 6 題**的答案為 **D**。

♦ 接著讀 G 段落，When Lu Su **recounts** later to Zhou Yu about the entire incident, Zhou Yu feels astonished by Kong Ming's successful prediction.，其中 **recount=narrate**，這句等同題目的 narrates a certain event to someone important，someone important=周瑜，可以馬上答**第 8 題**答案為 **E**。就這樣很快答完這 8 題，接著請馬上看摘要題。

♦ 摘要題放最後答，因為有時候出題者集中在某幾段出題，有時候又很分散，也可以在閱讀文章第一段的時候就也先掃描摘要題的部分，邊寫邊答這三類型題目。

♦ 先看**第 9 題**，such as 後有兩項列舉的項目，加上答題規範所以第 9 題有兩個答案，試題第一句對應到 A 段落首句 Kong Ming plays a pivotal role in later successes of the Shu empire，接續讀到 As the fiction progresses, several successful predictions and great feats of major events, such as borrowing **arrows** from the enemy and praying for an eastern **wind** at the Altar of the Seven Stars, **consolidate** his role as a military adviser and most important of all in the mind of people who read about him. ，consolidate 對應到試題的 condolidation，然後兩個 component 可能是套色標示的 arrows 和 wind，其實主要就是**借東風**和**草船借箭**，風和箭這兩樣顯示出孔明的智慧，所以第 9 題為 **arrows** 和 **wind**。

- 再來看**第 10 題**，Stratagems are used consecutively. The first one is employed by Zhou Yu 看到這兩句其實對應到 B 段落，蔣幹重了周瑜的計謀，緊接著 Upon viewing the letter, Cao Cao **acts merely on impulse**, making a regrettable decision. He beheads both Cai Mao（蔡瑁）and Zhang Yun（張允）, two major **commanders** of marine warfare. ，這兩句對應到第 10 題，其中 **acts merely on impulse = sudden thought**，**beheads...two major commanders = makes him lose two...**，所以**第 10 題**答案為 **commanders**。

- 再來看**第 11 題**，Zhou Yu is so pleased to learn the news that two major threats are long gone, but he later realizes the real menace is Kong Ming because Kong Ming is too smart. 對應到題目的 While some threats will pose no more harm to Zhou Yu's army, a closer look can reveal that the actual....，其中 **pose no more harm = major threats are long gone**，**can reveal that actual....remains = realizes the real menace**，故**第 11 題**答案為 **menace**。

◆ 緊接著是第 **12** 題，**請運用【跳讀】和【關鍵字定位】**，用試題的 **only ten days** 定位到 C 段落 He sets a **deadline**, which is **only ten days**, and under the military law. ，對應到 there is a _____，其實是出題者將兩個訊息拆開敘述，思考一下就可以推測出緊接著是要說 10 天期限後，是有 deadline 的，所以**第 12 題**答案為 **deadline**。

◆ 再來是最後一題，答題時間有限**請運用【跳讀】和【關鍵字定位】**，先用 **twenty boats** 定位到 Now **twenty boats** are linked together by a long rope, sailing to the North coast.和 About 3 a.m to 5 a.m **twenty boats** are approaching the North coast, very close to where Cao Cao's navy force reside.

◆ 然後迅速接續讀文章，Around ten thousand **crossbowmen** are responding to the surprise attack, **firing** as many arrows as others can imagine. Within a few minutes, **Kong Ming's boats** are peppered with arrows. ，試題中 Kong Ming's boats 對應文章，然後 are peppered with arrows 為 have gathered 的同義轉換 enough arrows，答案就在這附近，緊接著看到 discharged by Cao's 13._____，代表由曹操所發射出的，discharged by = firing，而**執行這個動作的一定是人**，所以別誤選其他名詞像是 arrows，所以可以推斷是由 **crossbowmen** 所執行這個動作的，故這題答案為 **crossbowmen**。

◆ 額外補充的部分是，其實遇到像是引導副詞子句的連接詞像是 if, when, since, unless 等等，可以直接跳讀主要子句（但如果是過於細節性的部分還是建議選擇不要跳讀），其實只看主要子句會快非常多，主要子句描述的一定是重要的訊息，**【副詞子句連接詞+S+V....，S+V...】**，直接跳讀後面套色部分（**S+V...**），可以大幅刪減掉許多訊息，尤其在某些文體時可以讀得更快。

◆ 在這篇文章中還出現蠻多副詞子句連接詞的，❶ 像 A 段落的 As the fiction progresses, several successful predictions and great feats of major events…，其實 As the fiction progresses 可以直接刪除不看也沒有影響句子意思，只是陳述到隨著小說進展。

❷ Upon viewing the letter, Cao Cao acts merely on impulse, making a regrettable decision.，也可以刪除或略過不看**【介係詞引導的子句】**，即前面的 Upon viewing the letter，主要訊息還是在 Cao Cao acts merely on impulse, making a regrettable decision.。

❸ He beheads both Cai Mao（蔡瑁）and Zhang Yun（張允），two major commanders of marine warfare.，其實也可以刪除**【同位語補充說明】**的部分，例如 two major commanders of marine warfare，知道這兩個人物就夠了，可是摘要題的挖空有出到關鍵詞，其實定位後即使跳讀後還是能找到。

◆ ❹ **If** ~~Kong Ming is not able to gather one hundred thousand arrows~~, he will have to face the execution. ❺ **When** Kong

Ming sees Lu Su, he makes a complaint about the whole thing. ❻ **since** there is a heavy fog, he orders the entire army to remain impervious to the situation. ❼ **Within** a few minutes, Kong Ming's boats are peppered with arrows.

◆ ❽ **As** the sun is about to rise and the fog is about to be cleared up, Kong Ming orders all twenty boats sail back to the South shore. ❾ **As** the boat sails south, all soldiers on the boats roar "thanks the prime minister for the arrows". ❿ **When** Cao Cao realizes it is Kong Ming's stratagem, they have already sailed around twenty miles away from the North coast.等等的。

其實要注意一個大重點，剪枝技巧其實沒有掌握高階同義轉換和時間統籌等重要，當訊息都剪完後，或也都看懂每句話其實雅思閱讀 7 分以下的考生，所面臨的還是對應不到同義轉換的部分，而沒辦法選出答案或找到答案，可以多掌握書中或官方試題中所有同義轉換對應到的部分。

除了這些之外，還有一些在學術文章中常見的句型，其實也可以只迅速看**主要敘述句**例如：❶-❺ 的句型

◆ ❶ Like/Unlike
❶ 的句型的話，【Like/Unlike+S+V..., S+V…】刪除前面的部分，直接看主要子句的部分即可，重要訊息其實在主要子句。

如果句子演變得較複雜，有出現**形容詞子句修飾**的部分，其實形容詞子句也可以忽略不看，其實沒有影響主要子句的意思，僅補充說明前面敘述的部分，例如【~~Like/Unlike+S+V…~~, **who/which**…, S+V…】，句子中who or which引導的長句敘述再長都直接忽略，（如果要速讀盡快掌握文意的話），**看 S+V** 的部分就好了。

* ❷ To+V…, S+V…
  這個句型在雅思閱讀中也很常見，其實【~~To+V…~~, S+V…】刪除前面的部分，直接看主要子句的部分即可，不過有時候這類型的句子是**表目的**的句子，蠻多時候其實會影響像是答段落標題的題目，可以自己在斟酌。

* ❸ 過去分詞構句
  這個句型是【~~P.P.…~~, S+V…】，也是可以刪除前面修飾性的句子。

  分詞構句是由副詞子句簡化而來的，其中又分成過去分詞（即以p.p）和現在分詞（即以 v-ing），分別引導現在分詞構句和過去分詞構句。（現在分詞包含了主動意涵，而過去分詞包含了被動意涵），在閱讀考試中分秒必爭，其實看過就養成**跳讀**的習慣就好，看到一篇文章時，遇到這種句型，**直接看 S+V** 的部分是最省時的。

* ❹ 現在分詞構句
  這個句型是【~~Ving…~~, S+V…】，也是可以刪除前面修飾性的句子。

◆ ❺ 片語類的，例如：In addition to, apart from…。

這類句型在雅思閱讀中極為常見，也是刪除前面修飾性的句子即可【~~In addition to+ving...~~, S+V...】，前面的敘述並不影響後面的主要表達。

例如❶**Test 1 Reading Passage 3**，~~According to the bestseller *Give and Take*~~, there are three types, takers, givers, and matchers.【刪除According to...】。❷ **Test 1 Reading Passage 3**，~~Contrary to what readers might think~~, givers are actually the ultimate winner, ~~since others are benefited by them before~~.【刪除Contrary to...和since引導的子句】。❸ **Test 2 Reading Passage 2**，In addition to topics these above-mentioned two books explore, many books all mention the importance of saving money. ❹ **Test 2 Reading Passage 3**，~~In addition to grades~~, there are other criteria and it is quite impossible for ones to excel at everything. ❺ **Test 3 Reading Passage 3**，~~Apart from someone who has inherited a great deal of money or someone who was born with a silver spoon~~, people have to work to support themselves.❻ **Test 3 Reading Passage 3**，~~In addition to these factors that influence the degree of job satisfaction~~, there are other factors, such as the personality of the worker, the type of industry, and dexterity of the job content.

A. Kong Ming plays a pivotal role in later successes of the Shu empire. Kong Ming's success relies heavily on his own wisdom, and he has become a legendary figure for later generations. As the fiction progresses, several successful predictions and great feats of major events, such as borrowing arrows from the enemy and praying for an eastern wind at the Altar of the Seven Stars, consolidate his role as a military adviser and most important of all in the mind of people who read about him. In the time of a huge turmoil, every leader is in desperate need of finding great warriors and famous military advisers.

孔明在蜀國後期的成功上扮演著關鍵的角色。孔明的成功很大程度地仰賴著他本身的智慧，而且對於後代人們，他已經成了傳奇性的人物。隨著小説的進展，幾項成功的預測和主要事件的偉大功績，例如跟敵人借箭以及在七星潭神壇祈禱東風，鞏固了他軍師的地位，以及最重要的是在那些閱讀到關於他的人們心中所佔的地位。在極大混亂的時代中，每個領導者都迫切需要尋找優秀的戰士和知名的軍師們。

B. Jiang Gan（蔣幹）is fooled by a stratagem used by Zhou Yu（周瑜），bringing the letter back to Cao Cao （曹操）. Upon viewing the letter, Cao Cao acts merely on impulse, making a regrettable decision. He beheads both Cai Mao（蔡瑁）and Zhang Yun（張允）, two major commanders of marine warfare. Zhou Yu is so pleased to learn the news that two major threats are long gone, but he later realizes the real menace is Kong Ming because Kong Ming is too smart. Zhou Yu sends Lu Su（魯肅） to see whether Kong Ming knows the stratagem he employs.

蔣幹受到周瑜的詭計蒙騙，將信件帶回去給曹操。在看過信件後，曹操僅出於一時的衝動，造成了令人感到遺憾的決定。他將蔡瑁和張允兩人砍頭，兩位主要的海戰軍事家。周瑜得知消息兩個主要威脅都被除去後感到極為高興，但是他稍後馬上了解到真正的威脅其實是孔明，因為孔明過於聰明。周瑜派魯肅去檢視孔明是否知道他所採用的詭計。

C. Lu Su does not follow what Kong Ming has asked him. Instead, he tells Zhou Yu that Kong Ming knows everything. This prompts Zhou Yu's later attempts at killing Kong Ming. He puts forward the idea that the army needs one hundred thousand arrows to fight Cao Cao on the Great River. He sets a deadline, which is only ten days, and under the military law. If Kong Ming is not able to gather one hundred thousand arrows, he will have to face the execution. To which, Kong Ming replies that he will only need three days. The trap really makes Zhou Yu ecstatic, knowing that he can finally have an excuse of killing Kong Ming.

魯肅並未遵從孔明所要求他的去做。取而代之的是，他告訴周瑜，孔明知道一切事情的發生經過。這促使周瑜後來幾次採取行動行刺孔明。他提出了一個想法，軍隊需要 10 萬隻箭應對在黃河上與曹操的戰鬥。在軍令下，他訂了截止日期，僅僅 10 日的期限。如果孔明未能夠於時限內收集到 10 萬隻箭的話，他將會受處死刑。對於此，孔明說他僅需要三日作準備。這個陷阱真的讓周瑜狂喜，知道自己最終能夠有藉口殺死孔明。

D. Zhou Yu is intentionally uncooperative, not giving enough supplies. When Kong Ming sees Lu Su, he makes a complaint about the whole thing. He wants Lu Su to lend him twenty boats, and each with thirty men on it. On each boat, there are thousands of straw bales, covered by black cloth, on both sides of the boat. Two days have passed, and yet Kong Ming does nothing. This makes Lu Su and others more perplexed than ever. It is not until the third day around 1 a.m to 3 a.m that Kong Ming makes the move. Now twenty boats are linked together by a long rope, sailing to the North coast. The heavy fog permeates through the surroundings. On the surface of the river, the fog is even denser, making the boat entirely invisible to the enemy. Kong Ming orders the boat to hasten the speed. About 3 a.m to 5 a.m twenty boats are approaching the North coast, very close to where Cao Cao's navy force resides.

周瑜故意不配合，不給予足夠的供給。當孔明見到魯肅，他向魯肅抱怨了整件事。他想要魯肅借他 20 艘船，而且每艘都配有 30 個男性在船上。在每艘船上，都配有數千個草包束，以帆布覆蓋著，分置於船的兩側。兩天過去了，而孔明毫無動靜。此舉讓魯肅和其他人感到更為困惑。直到第三天凌晨一點到三點時分，孔明採取了行動。現在 20 艘船上都以長索連結在一起，航向北方海岸。濃厚的大霧瀰漫著周遭環境。在船的表面上，霧更為濃厚，讓船隻全然隱入敵方視線中。孔明命令船隻加緊速度。大約於三點至五點時分，20 艘船正迫近北方海岸，非常接近曹操的海軍軍隊棲息所。

E. To Lu Su's surprise, Kong Ming orders the sailors to beat the drums and make roars, not fearing the attack made by Cao Cao. Cao Cao interprets this attack as an ambush, and since there is a heavy fog, he orders the entire army to remain impervious to the situation. Around ten thousand crossbowmen are responding to the surprise attack, firing as many arrows as others can imagine. Within a few minutes, Kong Ming's boats are peppered with arrows. Kong Ming commands all the boats to turn around, making sure that all the other side of the boat also gathers enough arrows attached on the straw bales. As the sun is about to rise and the fog is about to be cleared up, Kong Ming orders all twenty boats sail back to the South shore.

令魯肅感到意外的是，孔明命令航行者擊鼓而且製造吼叫聲，完全不恐懼於曹操的攻擊。曹操將者攻擊舉動解讀為埋伏，而且既然有著濃霧，他命令整個軍隊對於局勢維持毫無所動。大約 10 萬名弓弩手回應這個意外突襲，發射其他人所能想像多的弓箭。孔明命令所有船隻都轉向，確保所有其他側的船隻也收集到足夠的弓箭，附著在草束包上。隨著太陽正要上升而霧正要被除去，孔明命令所有 20 艘船駛回南岸。

F. As the boat sails south, all soldiers on the boats roar "thanks the prime minister for the arrows". When Cao Cao realizes it is Kong Ming's stratagem, they have already sailed around twenty miles away from the North coast. On their way back to the south shore, Kong Ming tells Lu Su that three days earlier, he has already predicted that there is going to be a dense fog so that he is dared to promise Zhou Yu three days will be enough to gather all the arrows he needs. Upon hearing this, Lu Su admires Kong Ming even more.

隨著船隻向南航駛，所有船上軍人大聲喊出「謝謝丞相賜箭」。當曹操了解到這是孔明的詭計時，他們已經行駛了離北岸 20 浬左右的距離。在他們回到南岸時，孔明告訴魯肅，三天前他就已經預測出將會有濃霧，如此一來他就膽敢向周瑜保證，三天就足夠湊得他所需要的所有箭。在聽到這個時，魯肅更加欽佩孔明了。

G. When they are back to the South shore, Zhou Yu awaits there with five hundred soldiers there, waiting to check ten thousand arrows. On each boat, there are around five thousand to six thousand arrows, making the total amount more than ten thousand arrows. When Lu Su recounts later to Zhou Yu about the entire incident, Zhou Yu feels astonished by Kong Ming's successful prediction. He then compliments Kong Ming. To which, Kong Ming replies it's just a small trick and it's nothing, making Zhou Yu extremely unpleasant.

當他們駛回南岸時，周瑜帶著 500 位軍人在那裡等待著，等著欽點 10 隻箭。在每艘船上，有大約 5000 至 6000 隻箭，使得箭的總數超過 10 萬隻箭。當魯肅向周瑜重述整件事時，周瑜對於孔明的成功預測感到吃驚。然後他讚美孔明。對此，孔明回覆，這僅是小伎倆，而且這沒什麼，此舉讓周瑜感到極度不滿。

READING PASSAGE 2

You should spend about 20 minutes on **Questions 14-27**, which are based on Reading Passage 2 below.

Case Study:
Love Suggestions from Renowned Scholars to Younger Generations

A. In *The Return of the Condor Hero*, when Lu Zhan Yuan tells Li Mo Chou（李莫愁）she does not know what love is, this is probably true, but saying this drives Li Mo Chou into behaving insanely. Perhaps Li really needs to take a love lesson, but just don't tell this to her in person. Love is such a complex subject and there seems to be lot for us to learn. Using our entire life to learn what is love is simply not enough. This is not an exaggerated statement. Even people in love do not know what love is. Some people think they have found it, but they are not. Others have spent their entire lives out there searching, but cannot seem to find it. Thousands of movies, fictions, and books about love have produced to help us get closer to what love is, and some are quite helpful. Let's find out.

B. In our counseling session, Jane admitted to us that she wished she had read books, such as Helen Fisher's *Why Him? Why Her?*, and did all personality tests. During her twentysomething years, she had no problems getting a date from a guy, and she happened to meet several guys that was so great that even her girlfriends were jealous of her. Deep down, she knew they weren't the perfect fit for her. In fact, her had five relationships before she turned thirty. Most people around her would comment how picky she was because those guys were fantastic, but she knew pretty well that people might have a wrong idea about suitability and attractiveness. Those guys were great, but were not great enough for her, not suitable for her. Other girls may think having a guy drive a Porsche waiting for you outside the campus is great. Or having someone who is willing to pay bills for you at an expensive restaurant and take you to several countries is dreamy and romantic. She, on the contrary, finds it exhausting, having to adjust herself for a jet lag after a long travel at every major holiday.

C. Most of the time, she just wants to take a hot bath (sounds like what one of the housewives in the *Desperate Housewives* telling her husband what she would like to do at the Valentine's days.), watch some soap operas, pamper her dogs, or simply enjoy their time together. She just wants a simple life, and she did not want to disappoint her boyfriends. Every time she learned the news about their new travelling plans, she had to pretend how excited that was, another international trip to Europe, and she then went to the bathroom strangling the huge Teddy bear. Looking back, she thought that she had to be apologetic and kind of felt sorry for the bear, which has always been there for her when she had a mood fluctuation. Now especially after reading Helen Fisher's *Why Him? Why Her?* and our counselling sessions, she now has a clear view of what she wants in a man. A few months after our counselling sessions, she told us the big news that she has found the guy and they are getting married in two weeks.

D. While Jane's case is about who has no trouble finding a guy, Cindy is the girl who cannot seem to find a guy. She is already 35 years old, and she remains single all the time. It is not that she does not want to get married. She feels frustrated that she cannot get the guy because everyone in the workplace is either married or gay. Where are good guys, she lamented. She told us the funny thing that she has rehearsed the wedding vow a thousand times, and she has accumulated enough money to get married. She even listens to the advice of *The Ugly Truth* and throws away relationship books, such as *Men Are from Mars and Women Are from Venus*, but recently she bought another relationship book, *Get the Guy*, to see if this book can really help her before she hit 40. To us, Cindy seems like a fun girl to be with, and she just needs to relax for a bit. She seems overprepared like getting married is the most important thing in life. When the time is right, she will just find the person to start the next chapter of her life.

E. What can we learn from both cases is that lots of us are waiting for love. We all deserve to be with someone who respects us. Sometimes it is just about the timing. Sometimes it is about widening your social cycles. Hastily moving onto a relationship can do more harm than good. Relationship books sometimes help. They prevent us from overthinking and some really keep us optimistic about life, and We don't want her to find the perfect person because sometimes that person just does not exist. Or it is just like the line from *Ugly Betty*, "maybe perfect doesn't always look like you'd imagine." Cindy certainly needs more therapy sessions.

F. Dr. Jake and Dr. Sally 2019/3/17

Questions 14-17

Reading Passage 2 has FIVE paragraphs, A-E

Which paragraph contains the following information?

Write the correct letter, A-E, in boxes 14-17 on your answer sheet.

NB You may use any letter more than once.

14 mention of a person who has amassed enough currency

15 a description of one's temperament that swings

16 mention of a heroine who misconstrues the meaning of love

17 mention of a plaything that is used for venting

Questions 18-22

Look at the following statements (Questions 18-22) and the list of books or shows below.

Match each statement with the correct books or shows, A-G

Write the correct letter, A-G, in boxes 18-22 on your answer sheet.

NB You may use any letter more than once.

18 includes psychological quiz

19 leads a further decision to discard a book

20 can be the prospect of solving some issues for someone

21 expresses a view that is contrary to popular beliefs

22 contains a heroine who simply just wants to relax on a holiday

---

List of books or shows

A *The Return of the Condor Hero*

B *Why Him? Why Her*

C *Desperate Housewives*

D *The Ugly Truth*

E *Men Are from Mars and Women Are from Venus*

F *Get the Guy*

G *Ugly Betty*

Questions 23-27

Complete the summary below

Choose No More Than One Word from the passage for each answer

Write your answers in boxes 23-27 on your answer sheet.

Helen Fisher's *Why Him? Why Her?* provides an insight that helps Jane know herself better. During her twentysomething years, **23.**_____ from her girlfriends was something Jane had to deal with, since she was a catch. Those guys were incredible, but Jane knew that they were not ideal for her. She has a different perspective when it comes to the type of guys that is attractive. For example, driving a vehicle like **24.**_____ _____is considered great by the norm of other girls. Other instance includes taking international trips, but accustoming herself to a jetlag makes her **25.**_____. People might have a false assumption about **26.**_____ and **27.**_____ _____, and she knew pretty well about that.

試題中譯

問題 14 到 17

閱讀文章第二篇有 **5** 個段落，**A-E**

哪個段落包含了下列資訊？

在你的答案紙，**14-17** 答案欄中，寫上正確的字母 **A-E**

NB 你可能使用任何一個字母超過一次

14 提及一個人已經累積了足夠的錢

15 描述一個人的情緒擺動

16 提及一位女主角誤解了愛情的意義

17 提及一項玩物是用於發洩情緒用的

問題 18 到 22

看下列敘述（問題第 18 題到第 22 題）和以下列表中的書籍或節目

將每個敘述與書籍或節目，**A, B, C, D, E, F, or G** 進行配對

在你的答案紙，**18-22** 答案欄中，寫上正確的字母 **A-G**

NB 你可能使用任何一個字母超過一次

18 包含心理學的測驗

19 導致進一步丟掉書籍的決定

20 有可能可以替某個人解決一些議題

21 表達與大眾不同的觀點

22 包含一位女主角在假期時僅想要放鬆

書籍或節目列表

A 神鵰俠侶

B 我們為何戀愛？為何不忠？

C 慾望師奶

D 醜惡真相

E 男人來自火星，而女人來自金星

F 男人完全解密

G 醜女貝蒂

問題 23 到 27

完成下列摘要題

段落中的每個答案，請勿超過 1 個單字

在你的答案紙，**23-27** 答案欄中，寫上你的答案

海倫・費雪《我們為何戀愛？為何不忠？》提供了能幫助珍更了解自己的洞悉。在她 20 多歲時期，從她女性朋友的 23._____，是珍必須要去應對的，因為她是個尤物。那些男人都很棒，但是珍深知，那些男人並不適合她。當提及具吸引力類型的男人時，她有著不同的看法。例如，駕駛像是 24._____ 為交通工具者被視為是其他女生朋友覺得棒的標準。其他例子包含了，去國際性的旅遊，但是需要調適自我來適應時差使得她 25._____。人們可能對於 26._____ 和 27._____ 有著錯誤的想法，而且對於那些她相當清楚。

Step 1:迅速看題型配置,再定出解題步驟

這篇文章的題型有:❶配對_段落細節題(Which paragraph contains the following information)、❷配對_人物題和❸摘要題。 這三個題型的搭配為劍橋雅思常見的題型搭配,多熟悉這題型後其實答題會快很多。

配對_段落細節題敘述開頭常以...an example of/a reference of.../mention of...等等開始,名詞片語或子句有時候拉太長,這樣回推其實太慢,看到這類題目直接理解成,段落中**有提到、描述或列舉中那些資訊,並且以關鍵字快速定位回文章收詢**。

Step 2:腦海中浮現答題策略,開始答題

這篇既然有❶配對_段落細節題(Which paragraph contains the following information)、❷配對_物品和節目題,建議先答這兩個題型,並一併收尋這兩個題型的相關關鍵字,**逐題回去尋找資訊太浪費時間,請同步找**,所以掃描第 14 題到第 22 題關鍵字,只少腦海中要浮現 4-5 個關鍵點,例如 **enough currency**, **temperament that swings**, a **heroine** who **misconstrues** the meaning of **love**, a **plaything** that is used for **venting**, **psychological quiz**, **discard a book**, **prospect** of solving some issues, a view that contrary to popular beliefs, a **heroine** who simply just wants to **relax on a holiday**,掌握這些資訊後開始讀段落,除了這些資訊也注意每個**書籍和節目**,每個**書籍和節目**均可能是出題點。

◆ 在 A 段落的前兩句可以找到 Li Mo Chou（李莫愁）對應**第 16 題**的 heroine，**meaning = definition**，**does not know what is love = misconstrue**，所以**第 16 題**答案是 **A**。

◆ 緊接著很快看過這段，幾乎都是鋪陳的敘述。也**可以直接跳讀到 B 段落**，提到人物 **Jane** 和書籍 *Why Him? Why Her*，要特別警覺，因為很可能是出題點，讀到 all personality tests 時，可以迅速對應到第 18 題中的 includes psychological quiz，psychological quiz = personality tests，故**第 18 題**為答案 **B**。

◆ 然後可以**接著讀**也可以**跳讀**，接著讀的好處是等等摘要題時可以更快定位，因為至少有些印象，可以減少來回查找的時間，順便大概知道簡的狀況。

◆ 接著到 C 段落，要很注意的是，很多考生常會忽略（ ）內的敘述，但常常卻是出題者愛考的考點，所以跳讀時**請別忽略**這部分，很容易會跳過這訊息後通篇讀完還找不到答案在哪。

◆ C 段落中的 one of the housewives in the *Desperate Housewives* telling her husband what she would like to do at the Valentine's days，**housewives** 其實對應到 **heroine**，**holiday = Valentine's days** 的同義表達，**relax** 對應 **take a hot bath** 等等，迅速對應到第 22 題的描述 contains a heroine who simply just wants to relax on a holiday，故**第 22 題**答案為 **C**。

◆ 緊接著在 C 段落中間找到 she then went to the bathroom strangling the huge Teddy bear，其實要馬上能體會出隱含的意思，strangling the huge Teddy bear 其實是 as a way to vent，**Teddy bear = a plaything**，而 **strangling** 的行為 = **venting**，故**第 17 題**答案為 **C**。

◆ C 段落還沒結束，也請仔細讀，可能還有其他考點在同個段落喔，she thought that she had to be apologetic and kind of felt sorry for the bear, which has always been there for her when she had a **mood fluctuation**.，讀到 **mood fluctuation** 這裡時可以馬上對應到 one's temperament that swings，故**第 15 題**的答案為 **C**。要小心有時候同個段落出現好幾次關鍵字是正確答案喔。

◆ 在 D 段落中，可以找到 she has accumulated enough money to get married.，**money = currency**，**amassed = accumulated**，所以可以迅速答完這題，**第 14 題**答案為 **D**。

◆ 緊接著看到幾個書名和節目，也是出題考點，She even listens to the advice of *The Ugly Truth* and throws away relationship books, such as ***Men Are from Mars and Women Are from Venus***, but recently she bought another relationship book, ***Get the Guy***, to see if this book can really help her before she hit 40.，要注意描述跟別粗心選錯了，其中 **throw away relationship books = discard a book**，所以**第 19 題**答案為 **D**。接著看到 can really help her before she hit 40，**help = can be the prospect of solving some issues for someone**。Cindy 期盼這本書能解決她的問題，所以**第 20 題**答案為 **F**。

◆ 這兩類型題型就剩 21 題未答，題目描述其實**較隱晦**，但還是繼續讀，或跳讀到最後一個書籍或節目，因為很可能就是那個答案，如果時間太緊迫可以直接猜是尚未讀到的書籍或節目為答案。定位到 Or it just like the line from *Ugly Betty*, maybe perfect doesn't always look like you'd imagine.，其實有時候完美真的就是這樣，不見得要每項都符合條件，但在當下卻是最好的或最適合的，描述等同 **a view that is contrary to popular beliefs**，故**第 21 題**答案為 **G**。

◆ 接著盡快答摘要題，摘要題訊息有點散，剛才沒有跳讀的話其實很快就能定位好段落，有跳讀也可以盡快用關鍵字定位比較省時。由 **Helen Fisher's *Why Him? Why Her?*** 和 **twentysomething years** 為關鍵字快速定位到 B 段落，判斷**第 23 題**空格，依文法看動詞為 is，空格為主詞且為名詞。

◆ During her twentysomething years, 23._____ from **her girlfriends** is something Jane has to deal with, since she was **a catch**.和文章中的 During her twentysomething years, she had **no problems getting a date from a guy**, and she happened to meet several guys that was so great that even **her girlfriends** were **jealous** of her.對照看，**no problems getting a date from a guy = a catch**，**her girlfriends = her girlfriends**，很明顯是某個特徵當主詞，答案很常會出現詞性轉換不見得全部對應到，這裡要將 jealous 換成 jealousy，jealousy 當主詞剛好，故第 23 題的答案為 **jealousy**。【詞性轉換】

◆ 接著速讀 For example, driving **a vehicle** like 24._____ is considered great by **the norm of other girls**.，可以迅速對應到 **Other girls may think** having a guy drive a Porsche waiting for you outside the campus is great.，其中 **the norm of other girls = Other girls may think** 出題者沒有直接用 drive 去換字，而改成另一個表達去形容，a vehicle like _____ = 交通工具，**a vehicle = Porsche**，出題者常會用這個方式或用形容詞子句改寫，要多適應這樣的表達，所以**第 24 題**答案很明顯是 **Porsche**。【改寫後的表達】

◆ 緊接著看到 Other instance includes taking international trips, but accustoming herself to a jetlag makes her 25._____.，請使用 international trips 和 a jetlag 為關鍵字迅

速定位到 She, on the contrary, finds it **exhausting**, having to adjust herself for a jet lag after a long travel at every major holiday，這裡要注意的是答案對應到後要改成 **exhausted**，這些事使她感到疲憊，故**第 25 題**答案要填 **exhausted**。【感受詞要注意**-ed/-ing 結尾**】

◆ 最後看到 People might have **a false assumption** about 26._____ and 27._____, and she knew pretty well about that.這題比較難，其實訊息在 Porsche 之前，但題目有時候出題會移來移去，其實如果**一時真的找不到對應訊息切勿心煩，其實往前幾句或往後幾句找下就會找到了**。

◆ 往前面找可以找到 Most people around her would comment how picky she was because those guys were fantastic, but **she knew pretty well** that people might **have a wrong idea** about **suitability** and **attractiveness**.，注意對應到的部分 **she knew pretty well** 和 **have a wrong idea**，**a false assumption = have a wrong idea**，所以答案很明顯是這兩個名詞，故**第 26 和 27 題**答案為 **suitability** 和 **attractiveness**。【亂序的出題】

　　此篇可以**刪除**的部分有：

◆ ❶ In *The Return of the Condor Hero*, when Lu Zhan Yuan tells Li Mo Chou（李莫愁）she does not know what is love, this is probably true, but saying ....❷【刪除介係詞片語和 when引導的子句】In our counseling session, Jane admitted to us that she wished she had read books,...【刪除介係詞片語】❸ ~~During her twentysomething years~~, she had no problems getting a date....【刪除 During...】❹ ~~Deep down~~, she knew they weren't the perfect fit for her.【刪除 Deep down】❺ She, ~~on the contrary~~, finds it exhausting, having to adjust....【刪除 Deep down】❻ ~~Most of the time~~, she just wants to...., watch some soap operas, pamper ....【刪除 Most of the time】❼ ~~Every time she learned the news about their new travelling plans~~, she had to pretend....【刪除 Every time...】

• ❶ ~~Looking back~~, she thought that she had to be apologetic, ...【刪除 Looking back】❷ ~~Now especially after reading Helen Fisher's *Why Him? Why Her?* and our counselling sessions~~, she now has a clear view of .... ~~A few months after our counselling sessions~~, she told us the big news ....【刪除 especially after... 和 A few months after...】❸ ~~While Jane's case is about who has no trouble finding a guy~~, Cindy is the girl who....【刪除 while 引導的副詞子句】❹ She even listens to the advice of *The Ugly Truth* and ...,*Get the Guy*, to see if ... her ~~before she hit 40~~.【刪除 before 引導的副詞子句】❺ ~~To us~~, Cindy seems like a fun girl to be with, and ....【刪除 To us】❻ ~~When the time is right~~, she will just find the person....【刪除when引導的副詞子句】 ~~What can we learn from both cases is that~~ lots of us are waiting for love.【刪除 what 引導的名詞子句當主詞】

中譯和影子跟讀

🔘 MP3 011

A. In *The Return of the Condor Hero*, when Lu Zhan Yuan（陸展元） tells Li Mo Chou（李莫愁）she does not know what love is, this is probably true, but saying this drives Li Mo Chou into behaving insanely. Perhaps Li really needs to take a love lesson, but just don't tell this to her in person. Love is such a complex subject and there seems to be lot for us to learn. Using our entire life to learn what is love is not simply enough. This is not an exaggerated statement. Even people in love do not know what is love. Some people think they have found it, but they are not. Others have spent their entire lives out there searching, but cannot seem to find it. Thousands of movies, fictions, and books about love have produced to help us get closer to what love is, and some are quite helpful. Let's find out.

在《神鵰俠侶》中，當陸展元告訴李莫愁，她根本不懂情為何物時，這可能是千真萬確的，但這個說法卻讓李莫愁的行為變得瘋狂。或許李真的需要修一門愛情課，但是就是別當面跟她說就是了。愛情是門如此複雜的科目，對於我們來說似乎還有很多是需要學習的。利用我們的一輩子去學習愛情是什麼似乎都不為過。這不是誇張的陳述。甚至人們在戀愛中都不知道愛情是什麼了。有些人認為他們已經找到了，但是卻不然。其他人已經花費了一輩子在外尋找著，但是卻似乎找不到。數以千計關於愛情的電影、小說和書籍已經製成，用來幫助我們更進一步去了解愛情是什麼，而有些相當的有幫助。讓我們看一下。

B. In our counseling session, Jane admitted to us that she wished she had read books, such as Helen Fisher's *Why Him? Why Her?*, and did all personality tests. During her twentysomething years, she had no problems getting a date from a guy, and she happened to meet several guys that was so great that even her girlfriends were jealous of her. Deep down, she knew they weren't the perfect fit for her. In fact, her had five relationships before she turned thirty. Most people around her would comment how picky she was because those guys were fantastic, but she knew pretty well that people might have a wrong idea about suitability and attractiveness. Those guys were great, but were not great enough for her, not suitable for her. Other girls may think having a guy drive a Porsche waiting for you outside the campus is great. Or having someone who is willing to pay bills for you at an expensive restaurant and take you to several countries is dreamy and romantic. She, on the contrary, finds it exhausting, having to adjust herself for a jet lag after a long travel at every major holiday.

在我們的諮商期間，珍坦承告訴我們，但願她早點讀像是海倫・費雪的《我們為何戀愛？為何不忠？》，而且完成所有的個性測驗。在她 20 歲時期時，她不費力就有男子的約會邀約，而她也碰巧遇到幾個蠻棒的男性，甚至她的女性朋友都忌妒她。在內心深處，她知道那些男性並不適合她自己。實際上，在她滿 30 歲之前，她已經有過五段戀愛關係。大多數她周遭的人都會評論她多挑剔因為那些男子都很棒，但是她非常清楚，人們對於合適性和吸引力有著錯誤的想法。那些男子很棒，但是對於她而言沒有好到令她感到非常棒，不適合她。其他女性可能會認為一個男性開著保時捷在校園外頭等著妳是很棒的。或是有人願意帶妳去昂貴的餐廳用餐且願意買單和帶妳去幾個國家旅行是很夢幻和浪漫的。對她來說卻是相反地，她認為這很耗費力氣，在每個主要假期的長途旅途後，要調適時差。

C. Most of the time, she just wants to take a hot bath (sounds like what one of the housewives in the *Desperate Housewives* telling her husband what she would like to do at the Valentine's days.), watch some soap operas, pamper her dogs, or simply enjoy their time together. She just wants a simple life, and she did not want to disappoint her boyfriends. Every time she learned the news about their new travelling plans, she had to pretend how excited that was, another international trip to Europe, and she then went to the bathroom strangling the huge Teddy bear. Looking back, she thought that she had to be apologetic and kind of felt sorry for the bear, which has always been there for her when she had a mood fluctuation. Now especially after reading Helen Fisher's *Why Him? Why Her?* and our counselling sessions, she now has a clear view of what she wants in a man. A few months after our counselling sessions, she told us the big news that she has found the guy and they are getting married in two weeks.

大多數時候,她只想要泡個熱水澡(聽起來像是在《慾望師奶》中的其中一位主婦一樣,在情人節時她告訴她丈夫她在情人節時想要做的事。),觀看一些肥皂劇、寵寵她的狗或是僅僅享受他們在一起的時光。她僅想要簡單的生活,而且她不想要讓她的男朋友失望。每當她得知關於他們新的旅行計畫的消息時,她都必須假裝自己有多興奮,另一趟往歐洲的國際性旅遊,而她會接著走到浴室掐大型的泰迪熊。回想起來,她認為她必須感到有歉意,而且有點對於熊感到抱歉,當她有情緒波動時,她總認為熊在她需要時一直陪伴著她。現在特別是閱讀了海倫·費雪的《我們為何戀愛?為何不忠?》和諮商課程後,她現在對於她想要的男性是如何有著更清晰的想法。在我們諮商課程結束後的幾個月,她告訴我們一則大消息,就是她已經找到了對的男人,而且他們在兩周內就要結婚了。

D. While Jane's case is about who has no trouble finding a guy, Cindy is the girl who cannot seem to find a guy. She is already 35 years old, and she remains single all the time. It is not that she does not want to get married. She feels frustrated that she cannot get the guy because everyone in the workplace is either married or gay. Where are good guys, she lamented. She told us the funny thing that she has rehearsed the wedding vow a thousand times, and she has accumulated enough money to get married. She even listens to the advice of *The Ugly Truth* that to throw away relationship books, such as *Men Are from Mars and Women Are from Venus*, but recently she bought another relationship book, *Get the Guy*, to see if this book can really help her before she hit 40. To us, Cindy seems like a fun girl to be with, and she just needs to relax for a bit. She seems overprepared like getting married is the most important thing in life. When the time is right, she will just find the person to start the next chapter of her life.

珍的案例是關於她沒有找男人的困擾，而辛蒂卻是位似乎找不到男伴的女孩。她已經 35 歲了，而且她仍舊一直維持單身。不是她不想要結婚。她深感挫折，認為在辦公室內每個人不是已婚就是同性戀，所以她找不到男伴。好男人都去哪了呢，她悲嘆道。她告訴我們有趣的事就是關於婚姻誓言，她已經演練了幾千次了，而她已經累積了足夠的結婚基金。她甚至聽了《醜惡真相》的建議將關於感情的書籍，像是《男人來自火星，而女人來自金星》的書籍丟了，但近期她購買了另一本書《男人完全解密》，看是否能幫助她在 40 歲前結束單身。對我們來說，辛蒂似乎是個相處起來有趣的女孩，而她僅需要稍微放輕鬆點。她似乎過度準備，像是結婚是人生中最重要的事情。當時機對的時候，她就會找到能與她度過人生下個篇章的人。

E. What can we learn from both cases is that lots of us are waiting for love. We all deserve to be with someone who respects us. Sometimes it is just the timing. Sometimes it is about widening your social cycles. Hastily moving onto a relationship can do more harm than good. Relationship books sometimes help. They prevent us from overthinking and some really keep us optimistic about life, and We don't want her to find the perfect person because sometimes that person just does not exist. Or it just like the line from *Ugly Betty*, maybe perfect doesn't always look like you'd imagine. Cindy certainly needs more therapy sessions.

我們能從兩個案例中知道的是，大多數的我們仍等待著愛情來臨。我們都值得與尊重我們的人交往。有時候只是時機的問題。有時候只是關於拓展我們的社交圈。過於快速進入一段戀愛關係所造成的傷害其實大過益處。戀愛書籍有時候有幫助。它們避免我們過度思考，而且有時候真的讓我們對於生命抱持著樂觀的態度。我們不希望辛蒂找尋一位完美的男人，因為有時候那樣子的男人根本就不存在。或許就像是《醜女貝蒂》中所說的，或許完美有時候並不總是如妳所預想的。辛蒂確實需要更多的療程。

F. Dr. Jake and Dr. Sally
2019/3/17

傑克醫生和莎莉醫生
2019 年 3 月 17 日

You should spend about 20 minutes on **Questions 28-40**, which are based on Reading Passage 3 below.

Survival of Animals in the Desert and Their Defense against Detrimental Situations

A. The climate in the desert might be barren and arid, but the life here is just amazing as you can find in the tropical rainforest. Beetles roam on the surface of the desert despite the fact that the weather is extremely hot. Some are pretty swift, making desert chameleons unlikely to catch them, but with a little chase and the swiftness of the sticky tongue, chameleons can eventually enjoy the juicy meals, one after another. Some beetles will choose to shelter themselves under the plant, making them easier to be captured. Hiding in the desert really needs a little extra effort.

B. However, chameleons' life in the desert is not about eating beetles that are easier to capture. Sometimes they do feed on small lizards and other creatures in sight, but not all creatures are as submissive as the beetles. Some are very hard to tackle, such as black thick-tailed scorpions. The venom of black thick-tailed scorpions is quite deadly and does pose a threat to chameleons. Chameleons should really watch out the sting to their body parts or most importantly their eyes; otherwise, they might have to pay a heavy price for underestimating the black thick-tailed scorpions that are probably one-thirds of their body.

C. Chameleons in the desert are not quite as flexible as chameleons in another ecosystem. In the forest, for example, we are amazed by how chameleons catch insects, such as mantises, grasshoppers, and smaller insects, and we are able to witness chameleons swiftly escaping larger predators, such as ravens, and their tongues. In the desert, they have become as cumbersome as turtles. They even have to leave some creatures, such as wasps, alone. They kind of lose their charm and their magic.

D. Predators of chameleons make them even less intelligent. Footage of the desert wonderfully captures how the zebra snake outwits the chameleon. The chameleon senses a potential danger by knowing the zebra snake's presence, it runs away as fast as he can, thinking that he can escape, but still meets its doom in the end by getting chased down by the zebra snake. The bite of the zebra snake determines the outcome. The zebra snake stays motionless and waits for the venom to do its work. Such a remarkable moment.

E. The footage of the chameleon and the zebra snake makes us realize that the predator-prey relationship cannot be changed. It can also be found in other footage that a rattlesnake gets eaten by a king snake. It is not so much as a wonderful design of the natural world as the brutality of the natural world. Although the rattlesnake is packaged with powerful venom, the king snake is gifted with complex protein that protects itself from getting harmed by the rattlesnake. The fearsome rattlesnake eventually meets its nemesis.

F. In addition to the lurking danger that endangers creatures in the desert, heat in the desert can cause quite a damage in an instant. Most of the time, some animals bury themselves under the sand to protect themselves from getting excessive sunlight. Other creatures are nocturnal so that they can avoid getting exposed to the sun and save energy and water. Still others shade themselves under the bush, stay in the cave, or develop some mechanisms to counter with excess heat.

G. In places as barren as deserts, you can hardly find an arable land, luckily enough to find an oasis, or encounter massive thunderstorm rainfall all the time. The shortage of foods and scarcity of water make the desert an unlikely place to live, yet some creatures have acclimatized themselves to this arid land. Let's take a look at how camels adapt themselves into the surroundings.

H. Camels are widely known as creatures that have adapted into this kind of environments. Their endurance helps them survive long periods of drought without consuming a drop of water. Reliance on a single insulation method is clearly not enough for creatures living in the deserts, so camels have a thick coat that isolates them from sweltering heat and wind, and reflecting sunlight. In addition, they are also skillful at conserving water in the body. Exhalation of air will not cause any loss of water from camels' body because camels' nostrils help them preserve it. Also, they have an exceptionally powerful kidneys that help them regulate the use of water.

I. Because of camel's physiological adaptability, the role of camels has changed over the year. They are used for multiple purposes that elevate their values to local residents and the government. They are used as the transportation for local residents and tradesmen. Some are used as symbolic backgrounds for the wedding or a ride for the tourist. At other time, you can even get to witness the drinking of camel milk at a popular location. Whatever purposes that camels are used for, we certainly have to treat them well.

Questions 28-33

Reading Passage 3 has nine paragraphs, A-I

Choose the correct heading for each paragraph from the list of headings below.

Write the correct number, i-xi, in boxes 28-33 on your answer sheet.

List of Headings

i	Diversified roles encounter a time of change
ii	Chameleon's inability to outwit its predator
iii	Shrewdness diminishes when predators present
iv	Life in the deserts can be as wonderful as other places
v	The lurking danger that endangers creatures in the desert
vi	Different creatures counter with heat by employing different strategies
vii	Several characteristics that make camels acclimatize into the desert environment.
viii	Exhibiting dissimilar traits in various ecosystems
ix	Roles in the natural world remain unaltered
x	A lack of foods and water make the desert an unlikely place to live
xi	Camel's unique kidney makes them adapt into the desert condition

28 **Paragraph C**
29 **Paragraph D**
30 **Paragraph E**
31 **Paragraph F**
32 **Paragraph H**
33 **Paragraph I**

Questions 34-40

Complete the summary below

Choose No More Than One Word from the passage for each answer

Write your answers in boxes 34-40 on your answer sheet.

Life in the desert can be as incredible as other ecosystems. Characteristics, such as swiftness can make **34.**_____ less likely to be captured by chameleons. Chameleons do feed on other creatures, such as small lizards. The representative of the species that is harder to be dealt with is black thick-tailed scorpions.

Black thick-tailed scorpions possess **35.**_____, something that can do quite a damage to chameleons, if they undervalue its power. Sometimes chameleons outwit hunters, including **36.**_____, and remain unharmed. Other predator, such as the zebra snake outwits the chameleon by keeping on being **37.**_____ and letting the toxin do its work.

The dreadful creature, the rattlesnake, also encounters a bitter fight with its enemy. Although the rattlesnake has powerful venom, its predator contains **38.**_____ that makes it immune from the bite.

Several traits make camels adaptable to the desert environment. Two organs, such as **39.**_____ and **40.**_____ help them conserve water.

問題 **23** 到 **27**

閱讀第三篇文章有 **9** 個段落，**A-I**

從下列標題列表中，選出每個段落的正確標題

在你的答案紙，**28-33** 答案欄中，寫上正確的號碼

標題列表

i 多樣化的角色遭遇時代的改變

ii 變色龍無法智勝牠的掠食者

iii 精明隨著掠食者出現而減低

iv 沙漠中的生命跟其他地方一樣精彩

v 潛在的危險危及沙漠中的生物

vi 不同生物面對高溫採用不同的策略

vii 有幾個特徵讓駱駝適應沙漠環境

viii 在不同的生態系統展現不同的特徵

ix 在大自然的角色維持不變

x 缺乏食物和水讓沙漠成了難以生存的地方

xi 駱駝獨一無二的腎臟讓牠們適應了沙漠情況

---

28 Paragraph C

29 Paragraph D

30 Paragraph E

31 Paragraph F

32 Paragraph H

33 Paragraph I

Test 4

1
TEST

2
TEST

3
TEST

4
TEST

Reading Passage 3

問題 34 到 40

完成下列摘要題

段落中的每個答案，請勿超過 1 個單字

在你的答案紙，34-40 答案欄中，寫上你的答案

在沙漠中的生命和其他生態系統中的生命一樣驚奇。例如像是快速這樣的特徵，能夠使得 34.＿＿＿＿＿＿＿ 較不可能受到變色龍捕食。變色龍確實以其他生物為食，例如小型蜥蜴。較難應付的代表性物種是黑色粗尾蠍。

黑色粗尾蠍擁有 35.＿＿＿＿＿＿＿，能夠對於變色龍造成相當損害的裝備，如果變色龍低估牠的力量的話。有時候變色龍智勝獵者，包括 36.＿＿＿＿＿＿，以及維持完好無缺。其他掠食者，例如斑馬蛇智勝變色龍，藉由繼續 37.＿＿＿＿＿＿ 和讓毒素自我發揮功效。

可怕的生物，響尾蛇，也遇到了牠的敵人而陷入苦戰。儘管響尾蛇有著強而有力的毒素，牠的掠食者含有 38.＿＿＿＿＿＿ 使牠對於咬傷免疫。

幾個特徵使得駱駝適應於沙漠環境中。兩個器官，例如 39.＿＿＿＿＿＿ 和 40.＿＿＿＿＿＿ 幫助牠們保存水分。

Step 1：迅速看題型配置，再定出解題步驟

這篇文章的題型有：❶段落標題配對題（**Choose the correct heading for each paragraph from the list of headings below**）、❷摘要題。 這篇文章為這兩個題型的搭配。

段落標題配對題是某些考生懼怕的題型，因為選項除了同義改寫過外，有時候找不到，或選錯一個發生連續錯好幾題的情形，還有些在劍橋雅思試題中，需要更多層的理解才能選對，無形中耗掉考生很多時間，要特別注意。

Step 2：腦海中浮現答題策略，開始答題

這篇既然有❶**段落標題配對題**（**Choose the correct heading for each paragraph from the list of headings below**）、❷**摘要題**，其實在有**段落標題配對題**設計的文章中，不論搭配的其他題型為何，不管是不是摘要題，都可以先邊讀邊答這類型的題目，大概看完一個段落就能去選答案，有時候題目中會出現有的段落中已經有的答案，考生只要答某幾段，考生也可以自己拿捏要不要跳讀，沒被選中的段落或已經要答案的段落，可能於其他題型分配中出現考點，出題者大概都是這樣去思考，為了平衡每個段落考點出到的頻率。**段落標題配對題**最需要的其實是區分**主旨句**和 **supporting details**，supporting details 為干擾選項。

◆ 考生可以略看 A 和 B 段落，也可以**直接跳讀閱讀 C 段落**，第 **28**

題答案是 **viii**，**viii** Exhibiting dissimilar traits in various ecosystems，從 C 段落首句可以看出 chameleons in the desert are not quite as flexible as chameleons in another ecosystem.表示出變色龍在不同生態系統中有不同的特徵，此句為主旨句，只是以另一個方式表達。

◆ 另外需要**注意關鍵字 for example**，尤其是在有段落標題題型出現時，表列舉的詞像是 **for example** or **for instance** 等，通常可以只看該詞前面那句話即可，就能選出符合標題的選項，其他句可以跳過，省掉更多時間，有時候看完整句和列表中的選項反而受到很多干擾選項影響或是花太多秒才決定這題答案為何。如果不放心，進一步看後面的段落 **in the forest** 和 **in the desert** 就分別進一步闡述兩個不同生態系統中變色龍的差異，所以**第 28 題**答案很明顯是 **viii** Exhibiting dissimilar traits in various ecosystems。

◆ **第 29 題**答案是 **iii**，**iii** Shrewdness diminishes when predators present 是 predators of chameleons make them even less intelligent 的同義轉換。要注意干擾選項像是 **ii** Chameleon's **inability to outwit** its predator（**inability to outwit** 已經扭曲了意思，代表無法智勝，但是文意要表明的是聰明度降低或較不那麼聰慧，所以要多注意，別看太快選錯了，段落標題題很容易連錯）。

◆ 第 30 題答案是 **ix**，**ix** Roles in the natural world remain unaltered 是 footage of the chameleon and the zebra snake makes us realize that the predator-prey relationship cannot be changed 的同義表達，其中 **roles** 換成了 **relationships**，而 **cannot be changed** 換成了 **unaltered**。

◆ 第 31 題答案是 **vi**，**vi** Different creatures counter with heat by employing different strategies，段落中有列舉出幾項特徵，均表示了每種生物以不同的方式來應對沙漠的高溫，這題算是要消化過段落內容後選出答案。要注意 **v** The lurking danger that endangers creatures in the desert 是干擾選項。

◆ 第 32 題答案是 **vii**，Several characteristics that make camels acclimatize into the desert environment，**H 段落**中列舉了幾項駱駝的特徵，這些特徵是駱駝能適應沙漠環境的主因。**記得要選段落主旨句，而非選 supporting details**。**xi** Camel's unique kidney makes them adapt into the desert condition 就屬於**細節性資訊**，屬於干擾選項，可以直接排除，因為僅表示其中一項駱駝所具備，在沙漠中適應環境的能力之一。（**區分細節性訊息和主旨句是段落標題要檢測的考點**，過於細節性的敘述要記得都排除掉。）

◆ 第 33 題答案是 **i**，**i** Diversified roles encounter a time of change，**diversified** 和 **multiple** 為同義轉換。文中還提到了

the role of camels has changed over the year 和 They are used for multiple purposes 等等，故答案為 **i**。

◆ **第 34 題** Characteristics, such as **swiftness** can make 34.____ _____ **less likely** to be captured by chameleons.，可以對應到 A 段落的 swift，Some are pretty **swift**, making desert chameleons **unlikely to** catch them, but with a little chase and the swiftness of the sticky tongue, chameleons can eventually enjoy the juicy meals，空格中為某種生物，由 some 主詞往前回推，得知答案為 **beetles**，故**第 34 題**答案為 **beetles**。

◆ **第 35 題** **Black thick-tailed scorpions** possess 35._____ ____, something that can **do quite a damage to** chameleons, if they undervalue its power.由 **Black thick-tailed scorpions** 迅速定位到 B 段落 The **venom** of black thick-tailed scorpions is quite deadly and does pose a threat to chameleons. **Chameleons** should really watch out the sting to their body parts or most importantly their eyes; otherwise, **they** might have to **pay a heavy price** for **underestimating** the black thick-tailed scorpions that are probably one-thirds of their body.，其中 **underestimating = undervalue**，但還要再往前看到 The **venom** of black thick-tailed scorpions = **Black thick-tailed scorpions** possess_____，文章經由濃縮改寫後成題目，故**第 35 題**答案為 **venom**。

- 第 36 題 Sometimes chameleons outwit hunters, including 36._____, and **remain unharmed**.，注意 **unharmed**，這題是比較隱晦的表達，但是也可以快速定位到 C 段落，we are able to witness chameleons **swiftly escaping larger predators**, such as ravens，**swiftly escaping larger predators = remain unharmed**，而 **hunters = ravens**，題目改成 hunters, including 36._____，**escaping = outwit hunters**，**such as = including** 所以第 36 題答案為 **ravens**。

- 第 37 題，Other predator, such as the zebra snake outwits the chameleon by **keep on being** 37._____and **letting the toxin do its work**.對應到 D 段落 The zebra snake **stays motionless** and **waits for the venom to do its work**.，**stays motionless** 對應 **keep on being** 37._____而 **waits for the venom to do its work** 對應 **letting the toxin does its work** 故第 37 題答案為 **motionless**。

- 第 38 題，Although the rattlesnake has powerful venom, its predator contains 38._____that **makes it immune from the bite**.，對應到 E 段落的 Although the rattlesnake is packaged with powerful venom, the king snake is gifted with complex **protein that protects itself from getting harmed** by the rattlesnake.，其中 **protein that protects itself from getting harmed = makes it immune from the**

bite，題目規定只能答**一個**單字，故**第 38 題**答案為 **protein**。

◆ **第 39 和 40 題** Several traits make **camels** adaptable to the desert environment. **Two organs**, such as 39.＿＿＿＿＿＿ and 40.＿＿＿＿＿＿ help them conserve water.，由 **camels** 對應到 H 段落，再由題目關鍵詞迅速過濾掉其他訊息，找兩個器官，當中僅有 Exhalation of air will not cause any loss of water from camels' body because camels' **nostrils** help them preserve it. Also, they have an exceptionally powerful **kidneys** that help them regulate the use of water.，故答案分別為 **nostrils** 和 **kidneys**。

　注意像是 **However** 這類的承轉詞、**but** 這類的對等連接詞和像是 **in addition to, such as, including** 這類的片語，因為通常出現這些詞的時候，接續的描述或該句也是考官愛出題的考點，也可以看文章時迅速將這些詞都圈起來。（閱讀其他篇章時也可以多注意這類的詞，其實有考到一定雅思閱讀成績者，都很能掌握這些訊息的轉變和這類字的出現。）

◆ Some are pretty swift, making desert chameleons **unlikely to** 【第 34 題摘要題】catch them, **but** with a little chase and the swiftness of the sticky tongue, chameleons can eventually enjoy the juicy meals, one after another.

- Chameleons should really watch out the sting to their body parts or most importantly their eyes; **otherwise【第 35 題摘要題】**, they might have to pay a heavy price for underestimating the black thick-tailed scorpions that are probably one-thirds of their body.

- Chameleons in the desert are not quite as flexible as chameleons in another ecosystem. In the forest, **for example【第 28 題段落標題題】**, we are amazed by how chameleons catch insects, such as mantises, grasshoppers, and smaller insects, and we are able to witness chameleons swiftly escaping larger predators, **such as【第 36 題摘要題】** ravens, and their tongues.

- It is **not so much as** a wonderful design of the natural world as the brutality of the natural world. **Although 【第 39 和 40 題摘要題】** the rattlesnake is packaged with powerful venom, the king snake is gifted with complex protein that protects itself from getting harmed by the rattlesnake.

- **In addition to 【第 31 題段落標題題】** the lurking danger that endangers creatures in the desert, heat in the desert can cause quite a damage in an instant.

- **In addition**, they are also skillful at conserving water in the body. Exhalation of air will not cause any loss of water from camels' body **because**【第 39 題摘要題】camels' nostrils help them preserve it.

- **Also**【第 40 題摘要題】, they have an exceptionally powerful kidneys that help them regulate the use of water.

- **Because of** camel's physiological adaptability, the role of camels has changed over the year. They **are used for**【第33 題段落標題題】multiple purposes that elevate their values to local residents and the government.

A. The climate in the desert might be barren and arid, but the life here is just amazing as you can find in the tropical rainforest. Beetles roam on the surface of the desert despite the fact that the weather is extremely hot. Some are pretty swift, making desert chameleons unlikely to catch them, but with a little chase and the swiftness of the sticky tongue, chameleons can eventually enjoy the juicy meals, one after another. Some beetles will choose to shelter themselves under the plant, making them easier to be captured. Hiding in the desert really needs a little extra effort.

在沙漠的氣候可能是貧瘠且乾燥的，在此的生命卻是如同你能在熱帶雨林中找到那樣的令人感到吃驚。甲蟲漫遊在沙漠的表層上，儘管天氣是異常地炎熱。有些甲蟲相當快速，讓沙漠變色龍難以捕捉牠們，但是有著些許追逐和具黏性的快速舌頭，變色龍最終可以享用多汁的餐點，一隻接著一隻。有些甲蟲會選擇待在能遮陰的植物底下，讓牠們輕易地受捕捉。藏匿在沙漠真的需要一些額外的努力。

B. However, chameleons' life in the desert is not about eating beetles that are easier to capture. Sometimes they do feed on small lizards and other creatures in sight, but not all creatures are as submissive as the

Test 4

TEST 1

TEST 2

TEST 3

TEST 4

Reading Passage 3

beetles. Some are very hard to tackle, such as black thick-tailed scorpions. The venom of black thick-tailed scorpions is quite deadly and does pose a threat to chameleons. Chameleons should really watch out the sting to their body parts or most importantly their eyes; otherwise, they might have to pay a heavy price for underestimating the black thick-tailed scorpions that are probably one-thirds of their body.

然而，變色龍在沙漠中的生活並不只是關於食用易於捕捉的甲蟲。有時候牠們會以小型蜥蜴和其他能看的到的生物為食，所有的生物並不總是像甲蟲那樣順服。有些很難應付，例如黑色粗尾蠍。黑色粗尾蠍的毒性相當致命且對於變色龍來說是個威脅。變色龍應該要相當小心身體部位，尤其是牠們的眼睛，否則，牠們可能會因為低估僅是牠們身體大約 1/3 大小左右的黑色粗尾蠍，而需要付出沉重的代價。

C. Chameleons in the desert are not quite as flexible as chameleons in another ecosystem. In the forest, for example, we are amazed by how chameleons catch insects, such as mantises, grasshoppers, and smaller insects, and we are able to witness chameleons swiftly escaping larger predators, such as ravens, and their tongues. In the desert, they have become as cumbersome as turtles. They even have to leave some creatures, such as wasps, alone. They kind of lose their charm and their magic.

在沙漠的變色龍並不像其他生態系統中的變色龍那樣具有彈性。例如在樹林中，我們會因為變色龍如何補捉昆蟲，例如螳螂、蝗蟲以及較小型的昆蟲，而感到驚訝。我們也能夠目睹變色龍快速地逃避大型的掠食者，例如大烏鴉，和牠們的舌頭。但在沙漠中，牠們已經變得像烏龜那樣笨重。牠們甚至需要不去打擾例如黃蜂那樣的生物。牠們有點失去了牠們的魅力和牠們的魔法。

D. Predators of chameleons make them even less intelligent. Footage of the desert wonderfully captures how the zebra snake outwits the chameleon. The chameleon senses a potential danger by knowing the zebra snake's presence, it runs away as fast as he can, thinking that he can escape, but still meets its doom in the end by getting chased down by the zebra snake. The bite of the zebra snake determines the outcome. The zebra snake stays motionless and waits for the venom to do its work. Such a remarkable moment.

變色龍的掠食者讓牠們甚至變笨了。沙漠中的鏡頭中神奇地捕捉了斑馬蛇如何智勝變色龍的畫面。變色龍藉由斑馬蛇的出現而感受到潛在的危險，牠盡可能地逃跑，以為牠能躲過一劫，但是仍在最後被斑馬蛇追上而難逃一死。斑馬蛇的一咬決定了結果。斑馬蛇維持靜止不動等待著毒性發揮作用。多麼神奇的時刻。

E. The footage of the chameleon and the zebra snake makes us realize that the predator-prey relationship cannot be changed. It can also be found in other footage that a rattlesnake gets eaten by a king snake. It is not so much as a wonderful design of the natural world as the brutality of the natural world. Although the rattlesnake is packaged with powerful venom, the king snake is gifted with complex protein that protects itself from getting harmed by the rattlesnake. The fearsome rattlesnake eventually meets its nemesis.

鏡頭中的變色龍和斑馬蛇讓我們了解到掠食者和獵物間的關係不能改變。這也可能於其他鏡頭中看到，響尾蛇被王蛇吃了。這不是大自然世界的驚奇設計，而是自然世界中的殘酷。儘管響尾蛇配有著強而有力的毒，王蛇有著與生俱來的天賦，複合的蛋白質，能保護牠免於受到響尾蛇的傷害。令人懼怕的響尾蛇最終遇到了命中的剋星。

F. In addition to the lurking danger that endangers creatures in the desert, heat in the desert can cause quite a damage in an instant. Most of the time, some animals bury themselves under the sand to protect themselves from getting excessive sunlight. Other creatures are nocturnal so that they can avoid getting exposed to the sun and save energy and water. Still others shade themselves under the bush, stay in the cave, or develop some mechanisms to counter with excess heat.

除了潛在的危險危及著沙漠中的生物之外，沙漠中的高溫能夠於短時間內造成相當大的傷害。大多數時候，有些動物將自己埋藏在沙底來保護自己過度曝曬。其他生物是夜行性生物以至於牠們能夠避免於曝露在陽光下，而且能夠保存能量和水分。還有些動物利用灌木底下的影子來遮陽、待在洞穴裡頭，或是發展出一些機制來應對過量的高溫。

G. In places as barren as deserts, you can hardly find an arable land, luckily enough to find an oasis, or encounter massive thunderstorm rainfall all the time. The shortage of foods and scarcity of water make the desert an unlikely place to live, yet some creatures have acclimatized themselves to this arid land. Let's take a look at how camels adapt themselves into the surroundings.

在像是沙漠這樣貧瘠的地方中，你幾乎很難去發現能耕種的土地、幸運地找到綠洲或是總是遇到大量大雷雨的時刻。食物的短缺和水的匱乏讓沙漠成為難以生存的地方，可是有些生物本身卻已經適應了這塊乾旱的土地，讓我們來看一下駱駝是如何能夠適應這個環境。

H. Camels are widely known as creatures that have adapted into this kind of environments. Their endurance helps them survive long periods of drought without consuming a drop of water. Reliance on a single insulation method is clearly not enough for creatures living in the deserts, so camels have a thick coat that isolates them from sweltering heat and wind, and reflecting sunlight. In addition, they are also skillful at conserving water in the body. Exhalation of air will not cause any loss of water from camels' body because camels' nostrils help them preserve it. Also, they have an exceptionally powerful kidneys that help them regulate the use of water.

駱駝以已經能夠適應這樣的環境而聞名。牠們的忍耐力幫助牠們長時間的生存而不需要攝取一滴水。仰賴這樣的單一隔離方法是不足以讓一個生物能夠存活於沙漠這樣子的環境中，所以駱駝有著厚的皮毛，將熱和風隔離牠們身體，以及反射陽光。此外，牠們也精通於保存體內的水分。呼出的氣體不會造成任何駱駝體內水分的損失因為駱駝的鼻孔幫助牠們保存水分。而且他們有著異常強而有力的腎臟幫助他們調節水的使用。

I. Because of camel's physiological adaptability, the role of camels has changed over the years. They are used for multiple purposes that elevate their values to local residents and the government. They are used as the transportation for local residents and tradesmen. Some are used as symbolic backgrounds for the wedding or a ride for the tourist. At other time, you can even get to witness the drinking of camel milk at a popular location. Whatever purposes that camels are used for, we certainly have to treat them well.

因為駱駝的生理適應性，駱駝的角色幾年以來已經改變。牠們用於為數眾多的目的，來提升牠們對於政府和當地居民的價值。牠們用於替當地居民和商人的交通運輸。有些用於象徵性的婚禮場合或是觀光客的搭乘工具。在其他時候，你甚至可以在流行的地點目睹引用駱駝牛奶的畫面。不論駱駝的功能為何，我們都要確實地好好善待牠們。

參考答案

Test 1

Reading passage 1 (1-13)

1. True
2. True
3. False
4. False
5. E
6. G
7. B
8. D
9. C
10. venomous
11. raccoons
12. decomposers
13. competitors

Reading passage 2 (14-27)

14. C
15. C
16. F
17. E
18. F
19. D
20. H
21. G
22. C
23. E
24. A
25. resume
26. temperament
27. flight attendant

Reading passage 3 (28-40)

28. D
29. B
30. A
31. G
32. L
33. F
34. K
35. J
36. takers
37. womanizer
38. disloyalty
39. appreciation
40. forgiveness

Test 4

T E S T 1
T E S T 2
T E S T 3
T E S T 4
Reading Passage 3

Test 2
Reading passage 1 (1-13)
1. D
2. H
3. I
4. J
5. E
6. B
7. C
8. L
9. M
10. H
11. C
12. B
13. C

Reading passage 2 (14-27)
14. B
15. G
16. F
17. E
18. E
19. B
20. D

21. E
22. D
23. B
24. F
25. A
26. C
27. D

Reading passage 3 (28-40)
28. E
29. D
30. A
31. F
32. G
33. F
34. B
35. celebrities
36. evaluations
37. True
38. False
39. False
40. Not Given

Test 3

Reading passage 1 (1-13)

1. C
2. F
3. C
4. A
5. C
6. E
7. B
8. D
9. A
10. temptation
11. maneuvers
12. awareness
13. analogy

Reading passage 2 (14-27)

14. selfies, gourmets
15. Facebook, IG
16. watches, bags
17. prosecutor
18. random hook-ups
19. hidden
20. lightweight
21. obscene
22. brain
23. Programmers
24. transparency
25. fake
26. profiles
27. peers

Reading passage 3 (28-40)

28. D
29. B
30. D
31. C
32. True
33. Not Given
34. Not Given
35. False
36. success
37. trap
38. unhappy
39. repetitive
40. velocity

Test 4

Reading passage 1 (1-13)

1. B
2. D
3. D
4. E
5. A
6. D
7. C
8. E
9. arrows, wind
10. commanders
11. menace
12. deadline
13. crossbowmen

Reading passage 2 (14-27)

14. D
15. C
16. A
17. C
18. B
19. D
20. F
21. G
22. C
23. jealousy
24. Porsche
25. exhausted
26. suitability
27. attractiveness

Reading passage 3 (28-40)

28. viii
29. iii
30. ix
31. vi
32. vii
33. i
34. beetles
35. venom
36. ravens
37. motionless
38. protein
39. nostrils
40. kidneys

閱讀文章	參考書籍/影集	引述句子
Test 1 READING PASSAGE 2	*The Millionaire Fastlane*	"…go to college, get good grades, get good job, save 10% of your paycheck…." only leads you to walk on the slow lane. (MJ Demarco, 2011, ix)
Test 1 READING PASSAGE 2	*The Defining Decade*	"Interviewers want to hear a reasonable story about the past, present, and future." (Meg, 2012, p.63)
Test 1 READING PASSAGE 3	*Rich Dad Poor Dad*	"Give and you shall receive".
Test 1 READING PASSAGE 3	*Harry Potter and The Goblet of Fire*	"I owe you one for telling me about the dragons." (J.K., 2000, p.431)
Test 2 READING PASSAGE 2	*Rich Dad Poor Dad*	"More money certainly cannot solve more problems."/will not solve their problems (Robert, 1997,2011, 2017, p.32)

Test 2 **READING** **PASSAGE 2**	*The Millionaire Next Door*	"one earns to spend. When you need to spend more, you need to earn more" (Thomas and William, 1996, p.52)	
Test 2 **READING** **PASSAGE 2**	*Millionaire Teacher*	"You are (she is) the one in financial trouble" (Andrew, 2017, p.32)	
Test 2 **READING** **PASSAGE 2**	*The Richest Man in Babylon*	"money comes from those who save it"	
Test 2 **READING** **PASSAGE 2**	*Millionaire Success Habits*	"the success hack, however isn't as much about money as it is about confidence." (Dean, 2019, p.184)	
Test 2 **READING** **PASSAGE 2**	*The Millionaire Fastlane*	"The rich understand that education doesn't end with a graduation ceremony; it starts. The world is in constant flux, and as it evolves your education must evolve." (MJ Demarco, 2011, p.191)	

TEST 1

TEST 2

TEST 3

TEST 4

Reading Passage 3

Test 2 READING PASSAGE 2	*Secrets of the Millionaire Mind*	"Each month read at least one book" (T.Harv, 2005, p.187)
Test 2 READING PASSAGE 3	*The Third Door*	"Gates didn't impulsively drop out of college either" (Alex, 2018, p.134)
Test 2 READING PASSAGE 3	*Where You Go Is Not Who You Will Be*	"if you don't have perfect scores on every standardized test since the second grade, your visions of Stanford would be termed hallucinations." (Frank, 2015, p.39)
Test 2 READING PASSAGE 3	*The Millionaire Fastlane*	"The world is in constant flux, and as it evolves your education must move with it or you will drift to mediocrity." (MJ Demarco, 2011, p.191)
Test 2 READING PASSAGE 3	*Where You Go Is Not Who You Will Be*	"careers aren't built on the names of colleges." (Frank, 2015, p.30)

Test 2 READING PASSAGE 3	*Where You Go Is Not Who You Will Be*	"It is built on carefully honed skills, ferocious work ethics, and good attitudes." (Frank, 2015, p.30)
Test 3 READING PASSAGE 3	*How Will You Measure Your Life*	"Money acts as a highly accurate yardstick of success." (Clayton, 2012, p.37)
Test 3 READING PASSAGE 3	*The Millionaire Next Door*	"One earns to spend. When you need to spend more, you need to earn more." (Thomas and William, 1996, p.52)
Test 3 READING PASSAGE 3	*How Will You Measure Your Life*	"Many of my peers had chosen careers using hygiene factors as the primary criteria." (Clayton, 2012, p.35)
Test 4 READING PASSAGE 2	*Ugly Betty*	"maybe perfect doesn't always look like you'd imagine."

國家圖書館出版品預行編目(CIP)資料

一次就考到雅思閱讀7+/ 韋爾著-- 初版. --
新北市：倍斯特, 2019.07 面 ； 公分. --
（考用英語系列；18）
ISBN 978-986-97075-8-9（平裝附光碟）
1.國際英語語文測試系統　2.讀本

805.189　　　　　　　　　　108009637

考用英語系列　018

一次就考到雅思閱讀7+（附英式發音MP3）

初　　　版　　2019年7月
定　　　價　　新台幣480元

作　　　者　　韋爾
出　　　版　　倍斯特出版事業有限公司
發 行 人　　周瑞德
電　　　話　　886-2-8245-6905
傳　　　真　　886-2-2245-6398
地　　　址　　23558 新北市中和區立業路83巷7號4樓
E - m a i l　　best.books.service@gmail.com
官　　　網　　www.bestbookstw.com
總 編 輯　　齊心瑀
特約編輯　　洪婉婷
封面構成　　高鍾琪
內頁構成　　菩薩蠻數位文化有限公司
印　　　製　　大亞彩色印刷製版股份有限公司

港澳地區總經銷　　泛華發行代理有限公司
地　　　址　　香港新界將軍澳工業邨駿昌街7號2樓
電　　　話　　852-2798-2323
傳　　　真　　852-3181-3973